Death a
Danc
Snowman

Other books by Carol Westron

The South Coast Crime Series

The Terminal Velocity of Cats (Mia Trent)

About the Children (Tyler)

Karma and the Singing Frogs (Mia Trent)

The Fragility of Poppies

Cosy Crime

This Game of Ghosts

The Curse of the Concrete Griffin

Victorian Murder Mysteries

Strangers and Angels

Children's Picture Books

Adi and the Dream Train

Adi Rides the Night Mare

Adi and The Ghost Train (a Christmas Story)

Death and the Dancing Snowman

Carol Westron

ISBN 9798864191903

First published in the UK 2023

pentangle
press

Dedication

To Dot

Thank you for your unfailing friendship and support

Acknowledgements

Thanks to my brilliant beta readers: Dot Marshall-Gent, Lesley Talbot and Jo Halsall. I couldn't do it without you.

And thanks also to Marni Graff and Lizzie Sirett for your constant support and encouragement.

Immense gratitude to Jack Halsall of digital-thread.org for creating an incredible book cover and a brilliant book trailer, as well as designing my new website.

Thank you Denmead Writers; Havant & District Writers; Dunford Novelists and the members of Mystery People for your input and encouragement during three very difficult years.

As always, my love and thanks to my family, Peter, Jo, Jack & Adam, Paul, Claire, Oliver & Henry, Alan, Lyndsey, Thomas, Tabitha & Pippa. Thank you for being there for me. Without you nothing I achieve would be worthwhile.

Chapter 1

"Grace! Welcome back!" Maddie ushered her friend into her hall and shut the door. "You've brought some lovely weather with you. I wouldn't be surprised if it snowed."

"I'm sorry." Grace looked nervous. Maddie wondered whether she was apologising for the December weather or feeling guilty that her 'few days away' to visit relatives had turned into several weeks.

For that matter, Maddie still wasn't sure how she felt about Grace's desertion soon after their Hampshire senior citizens' estate had been thrown into turmoil by blackmail, violence and death. Maddie had been hurt that Grace had left so abruptly at a time when she'd have appreciated her support, but she'd told herself not to be pathetic and tried to get over it. Everyone had their own coping mechanisms and she should have guessed that Grace's would be to withdraw. There had been several days when reporters hung round the estate and Grace hated any trace of notoriety.

She smiled at her friend, "Come and sit down, I've just made a pot of tea. If I'd known you were coming I'd have baked a cake." She bustled into the small kitchen that adjoined the sitting room and returned carrying an iced Victoria Sponge. "What do you know? I did bake a cake. I saw you drive round The Green a couple of hours ago."

"Thank you."

"Have you collected Tiggy from the cattery yet?"

"No, I've arranged to get him tomorrow morning. Are your family all well?" Maddie thought the enquiry sounded polite rather than engaged.

"Fine. Libby and the boys are away this week. They won a Christmas competition and the school gave them permission to go."

"How nice."

"Is your aunt okay?" Maddie wondered if she'd wronged Grace and her extended stay was because her aunt was seriously ill.

"Quite well. Frail and rather forgetful, but then she's over ninety." Grace sipped her tea.

"You were away longer than I expected." Maddie knew that Grace's long-estranged cousin had seen her mentioned in a newspaper report and invited her to visit but she hadn't anticipated the absence would be so long.

"I know but I felt I owed it to my aunt. After all I hadn't seen her for over forty years. Father quarrelled with her at Mother's funeral and never allowed any contact with her again. At first she wrote and sent Christmas and birthday cards but he tore them up and forbade me to answer them." Grace hesitated, and Maddie thought she looked uncomfortable, almost shifty. "I'm not sure what to do. My aunt has asked..."

A loud, drawn-out moan echoed around the room. Grace jumped, sloshing tea into her lap. "What was that?"

"Nothing to worry about," said Maddie, at her most nonchalant, "just Hatty, my new next-door neighbour, summoning the dead. I'll get you some kitchen towel to mop up that tea."

Grace accepted the paper towel and dried her dark grey trousers with swift, nervous dabs. Another howl, louder than the first, made her wince. "What do you mean, summoning the dead?"

Maddie struggled not to laugh. Grace, with her High Anglican beliefs and conservative attitudes was not going to like this. She suspected Grace's time away

2

had robbed her of the burgeoning sense of humour that Maddie had worked so hard to cultivate.

"My new neighbour is a medium, at least she says she is, and she's trying to raise dead spirits and release them from whatever captivity they're in on this spectral plane."

Grace sat stiffly upright, her face cold and rigid, all her features turning down. "That's sacrilegious nonsense!" She spat the words. "She has no right. No authority. Such things should be left to those priests who have God's blessing to do such work."

Maddie sighed. She'd known Grace wouldn't be happy about a ghostbuster moving onto the estate but she hadn't anticipated a full-scale tantrum.

"Hatty's a bit noisy," she admitted. "In fact, considering how well insulated these cottages are, you could say she's downright rowdy. But she only does it for ten to fifteen minutes most days. I've asked her not to do any loud spirit-contacting after six o'clock or when my grandsons are here. Once you get used to her she's no problem. In fact she's a lot pleasanter neighbour than old Norman ever was."

"That's not the point." Grace sniffed disdainfully.

Maddie's amusement vanished. Who did Grace think she was to take herself off for six weeks, when she could have been helpful, and then come back and lay down the law?

"What is the point then?" she snapped.

"There's no need to get cross about it, Maddie. You must know as well as I do that it's wrong to meddle with spiritual matters. And it's dangerous."

Maddie had been a bit concerned about that herself. She'd wondered whether her neighbour's forays into the supernatural could cause psychological and emotional damage to herself and the people who believed in her psychic powers. When people had been bereaved they could be desperate and very vulnerable.

"It's not just that the woman's endangering herself," continued Grace, "she's opening up portals to the unknown. The evil she releases could contaminate the whole estate."

Maddie stared at her. "Did you just say portals? What sort of films have you been watching? Have you and your old aunt been binging on back-to-back Ghostbuster movies?" She began to sing the Ghostbuster theme.

"Stop being silly! This is serious." Grace shuddered. "Is that woman going to keep on making that noise for ever?"

Maddie murmured one final, defiant, "Ghostbusters," then turned her attention to the keening that was still intruding from next door. "Is she putting you off your cake?" she enquired. "I'm sure she'll run out of steam soon. It's getting towards dusk now and, like I said, she's very considerate about not moaning for too long or too late."

"Considerate!" Grace glared at her. "I'm surprised you've got a new neighbour so quickly. I thought the management would have had problems selling that cottage. There are others available and a man met a violent death in that one."

Maddie was tempted to explain that for Hatty recent violent death had been a positive selling point, but she suspected her Grace-baiting had gone far enough. "I think it was cheaper than the new-builds. I'm not sure she's that well off."

For all her stuffiness, Grace was kind-hearted. "Poor woman. It's not easy to manage on a small income. You called her Hatty. I assume her name's Harriet?" It was clear she approved of this as a sensible name.

"Well no." Maddie abandoned her good resolutions. In fact she paused for a moment to savour the coming reaction. "Don't tell anybody else on the estate but actually she calls herself Hatshepsut."

"What?" Grace's voice rose to a squeak.

Maddie struggled to keep a straight face. "Hatshepsut, the first female Pharaoh of Egypt. Her name means 'foremost noblewoman'."

"The woman's mad!" Grace spoke with deep conviction.

Maddie got up to make more tea. She glanced in the mirror that hung over the fireplace. It was an art deco style mirror, edged with coloured glass. It had belonged to her grandparents so it wasn't surprising that it was slightly tarnished in a few places, but it was still fun. She saw her own reflection: plump and her face somewhat lined, but her purple-dyed, spiky hair had an extra powdering of glitter to celebrate Christmas and her red reindeer jumper with its embedded lights twinkled merrily. "There's nothing wrong with crazy," she remarked.

A piercing scream sounded from next door. "But there's something wrong with that!" she exclaimed, and headed towards the door.

Chapter 2

Outside, it was almost dark and the threatening snow had turned to icy rain. Grace grabbed her coat and struggled into it as she followed Maddie to the next-door cottage. Even though it was a short distance she worried about Maddie, whose fluffy slippers must be soaking up the wet.

Maddie banged on Hatty's door and rang the bell. No answer. She opened the letter box and bent down to peer through. "Hatty!" she shouted through the opening. "Hatty! It's Maddie. Are you okay?"

Grace felt something soft and damp wind round her ankles and shuddered. Looking down she saw a grey, long-haired Persian cat leaning against her and looking hopefully at the door.

"That's Toly," said Maddie

"Toly?"

"Short for Ptolemy. He's Hat's cat. And, before you say anything, it's no weirder than you calling your cat Tiglath Pileser the Third."

Grace was tempted to argue that calling your cat after a Biblical monarch was totally different but she realised this wasn't a suitable time or place. She remembered how, two months ago, they had twice been compelled to enter neighbours' cottages when they feared something was wrong. One neighbour had recovered after a stay in hospital, the other had not. She shivered. "I've got a bad feeling about this, Maddie."

"I didn't think you believed in premonitions. I've got a key to Hat's house in case of emergencies. Could you nip back and get it Grace? It's in the drawer of the small table by the front door. I'll stay here and keep calling to her." She passed Grace her keys.

Grace didn't argue, but, as she splashed her way through the puddles back to Maddie's cottage, she wondered if the emergency key exchange between neighbours was mutual and this Hatty woman now had Maddie's key. If so, it was the key that Grace had temporarily returned when she accepted her aunt's invitation to visit her. The thought caused her a pang of loss, mixed with jealousy.

She collected the single, labelled key and grabbed Maddie's coat from the hook. As an afterthought, she picked up her own handbag, in case she wanted to go home before Maddie was ready to leave her new, strange friend. Then she hurried back to where Maddie was waiting and handed her Hatty's key and Maddie's own keyring.

"Thank you." Maddie smiled as Grace draped the coat around her shoulders.

Maddie turned the key and opened the door. "Hatty," she shouted. "It's Maddie. I've let myself in." She stepped inside, preceded by Ptolemy and followed by Grace. The house was silent, save for the steady tick-tock of the grandfather clock that stood just inside the door.

Grace felt herself shaking. She could hear Maddie's breath coming in short, nervous gasps and knew she shared her fear that they were about to discover another body in this house.

Maddie called again. "Hatty, it's Maddie. Are you okay?"

No answer.

Grace could see Maddie's hand shaking as she reached out to open the sitting room door, and placed her hand gently on her friend's arm, although she was aware that she too was trembling.

Just as Maddie touched the handle, the door opened, and a woman stood there. She looked shaky and dishevelled, although Grace was uncertain how much of her bedraggled appearance was natural. She was a short, plump woman, dressed in a bright turquoise kaftan, topped with layers of shapeless cardigans in clashing colours. Her hair was long, grey and straggly, and blood was running down her face from a cut on her forehead.

"I've got my First Aid kit in my handbag," said Grace.

"Of course you have." Maddie's smile removed the sting from her mocking words. She took Hatty's arm and led her back into the dimly-lit room, then eased her gently into an armchair.

"Hatty, what happened?"

"I was attacked." The words were hardly more than a whisper.

"Attacked!" Grace looked around nervously in case the assailant was still lurking in the shadows.

The room was crowded with the heavy, old-fashioned, shabby furniture, which she recognised from Norman's time. Presumably, the lawyers administering Norman's estate had been happy to sell it to Hatty when she bought the cottage. However, Grace was certain that Norman had never possessed an array of multi-coloured, floating draperies embellished with esoteric symbols. Not to mention the dream-catchers in many designs that dangled everywhere and the medley of crystals and strange eastern statuettes that adorned every surface. Grace shuddered.

"If somebody attacked you we need to call the police!" exclaimed Maddie.

"No! That would be a betrayal of a Sacred Trust!"

"Do you mean you know who it was that hit you? Where did he go?"

To Grace's ears, Maddie sounded as though she'd reached the end of her patience but Hatty seemed unaware of this. She smiled as she replied, "He vanished. Into the ether."

"The ether?"

Hatty drew herself up to her full, not very impressive height. "I was attacked by a Being from the Other Side," she announced.

Chapter 3

"You're saying a ghost attacked you?" Maddie felt like an extra in a spoof, paranormal film. She couldn't imagine what Grace was thinking, ghostly apparitions and Grace just didn't mix. Apparently Grace agreed. She marched into the kitchen area without saying a word.

"I was looking into my crystal ball, summoning the spirits, and I saw him. He appeared. The apparition." Hatty sounded proud. She looked up at Maddie as if she expected congratulations.

Grace came back from the kitchen with a glass of water, which she handed to Hatty with the terse command, "Drink this." Then she came round the other side of the chair, balanced a bowl of water on its arm, switched on a nearby reading lamp and slanted it towards Hatty's face. That done, she started to bathe the wound with a pad of lint. Maddie noticed that she was wearing thin vinyl gloves. Grace really was very good at First Aid and Home Safety and all those practical things. It was good to have her back, assuming she was back for good. Maddie turned her thoughts firmly back to the present predicament and asked a question she knew she'd probably regret. "What happened then, Hatty?"

"I spoke to him, of course. I asked him who he wanted to contact. He didn't answer. I repeated my question and asked what I could do for him, sometimes apparitions need encouragement. I fear I must have angered him, because he levitated the crystal and smashed it into my face. And then I did something terrible. I struck out at him. I'm so ashamed that I did that. It caused him to dematerialise."

"You mean you lost consciousness?" said Maddie.

"The Psychic Power was so strong that it overwhelmed me."

Maddie stared at her. The first word that sprang into her mind was short and crude, and would offend both Hatty and Grace. She chose a diluted version. "Rubbish! You blacked out."

"That's not true! I..."

"It's more likely she fainted from fright than lost consciousness from concussion," said Grace, "the wound is very superficial, hardly more than a scratch." She finished her ministrations and moved back, broken glass crunching beneath her feet.

"Oh please be careful!" exclaimed Hatty. "I've got to gather up every piece separately and perform the rituals that will prevent evil from befalling. And of course I didn't faint from fright. An experienced medium would never do that. I was overcome by the Psychic Power."

In frosty silence Grace stepped clear of the shattered ball. "I've cleaned the wound. It doesn't look serious, but you should go to hospital and get it checked."

"Oh no! I can't leave this place. I must try to contact that poor, disturbed apparition. There must be something that he needs from me. Thank you for all you've done but now I must consult my reference books. I've never heard of a spectre quite like that."

"Like what?" asked Maddie.

"He was a snowman," said Hatty. "Staring out at me from my crystal ball."

"A snowman?" repeated Maddie. "Hatty, you need to go to hospital. You're imagining things."

"No, I'm not. I know what I saw. I saw his white face and coal black eyes and orange pointed nose. But I can't work out what it means or who he was or what he was trying to tell me. Please, leave me now."

Neither Grace not Maddie spoke until they were well clear of Hatty's cottage and Maddie was opening her own front door.

"Can't work out what it means indeed!" exploded Maddie. "I'll tell you what it means. The woman's completely crazy. You were right and I was wrong. I've swapped living next to a miserable old miser for close proximity to a loony who imagines spectral snowmen. Lucky me!"

"I'm not sure she imagined it," said Grace.

"Seriously? You're joking aren't you? Best case scenario, she was holding that crystal ball above her head, the way she often does when she's being melodramatic, and she saw something reflected in it that startled her and she dropped it on her head. Like I said, she's delusional. Snowmen indeed!"

"Don't take your coat off," said Grace. "Put your boots on and follow me." She rummaged in her handbag, got out a small torch, switched it on and led the way into Maddie's back garden.

"What are we doing?" asked Maddie.

"Hunting for Hatty's ghost."

"It's way past Halloween and I'm not going trick-or-treating with you." Despite her protests, she followed Grace out of her garden and into Hatty's. "I hope Hatty doesn't see us. She'll think we're more ghosts come to visit her."

"She won't see us. Her blinds are down and her windows are shut and latched. I did that when I was getting the water."

"You mean the windows weren't all shut before?"

"No, the blind was up and the kitchen window was pulled to, or maybe pushed to, but not latched. I shut it properly because it felt safer that way. I put on gloves to close it, just in case there were fingerprints. I thought it was best to preserve evidence of the break-in and I didn't realise she'd refuse to call the police." She directed her torch under the kitchen window. "Look, there are footprints in the mud, you can see where somebody jumped down."

"And there's one on the windowsill, so they got in that way too." Maddie got out her phone and took photos of the prints. "Not that Hatty's going to believe us. She'd rather think it's a spooky snowman than a fancy-dress burglar. What's that?" As she took a final flash photo something orange caught her eye. She bent down and picked it up. "It's a material carrot."

"From a snowman's fancy-dress outfit," said Grace triumphantly.

They hurried back into Maddie's cottage and she poured them each a glass of sparkling wine.

"We need a toast," she said. "Isn't it funny how the second you turn up we've got a mystery to solve. Here's to The Mystery of the Spectral Snowman."

"When you talk like that I know you've been watching too many cartoons with your grandsons," retorted Grace.

Maddie grinned at her, happy that their friendship was moving back on track. "Scooby-Dooby-Doo," she said. "Now you know you're home."

Chapter 4

"So where do we start?" asked Grace. Although she still had a major decision to make about her future, she was glad to postpone it. Anyway, it was her duty to persuade Maddie not to encourage her strange new neighbour in such undesirable behaviour.

"I start by changing my soggy socks and damp jumper and going over to the Nursing Home. The Manager agreed to allow the Main Hall to be used for rehearsals of the Clayfield Carnival Dancers and I'm helping out."

"You've joined some Morris Dancers?" Grace knew Maddie was eccentric but she couldn't believe she'd cavort around in a strange costume wearing bells. Although, on second thoughts, that was easier to imagine than the prospect of Maddie being willing to keep in step with seven other people.

"And why not?" demanded Maddie. "Dancing is good exercise."

"But you suffer from arthritis!"

"Movement is good for it. Anyway, my costume doesn't allow for much in the way of high kicks, as well as concealing a multitude of self-indulgent sins. I'd rather pop a couple of painkillers and keep dancing than turn into an old fogey."

Grace wasn't sure whether to take that comment personally but decided it was better not to ask. "Surely Morris Dancers are all men?"

"We're not Morris Dancers. We call ourselves Carnival Dancers. The girls who've choreographed our dances say that's a name used for female Morris Dancers, although our dances aren't traditional. Another name for women dancers is Fluffy Dancers, but for some reason the guys from Freddie's pub darts team were even less keen on that than the women were." As she was talking, Maddie was stripping off her rain-soaked socks and jumper and replacing them with garments warm from the radiator.

Grace battened onto the one name with which she was familiar. "So this was one of Freddie's bright ideas? I can't say I'm surprised." Freddie Fell lived in the cottage directly opposite to Maddie's, across the stretch of grass shared by the residents and known by them as The Green. He was a good-natured and generous man, but too eccentric for Grace to feel totally at ease with him.

"After what happened in the autumn, he thought we needed something to cheer us up and to help the people on the estate make links to the village, and I agree with him."

"If you're making links with the village, you should have made the effort to use the church hall." When she had moved into the Clayfield Estate, Grace had been disappointed at how few of her fellow residents regularly attended church or supported church events, and, over the last fifteen months, her disappointment had turned to disapproval verging on resentment.

"We can't. A coach carrying a visiting choir misjudged the corner and took out half the north wall. Fortunately nobody was hurt but the church hall's propped up with support and scaffolding and no-one's allowed in until it's rebuilt and that won't be until the insurance companies get their act together."

"That's terrible! What a disaster!"

Maddie nodded. "God moves in a mysterious way."

Her voice was solemn but Grace knew she was mocking her.

"Anyway, that's why Freddie and Mrs Mountjoy negotiated with the Manager to let us use the facilities in the Nursing Home at cut price residents' rates. It was that or the school hall and the Brownies and WI had first dibs on that. And half of any profits our entertainment makes goes to the Church Hall Restoration Fund and the other half to a charity for disadvantaged children."

"If you make any profit." Grace knew she was being grudging but it was hard to accept that nobody seemed to have missed her. It was as if, the moment she left, her space had come together and sealed without a mark to show where she'd been.

"I don't see why we shouldn't make some money. We may not be the coolest or most graceful dancers around but we're pretty funny, and we've kept costs down by donating materials and expertise. I painted any backdrops we needed and designed the costumes, and Rose and Nell sewed them and Amy did anything that needed knitting, and Mrs Mountjoy helped compose some music and wrote some original songs with a bit of help from Freddie and a couple of local kids. For a woman who's over ninety, Mrs M has a wonderful singing voice."

Grace was feeling more miserable and left out all the time. She was tempted to repack her cases and go back to her aunt's large and luxurious house. At least there she had a role, albeit a utilitarian one. But there was Tiggy to consider. She had left him in the catteries far longer than she'd intended. Of course, he'd probably have forgotten her, or be so cross that he refused to acknowledge her. If so, it would be her own fault. He was her darling cat and she loved him, and it was her duty to look after him, even if he rejected her.

"What are you thinking?" asked Maddie.

"I was wondering if we should have left your neighbour alone," said Grace, and felt shocked at the ease with which the lie had tripped off her tongue. "She didn't appear to be badly hurt but still..."

"I'll drop in after the rehearsal and check on her. I don't think there's much wrong apart from an over-active imagination and hysteria. I've warned her about holding that crystal ball over her head. She looks up at it as she turns round and round. It's not surprising if she got dizzy and let it go. It was an accident waiting to happen."

"Is she part of your entertainment group?" asked Grace.

"No, I invited her to join us but she said she didn't like that sort of thing. I don't think our Hatty is much of a team player."

That made Grace feel a bit better. She wondered if there was anything she could do to be part of the Clayfield Carnival Dancers? Not appearing on stage, Grace was terrified of people looking at her and the thought of making a fool of herself made her shudder but maybe she could help behind the scenes.

"I know it's your duty not to let the rest of the dancers down," she said, "but it's a pity we can't start investigating tonight."

Maddie gave her a curious, sideways look. "Who says we can't?" she replied.

Chapter 5

"Lovely to have you back, Grace. We'll have a good chat later. Perhaps we can arrange a get-together for Tiggy and Percy, he's missed his favourite playmate. I can't stop, I must talk to Maddie about the way my antlers wobble when I bob up and down."

Freddie beamed at Grace and bustled back into the throng of people all busy with their own tasks. Some were sorting clothes, others assembling props, while dancers practised their steps and musicians tuned their instruments. As soon as they'd arrived, Maddie had disappeared into the crowd without a second thought for Grace or the mystery they had to solve.

Grace stood at the edge of the hall, uncertain what to do. Most of her neighbours had waved and called how good it was to see her, but the only invitation she'd received to visit anyone was Freddie's request that his Pekingese could have a play date with her cat. And what was all that nonsense about his antlers? Did Carnival Dancing have a dark side? Perhaps a connection with devil worship?

Mrs Mountjoy walked slowly across the room towards Grace. The solid mass of people gave way before her, leaving a channel for her to progress through. Grace wondered if that was out of respect for the old lady's great age or a tribute to the power of her personality.

"Good evening, Grace. So you've decided to come back?"

"Yes. I stayed longer than I intended. My aunt was very pleased to see me."

Mrs Mountjoy didn't reply but her silence was as eloquent as any spoken words.

Grace searched her mind for something uncontroversial to say to break the ice. "This all looks very busy, very exciting. Who arranged it all?"

"Maddie, of course, along with Freddie. He has the big ideas but she's the one with the eye for detail who carries it through. Mind you, it was very kindly intended on his part. I'm sure he thought it would bring her out of herself after the terrible experience she had in October. Freddie's a clever man for all his funny ways and he's very fond of Maddie. He knew, if she was given something to do, she'd throw herself into it and make it work."

Grace's comment about the entertainment hadn't taken them as far away from a discussion of her failings as she'd hoped. But she suspected Mrs Mountjoy would have made sure all conversational roads led back to her desertion of her best friend at a time when she was needed.

"There are a lot of people I don't recognise," she said, "and most of them look too young to be new residents."

"A few of them are people Freddie met at the pub. He joined their darts team, in fact he drove me down a couple of times to have a game."

"Really?" Grace imagined Mrs Mountjoy, armed and dangerous, and shuddered.

"We're thinking about setting up a darts team here but the wretched Manager is being obstructive. She keeps bleating about Health and Safety. As if there weren't enough things in everyday life that any determined person can use to kill or injure their victims."

"I suppose there are." Grace wondered she should interpret this as a threat. "Are those young people some of the residents' grandchildren?"

Mrs Mountjoy followed her gaze to where two tall, slim girls dressed as elves stood laughing with a fair-haired, short young man. They were all clutching musical instruments. "No, they're from the local college. They've formed a quartet. Appearing with us is useful for them to get points for their Performing Arts qualification. I gather that we qualify as a Community Project."

Grace didn't want to be controversial but her passion for accuracy couldn't let this pass. "There's only three of them."

"So I observed. Kyle's late again."

Grace thought Mrs Mountjoy sounded remarkably tolerant of this tardiness but a tall, slim, dark-haired woman, who was standing nearby, said, "That boy! He's so unprofessional! I've told Tempest it's time they threw him out of their quartet."

"That would be a pity," said Mrs Mountjoy, "he's the most talented musician of the lot."

The woman's frown became a scowl. Grace had been thinking she was in her late twenties but now she revised her estimate up by at least ten years. "Tempest is just as talented," she said.

"They're all good musicians," agreed Mrs Mountjoy, "but Kyle is exceptional. I'm sure Temp would agree with that."

The scowl grew more ferocious. "Tempest is obsessed with the wretched boy! I hope she'll grow out of him soon and see how ridiculously unreliable he is."

Mrs Mountjoy didn't look angry but there was a steely quality in her steady gaze that made Grace shiver. "Kyle is the only one of the quartet who isn't still living at home with at least one parent to support him. Cared for children have it hard but it can be even tougher for care leavers."

"Whatever." The woman became aware of Grace listening and glared at her. "Do you mind? This is a private conversation."

"As was the conversation you barged in on," retorted Mrs Mountjoy. "Grace, allow me to introduce Janetta Briar. She's a dance teacher and she's going to appear alongside her pupils. Her daughter, Tempest, is part of the quartet we were discussing. Janetta, this is Grace Winton, one of the estate residents. She's got a lot of influence with the Manager, so you'd better mind your manners or she could have you banned and you'll lose your chance to prance around showing off."

Grace had thought today couldn't get any more confusing but this brought it to new heights. Occasionally, she had mediated with the Manager regarding matters on the estate but getting people banned was definitely outside her remit. The rigid High Anglican part of Grace wanted to deny this untruth; the cowardly part didn't want to cross Mrs Mountjoy; and the human part embraced the way this unpleasant new acquaintance had been put in her place. And what sort of name was Janetta anyway?

"I'm sure the Manager values the volunteer work my sister and I do far too much for that." Janetta tossed her head in a pettish gesture that sent a ripple through her shoulder-length dark hair. She met Mrs Mountjoy's unrelenting gaze and turned back to Grace. "Sorry, didn't mean to snap. Nice to meet you. I haven't seen you around before?"

Despite the politer words, Janetta still looked discontented. Grace wondered whether it was Mrs Mountjoy's rebuke or her remark comparing musical talent that still rankled.

"I've been away. I've only just got back," she said.

"Lucky you, fitting in a winter holiday. Have you been somewhere nice?"

"Visiting my aunt. I felt it was important to spend some time with her."

"Your aunt?" repeated Janetta. "I can understand you'd want to keep in with her. She must be ancient. I guess she won't be around much longer."

Grace knew she could be over-sensitive. Why should a stranger go out of her way to imply that Grace was so old that any of the generation above her must be drawing their last breath. She was sixty-eight but surely she didn't look so decrepit? Then she realised the implication of 'keeping in,' and guessed the woman thought the only good reason for visiting an elderly relative was the expectation of inheritance. She stared at her, uncertain what to say.

Mrs Mountjoy had no such inhibitions. "Of course, as you see, Grace, opening up our activities to outsiders does have some drawbacks. The youngsters are delightful but some of the middle-aged volunteers are very ill-bred."

So war was declared! Grace saw Janetta Briar's face stiffen and blanch with anger, so that the artificial colour on her stood out like a clown's make-up. Whether she was more enraged by being called ill-bred or middle-aged was unclear, but an explosion was definitely imminent. Grace realised she was about to find herself in the middle of the sort of vulgar scene she'd do anything to avoid.

Chapter 6

Maddie had suspected that taking Grace to the rehearsal could be a mistake but she didn't know what else to do with her when she was in such a prickly, defensive mood. If Maddie told her she was busy and she'd see her tomorrow Grace would decide she wasn't wanted; but the chaotic free-for-all of the average rehearsal was the sort of thing she loathed. A lot of the time, Maddie wasn't too keen on it either but consoled herself with the thought that sometimes disorder was a necessary part of the creative process. As a knitter, Grace would never let her wools get tangled, she kept them as firmly regimented as she did the different aspects of her life. As a painter, Maddie tried to prevent her colours merging into a soggy splodge but she knew that sometimes the best effects appeared by chance.

Of course, sometimes the splodge remained just that and the painting had to be abandoned, but that happened less frequently the more experienced an artist became. Unfortunately, Maddie's only experience in running a Christmas entertainment was when she'd been a teacher and that was in a more structured environment. She sent a silent apology to all the children she'd had hard thoughts about in the past. Compared to the residents of the Clayfield Estate and their hangers on, even the most refractory nine-year-old appeared angelic. She was increasingly convinced that, far from emerging as a dazzling show, this entertainment was going to remain a dreary, ill-tempered splodge.

Maddie planned to examine the costumes before any of the other ladies, who called themselves the Wardrobe Staff got there. She worked her way towards the corner of the hall where they were stored, but en route she had pause to deal with various queries. She knew if she didn't satisfy the questioners they'd follow her and the last thing she required was an audience. In this estate, gossip spread like wildfire and grew more extravagant every time it was told. If her suspicions proved true, the only onlooker she could trust to keep quiet was Mrs Mountjoy. Unfortunately it would look odd if she asked a lady in her nineties to bend and stretch to sort out the clothes, and within seconds Mrs Mountjoy's daughter, Nell, and half a dozen other ladies, would be there fussing and interfering and listening to every word they said.

When Grace was onside, she'd be Maddie's first choice to help sort things out and use as a sounding board. Nobody would wonder about Grace helping Maddie with the costumes, but Grace was standing at the edge of the room, looking disapproving. If she didn't up her game, Maddie had a strong suspicion that Mrs Mountjoy would tell her exactly what she thought of people who disappeared with the flimsiest of excuses just when their friends needed their support.

"Maddie!" Amy Bunyan hurried over to catch up with her. She looked as harassed as Maddie felt. "Ron asked me to tell you that the papier-mâché on the snowballs for the snowman dance isn't dry yet. He's got them at home, in front of the fire, but he doesn't want to leave them in case they go up in flames."

Maddie suspected it was more a case of Ron not wanting to leave the fire on a cold, sleety night, but there was no point in saying so. Any harsh words would upset Amy and, if he heard about them, would antagonise Ron, who'd helped a lot more than Maddie had expected him to.

"Don't worry, Amy. I ordered some polystyrene practise balls, they can use those."

"Thank goodness! You're so efficient. If you don't need me at the rehearsal, I'll go home and start running the hairdryer over Ron's balls."

Blissfully unaware of having said anything untoward, she rushed away.

Maddie had hardly recovered her composure when Amy was replaced by Rose Barton, another resident whose ability to twitter and dither tried Maddie's patience to its limits.

"Maddie, do you need me this evening? I was hoping to go home."

"Of course you can go, you don't need my permission."

"I know, but I wouldn't want to let you down."

"You won't. You're not a performer and you've done plenty making the costumes along with Nell." She noticed that Rose's eyes were red-rimmed and she looked very pale. "Are you okay? If you feel poorly I can get somebody to walk you home."

"Oh no! I'm fine. It's Snowy. She got out when I opened the door to come over here and I hate to think of her locked out on such a cold, wet night. She'll be so cold and afraid."

In Maddie's opinion, Snowy was a born survivor as well as an escape artist who could show Harry Houdini a trick or two. Also she was the most pampered cat in Hampshire.

"I'm sure Snowy will be fine." She tried to sound sympathetic. Rose would be hurt if she realised what was in Maddie's mind. She was a lonely woman who adored her pet and Maddie hoped the little runaway would be sitting on the doorstep when Rose got home.

"If I find Snowy and get her inside I can come back," offered Rose.

And, as soon as Rose opened the door, Snowy would escape. Then Rose would return to the hall to explain why she couldn't stay and the whole scenario would start again. "No, it's fine. Stay home in the warm with Snowy."

A glance across the hall showed her that Mrs Mountjoy had cornered Grace, but that was inevitable and Maddie had no intention of stepping between the old lioness and her prey.

She managed to take eight more steps towards the costumes before an apologetic voice said, "Excuse me, Maddie."

She forced herself to smile. "Hi Stan. What can I do for you?"

Of all the older performers who'd volunteered to take part in the show Stan Godwin was the one she knew least about. He was a shy, inarticulate accountant, nearing retirement, and Maddie thought he was lonely since his wife had died, nearly three years ago. He lived some miles from Clayfield but his sister was in the nursing home that was part of the estate.

"I just wanted to let you know that I'd like to miss the next rehearsal, if that's all right with you. At least, it's not that I'd like to, but there's somewhere else I want to be."

"Of course it's okay." Maddie wished everyone would stop coming to her for permission when they wanted to skive. "Are you going somewhere nice?"

"My grandson is having his seventh birthday party and I've been invited."

"You can't miss that. We can always call a separate rehearsal for your polar bear dance. I'm sure we can work something out." She still found it strange that a man who seemed as diffident as Stan could be such an accomplished tap dancer. In their duet he supplied the skill and she provided the comedy.

"Thank you. It's the first time my daughter-in-law has invited me to anything with the children, although, when she was alive, June always used to go."

"Perhaps your daughter-in-law was afraid you wouldn't be interested. You'll have to show how much you're enjoying it and then you may get more invitations. You could invite them to our show."

"Now that's an idea. I wonder what the children would think of their grandpa as a dancing polar bear?"

"They'll love it. It's good of you to give up so much of your time to help us."

"It's a pleasure. I'm usually here at least three times a week to see my sister." He pulled a rueful face. "Not that she usually knows who I am. As long as the nursing staff remember to dress her up in her frills and flounces and put on all her jewellery she's usually content enough."

"That's good." Maddie couldn't think of anything else to say.

"Mind you, when her favourite ruby pendant was misplaced she raised merry hell. Screamed the place down. Thank goodness they found it again." He smiled apologetically. "Sorry, I shouldn't keep boring on. I know you're busy." He hurried away.

Another quick look at Grace revealed that she and Mrs Mountjoy had been joined by Janetta Briar. Now that was definitely a cruel and unusual punishment for Grace's defection.

"Maddie, my costume's split but you weren't here last time," complained the podgiest snowman.

"Tell Nell!" she snapped. Doug had been introduced to the entertainment via Janetta Briar. He knew the protocol for costume repairs but he preferred to think the rules didn't apply to him.

Doug pulled a sulky face and slouched away in the opposite direction to Nell who was inspecting the contents of the costume basket. Maddie managed resist the temptation to aim a kick at his ample backside but it was a close-run thing.

"Maddie, I need to talk to you."

"And I need to talk to you, Freddie. This entertainment is getting completely out of control. What happened to a couple of dance routines and a few Christmas songs?"

"It's grown out of all recognition hasn't it?" Freddie beamed at her. "Who would have thought we had so many talented people in Clayfield? Isn't it wonderful?"

Clearly this was not the time to convince him that his entertainment had to be scaled back.

"Come for lunch tomorrow."

"Thank you, my dear, I'd love to. Now about my antlers..."

"Freddie, I don't give a damn about your antlers."

Nell had beaten her to it and was already unpacking costumes and shaking them out, but Maddie kept going towards that corner, Freddie trailing behind her. She could hear raised voices on the other side of the hall. A quarrel in Grace's vicinity was just what she needed to make her homecoming complete.

"Oh dear! Mrs Mountjoy and Ms Briar seem to be having words!" exclaimed Freddie. "Maddie, do you think you ought to intervene?"

"Not my problem. You were the one who allowed Janetta Briar and her sister to wheedle their way in, so you can deal with it. My money's on Mrs Mountjoy for a Knock Out anyway."

Freddie gave her a reproachful look and started to thread his way back through the hall.

Maddie watched him without the slightest twinge of guilt, but when she saw how stressed Grace looked she knew she'd have to rescue her. Fortunately that didn't require super-ninja skills, just a penetrating voice.

Chapter 7

"Grace, can you come and give me a hand, please?"

Never before had Maddie's voice sounded so welcome to Grace.

"Coming!" As swift off the mark as a professional sprinter, Grace weaved her way through the performers to where Maddie was standing beside a large clothes rail, heavy with an extraordinary array of garments. Beside her, Nell Mountjoy was bending over a large basket and rummaging through its contents.

"What can I do to help?" asked Grace.

"You can help us sort through these costumes. We're behind schedule this evening because I wasn't at the last dress rehearsal. I had to look after the boys while Libby did Parents' Day and Freddie didn't manage to get the costumes put away in good order."

"I'm afraid that was our fault," said Nell. "Mother was tired and Freddie helped me push her wheelchair back to our house, then we invited him in for a drink. Amy and Ron had already gone, you know how he complains if he's kept up late, and Rose would never be able to boss the snowmen the way you do. Not that I mean you're bossy."

"But if the cap fits I might as well wear it," said Maddie. "I'd rather be a bossy cow than a bleating rabbit."

"Rabbits don't bleat," said Grace.

Maddie grinned. "I know. I put that in just to give you the pleasure of correcting me. Come on, we're running out of time to sort these costumes. We have to make sure they're all in good condition. If any need a lot of work, we put them aside for Rose or Nell to mend, preferably before they rip beyond repair.

Smaller jobs, like loose buttons or decorations, go in a different pile for Amy or me to do. Anything that needs washing goes in that big plastic washing basket for Freddie to deal with."

"Freddie does the washing?"

"Don't sound so surprised. This is the 21st century and Freddie is the nearest thing to a New Man that this estate can run to."

"And he wields a pretty skilful iron," added Nell, clambering to her feet. "The polar bear needs a bit of attention, but it should hold out until after this rehearsal without too much damage and Doug's seams need repairing and reinforcing all over. I'll take them home with me after the rehearsal and then pass them on to Freddie to wash."

She glanced across the hall. "Speaking of Freddie, he doesn't seem to have defused the situation. I'd better go and distract Mother before she bops that annoying Briar woman with her stick." Despite this dire prediction, she sounded remarkably cheerful. "It's nice to have you back, Grace. You must come round for tea as soon as you've settled in." She hurried across the hall.

"Nell looks happy," said Grace.

"Yes, I think that's because she's got a lot to do, which makes her feel useful. And her mum's so much better since her medication was sorted out, so Nell doesn't have to worry so much. In fact Mrs M. seems to get more on the ball all the time."

"I noticed," agreed Grace ruefully.

"But it's also because this entertainment seems to have brought the estate together. Everybody is so enthusiastic. Unless the others are all incredibly good actors, which doesn't seem likely from what I've seen of their stage performance skills, I think I'm the only person who's afraid we've been too clever and taken on too much for our own good. Even Ron has been helping out, painting scenery and making props, at his own pace of course."

"That's amazing."

"Well Amy had promised to help out and he didn't like the thought of having to sit at home without her. You know how he sulks if he isn't the centre of attention. We've got way too many divas involved with this show. But one good thing, the new couple who moved in next to Joel, that we thought were snobbish, are really pleasant when you get to know them. He's brilliant on the piano and she's got a lovely voice, so they've promised to lead the community carol singing."

"What about the two Scrabble ladies?" Grace felt she was on firm ground there. The two ladies were so Scrabble obsessed that they spent a lot of time travelling to tournaments and would have no room in their lives for something as trivial as a Christmas entertainment.

"No, they're not performing with us, although they've promised to come and watch. And they're going to run a raffle and they're donating the prizes, apparently they often win things they've got no use for at the social evenings after their tournaments. Freddie can be very persuasive when he tries."

"I can imagine." Grace felt as if the fifteen months in which she'd been a part of this community had trickled away as if they'd never existed. It seemed as if all the residents of the Clayfield Estate had become embroiled in this Christmas pageantry, along with a lot of people she'd never met. There was only one person Maddie had not mentioned: a man of intellectual aspirations, with a strong sense of his own dignity, who would never caper around in a fluffy costume. She clung to this lifeline. "I can't believe that Joel has agreed to be part of this?"

Maddie laughed. "Oh no, Joel's far too pompous for that. He refused 'to prance around masquerading as a penguin or polar bear'," she made quotation signs with her fingers as she spoke, "but he didn't want to be left out so he's offered to do a separate performance, reading extracts from Victorian Christmas stories, and he's hired a Victorian outfit to add 'gravitas to the performance'." She giggled.

"I see." Grace could hear how flat her voice sounded and tried for a slightly more upbeat note. "What did you want me to help you with?"

"I thought you'd appreciate being rescued from the war between Mrs M. and the abominable Janetta."

Grace had to admit she was relieved to be away from the embarrassing scene but she was hurt that Maddie regarded her as so useless she wasn't even needed to help sort out costumes. She thought that the decision she'd been dithering over was being made for her.

"Also, I wanted you to help me go through our snowman costumes as discreetly as possible," said Maddie.

Grace stared at her. "Snowman costumes? You mean you knew all along that the intruder in your neighbour's house had got his outfit from your costumes?"

"Not actually knew, only suspected. After all, at this time of year there are lots of itinerant snowmen wandering round."

"Itinerant snowmen indeed! You were deliberately not telling me because..." Grace stopped mid-sentence as Maddie's hand clenched on her arm. She became aware of a tall, thin woman standing behind her and turned round to face her.

"I'm sorry, I didn't mean to interrupt. I just wanted to apologise to your friend if Janetta said anything to upset her. Janetta isn't really rude but she gets highly-strung before a performance and says things she doesn't mean."

"Apologise away," said Maddie. "Grace Winton, meet Elouisa Briar, Janetta's sister."

Given that information, Grace could see the resemblance in their features, although Elouisa's dark hair was streaked with grey and her face was lined. Grace thought that either she was much older than her sister or she spent a lot less time and money on clothes, hair stylists and make-up.

"How do you do?" She wondered why both Briar sisters seemed to bring out the rigidly formal part of her nature.

Elouisa smiled at her. "It's nice to meet you. I do hope you didn't get the wrong impression of my sister?"

"No, I don't think I did." To her own surprise, her voice had a sarcastic undertone. It wiped the smile from Elouisa's face.

"Well, if Mrs Mountjoy hadn't been so rude about Tempest's musical ability, Janetta wouldn't have been provoked."

"It isn't rude to express the opinion that another young person is even more talented."

Grace expected a similar tantrum to the one Janetta threw but Elouisa merely sighed. "Oh dear! I'm sorry. Janetta was devastated when Tempest grew too tall to be a dancer, although I suppose it was inevitable, as a family we're all quite tall. But having a dancer for a daughter was Janetta's dearest wish and now she's desperate for her to succeed in her chosen branch of the arts."

She dabbed at her nose with a tissue and winced as the paper touched skin that already looked inflamed.

"If you've got a cold, it would be a good idea to go home and keep it to yourself," said Maddie. "There are lots of vulnerable older people here and Janetta won't be happy if you pass it on to her dance pupils just before the show."

"It's not a cold, it's an allergy," snapped Elouisa. "Excuse me, I must go and help Janetta prepare her little snowflakes for their rehearsal."

She hurried away to a corner of the room where a dozen small girls were being corralled if not controlled by Tempest and her fellow musicians.

"That's good," said Maddie, "between us we got rid of her in record time. Let's look at the snowman costumes before somebody else comes to interrupt us."

She rummaged through the hamper tossing the costumes to Grace, who held them up and inspected them for damage and then put them to one side.

"There are seven here," she said when Maddie finished hunting, "and they've all got their noses."

"There should be eight. Did you notice what size they are?"

"Four for quite tall people of average build, one that needs mending for a tall, very plump person, and two for smaller people, although one costume has more give to it than the others."

Grace held up the costumes for Maddie's inspection as she spoke. She felt proud of her own efficiency and hoped for congratulations. None came. Looking round, she saw Maddie's expression. "What's wrong?"

Chapter 8

Maddie realised she'd given herself away. Now it came to it, she wasn't sure how much she should tell Grace, who could be extremely self-righteous. There was no certainty that Grace would allow herself to be guided into keeping quiet until Maddie had discovered whether the truth was as bad as she feared.

"Nothing's wrong. I was just thinking what a nuisance it was that one of the snowmen dancers has been careless with their costume. Not to mention Doug splitting his seams again. Nell and Rose have better things to do with their time than keep making replacements. The snowmen won't be on until later, one of the girl dancers is a doctor and another one's a physiotherapist and they warned me that their shifts tend to drag on. I think I'll tell the snowmen to rehearse in ordinary clothes today."

She had a bad feeling she was prattling too much and Grace's sceptical expression confirmed this.

"You know who the missing costume belongs to, don't you?"

Grace spoke softly, which gave Maddie some hope that she'd be discreet. Anyway, it was clear her bluff hadn't been believed and she had to tell her something. She nodded. "One of the musicians," she said. "Both of the boys have agreed to dance as well as play with their quartet. Although you can't see the difference when they're performing, Nell made their costumes of a lighter more flexible fabric so it's easier to play their instruments while wearing them."

She saw Grace look across the hall to where the three young musicians were still doing battle with the rampaging snowflakes and then back to focus on the smallest snowman costume.

36

"I presume that the missing costume belongs to the other male musician? The one who's also missing?" she said.

"Not missing, just late. Kyle has a lot going on in his life."

"So Mrs Mountjoy mentioned. I must admit I was surprised. I know you're a soft touch when it comes to young people in trouble, even if they have misbehaved, but I thought Mrs Mountjoy was made of tougher stuff. After all, it's obvious that a boy from a bad background is more likely to go astray and you can't deny that the missing costume is his."

Maddie knew, when Grace accused her of being a soft touch, she was referring to an incident that had occurred just before she'd gone to stay with her aunt. She was tempted to point out that, while she had led the rehabilitation mission, Grace had also helped the young woman to sort out her life before desperation caused her to stray any deeper into crime. Maddie knew the chances were low that Grace could be persuaded to take such a lenient view again. She valued her friend's fundamental kindness and decency but Grace had been brought up in a rigidly religious straitjacket and struggled with the concept of the quality of mercy not being strained. It seemed probable she'd dig her heels in when it came to giving Kyle the benefit of the doubt.

"Mrs M. may not be a soft touch but she's a great believer in fair play. She and I agree that giving a dog a bad name and hanging it may be an easy solution but it's not fair."

As she expected, the harsh term made Grace wince.

"I don't know what you mean by that," she said stiffly.

Maddie lost her temper. "I don't expect you know about negativity bias either," she snapped, "or

37

confirmation bias come to that. But, after all those years of teaching Sunday School, I'm sure you know about the concept of a scapegoat."

Grace stared at her. "You feel really strongly about this, don't you?"

Her bemused tone tickled Maddie's sense of humour and her anger evaporated. "Well done for noticing that," she said.

"I suppose there's no reason to assume that the boy took the costume just because it's his one that's gone missing," conceded Grace.

"That's true. In fact it makes sense that anyone who wanted to use the costume to do something dodgy would choose Kyle's because he and Sam have lighter material."

"And the other boy's costume would only fit somebody who was five-foot-six or smaller," said Grace.

"So let's do some investigating before we start accusing anyone," suggested Maddie.

"Yes," Grace smiled at her. "We won't let any dogs get hanged today."

"And no goats sent into the desert loaded with sins," agreed Maddie.

"Hey! Are we doing any rehearsing or are you going to stand around gossiping all day?" complained Doug.

"We wouldn't be so behind if you'd all put your costumes back neatly even when I'm not there to watch you," retorted Maddie. "It's worse than clearing up after a class full of infants. I see that Janetta is ready to go, so we'll start off with the snowflakes. Then the children can go home, we don't want to keep them out too late."

"When are we going to get to the snowman dance?" grumbled Doug. "I've got other things to do than hang round here."

"Then go and do them. We've got a good understudy that can take your place." Maddie kept her fingers crossed that Doug didn't take her at her word. Stan was an obliging understudy and a better dancer than most of the older snowmen, although he didn't have Doug's comedy value, but if Kyle didn't turn up, they'd need Stan to fill in there.

To her relief, Doug grumbled a bit under his breath but followed the other adults across the hall to sit and watch the snowflakes.

Maddie didn't bother to watch the children dance. This was Janetta's province and she'd make sure the performance did her and her dance school credit. However irritating Maddie found Janetta, she had to admit the children would bring in parents and grandparents from the village and would appeal to a lot of the older residents. Although a glance at Mrs Mountjoy informed her that the formidable old lady looked far from enraptured.

Maddie grabbed her costume from the rack and retired behind a screen to get changed. It was a matter of moments to strip down to the leggings and tee-shirt she was wearing under her jeans and jumper but more of a struggle to get her costume sitting squarely with all of the padding in the right places. When her costume was as comfy as it was liable to get, she remembered she'd put her mobile on silent and muttered to herself about her own stupidity. This wretched show was taking up all her time and energy, so she was forgetting the most routine things. She got her phone out of her jeans' pocket and checked it. To her relief, there was a message from Kyle: ON WAY. Not exactly informative, but at least he wasn't on the run after biffing Hatty with her crystal ball.

Her reappearance from behind the screen coincided with the snowflakes taking their curtsies, a

39

procedure that could go on for longer than their scheduled performance unless curtailed. Maddie was about to usher them off the stage when the hall door opened and Kyle slipped inside. He looked breathless and overheated despite the icy weather. Maddie pushed her way across the hall to greet him, although she was beaten to her target by Tempest, who was fifty years younger and had much longer legs.

"Where have you been?" demanded Tempest. "We've been waiting for you and everyone's furious."

"More worried than furious," interposed Maddie. "Are you okay?"

"Yeah. Well no, not really. My bike's been nicked. I had to get a bus as far as Waterlooville and jog from there."

"Oh, poor you!" Tempest hugged him, then wrinkled her nose in disgust. "You're all sweaty!"

"Like I said, I jogged."

"Where was it stolen from? Have you told the police?" asked Maddie.

"Down the city centre and no, there's no point telling the police, They won't do anything."

"Probably not, but it might turn up."

"But he'd have to tell the police what he'd been doing and he wouldn't want that." Janetta's voice was shrill enough to reach the furthest corners of the hall. The look she directed at Kyle was a curious mixture of venom and triumph.

"What do you mean?" It was Tempest who took up the challenge. She glared at her mother.

"I've seen what he's been up to in Portsmouth, in the shopping arcade." Now Janetta sounded triumphant. "He was there with his fiddle, begging, wearing that snowman outfit he stole."

Chapter 9

Maddie knew it was up to her to take control. Janetta's accusations were certain to inflame many of her listeners, the majority of whom were elderly, middle-class and reasonably affluent. Begging and stealing were anathemas to them and it seemed unlikely that Kyle was going to speak in his own defence. It was a long time since Maddie had felt so inadequate. She wished she was still in her ordinary clothes. What chance did a short, plump penguin, with extra stuffing, have against a tall and toxic snow queen?

"Busking isn't the same as begging." Apparently Freddie felt no such reservations about his reindeer costume, even though his antlers wobbled violently as he pushed his way through the onlookers to join them. "Busking is standing outside in all weathers, offering one's talent to people and hoping that some of them are generous enough to pay a few coins for their entertainment."

"And borrowing is not the same as stealing." Mrs Mountjoy did not need to force her way to the centre of action. She too had taken advantage of the snowflake dance to change into the costume she had designed and Nell had made. As a tree of the forest, about to be decked with garlands, she was awe-inspiring. Always a commanding figure, her swishing, long, green skirts gave her a primitive magnificence, the regal effect enhanced by her daughter and another helper scuttling behind her, holding up the trailing tinsel like a glittering train.

"I saw Kyle wearing the snowman suit on one of his busking gigs and very good he was too," said Freddie, "but we can't have people walking off with the costumes for their own purposes and I explained that to him. If that happened, people would forget to replace them and we'd end up with a performance more like The Full Monty or Hair, and let's face it, most of us are too thin on top to get away with that nowadays."

Maddie tried to imagine the Manager's face if they introduced nudity into what she referred to as their 'dear little show.' The prospect of her horror almost reconciled Maddie to the thought of all those flabby, wrinkled, old bodies on public display.

"We can always hire wigs," she murmured, but fortunately not loud enough for anyone to hear.

"There you are!" announced Janetta triumphantly. "It's not just me who has seen him masquerading as a snowman in that stolen costume."

"Will you kindly stop trying to make trouble!" snapped Maddie. She was tempted to stamp her foot for emphasis but remembered in time that the orange webbed flipper would add farce not power. "Freddie, did you insist on Kyle returning the costume to the box?"

"No, I got him to return it to me and I washed and dried it and checked it for damage. It was in good condition so I put it back in the box myself, three days ago."

"I didn't steal it." Kyle found his voice for the first time. "I wasn't going to keep it. Like Mrs Mountjoy said, I borrowed it."

"And who's to say you didn't borrow it again once Freddie had cleaned it up?" said Doug from his place amongst the onlookers. "There's too many of these buskers hanging round, blocking up the pavements, taking money from legitimate shopkeepers by lowering the tone of the neighbourhood."

"I don't need to borrow the snowman costume anymore, I've got a good one of my own," announced Kyle.

"Another snowman costume?" asked Maddie, thinking of Hatty's assailant and praying there weren't two such rogue outfits sculling round the estate.

"No, it's a pied piper's coat, multicoloured. I made it from scraps of velvet I had left over," said Nell. "It was rather fun to do after all the white fleece and fur I had to sew for the snowmen and polar bear." She realised that everybody's eyes were on her and blushed.

"Freddie gave me a top hat too, and it pulls in a lot more punters than the snowman outfit did," said Kyle, "and I can wear it other times than just Christmas."

"My suggestion," said Mrs Mountjoy proudly.

"Of course it was," said Maddie, grinning at her.

"But Nell's the design and sewing genius," continued Mrs Mountjoy. "No need to look so flustered, my dear, you know it's true. When Freddie told me about the busking, I thought straight away that what Kyle needed was a bright outfit that grabbed the audience's attention but with lots of variety so it could get plenty of use but practical so it didn't show the dirt."

Maddie fished her mobile from the concealed pocket that she'd assured Nell all well-dressed penguins required and checked the time. Nearly an hour gone and the adults hadn't even started rehearsing. "Hopefully, whoever's taken Kyle's snowman costume will return it," she said, "the snowmen can dance in their ordinary clothes if they prefer." She glanced across at a tall, slender woman standing at the back of the group. "As long as that's okay with our Carnival Dance choreographer?"

43

The young woman shrugged. "No problem as far as I'm concerned."

"I would advise you to rehearse wearing costumes, those of you who haven't misplaced them, that is," announced Janetta. "Professionals like myself may be able to carry off a convincing performance without costumes but amateurs need all the help they can get."

"Janetta's right," chimed in Douglas, "start as we mean to go on, that's what I say. When we've got such a talented dancer to guide us, we ought to listen to every word she says."

"You mean hang on her lips like you do?" said Mrs Mountjoy acidly.

Maddie felt control of the situation slipping away from her again. "Everybody who has a costume to wear and wants to wear it, get changed now. I'm sure Kyle is sufficiently professional that he'll manage a great performance until we recover his costume or make another one. But I warn you, if we don't start the rehearsal in the next five minutes, I'm cancelling it and going home. As Doug pointed out, most of us have got better things to do than stand round here."

Freddie leapt into action. "Maddie's right! We're wasting time! Places, everybody! Let's get this show on the road!"

As nobody had remembered to give out a rehearsal schedule, this flurry of commands was met by bemused silence, broken only by an uncertain shuffling of feet.

Maddie braced herself to try and take command yet again when an apologetic voice spoke from the doorway. "Oh dear! I hope we're not interrupting anything?"

Amy edged her way through the parents who'd collected their young dancers and stayed around to enjoy the drama. She scurried in, pulling a tartan shopping trolley, followed by her husband, Ron, leaning heavily on his stick.

"Are we in time for the snowman dance?" she continued. "The papier-mâché balls have all dried nicely so we brought them over. Say what you like, polystyrene balls just aren't the same."

Chapter 10

Grace was longing for some excuse to escape the rehearsal. In fact she wanted to avoid the whole business of the show, which she feared would be a disaster. She'd do a great deal to avoid placing herself in embarrassing situations and she found the sight of other people making fools of themselves deeply distressing. Now was clearly a good time to leave. She headed towards Maddie to say she was tired after her journey and would see her tomorrow but Freddie thrust a clipboard, with paper and pen attached, into her hands.

"Grace, it would be wonderful if you could take some notes of the performances. Just write down anything that needs altering or that we need to focus on. You're so efficient, I know you'll be a great asset. We're all so glad you got back in time to be part of this."

Grace had no choice. She had to accept her new role. "I'll do my best, but I'm not sure what I'm doing."

My dear, none of us have the foggiest idea what we're doing, so you'll fit right in."

That was definitely not reassuring! Everything inside Grace cringed. She wished she had a time machine that would transport her instantly back to her aunt's carefully controlled house where nothing unexpected ever happened.

To Grace's surprise, the entertainment was not the ordeal by mortification that she'd anticipated. It was clearly an amateur production but the musicians were excellent and each of the adult dance acts had a certain humorous charm. When the performers weren't actually appearing they came down to sit in the front to be part of the audience. The constant shift of people made it hard for Grace to focus, especially as she knew the names of only a few of the performers and found it hard to identify people behind their masks. All of the acts were linked by the penguin and the reindeer, aka Maddie and Freddie, who bobbed in and out, sometimes mimicking the dancers, sometimes doing their own thing. Freddie was undeniably sprightly and Grace was not convinced that even seamstresses as talented as Nell and Rose could prevent his antlers from wildly waggling; nevertheless she made a dutiful note of it. Maddie made an adorably cheeky penguin, and the dance where the tall, thin polar bear tried to teach the short, plump penguin to tap dance had all the audience laughing and clapping in time to the music.

She moved to the back of the audience, where she could get a better view, and tried to concentrate. Alas for her good intentions, within seconds she was joined by Elouisa Briar.

"It's such a pity, isn't it?" she whispered loudly. "So foolish of them. When they have a performer as talented as my sister available, they should have asked her to star in the whole show and direct it too."

"But this makes it a lot more varied. And it's supposed to be an event for the whole village," protested Grace, flinching away from the warm, moist hissing of Elouisa's breath in her ear. She glanced to where Janetta was sitting with the large man who had supported her view about busking, then she tried to concentrate on the action on the stage, where Freddie the reindeer had jived into view and was trying to woo the Maddie penguin to abandon the polar bear and dance with him.

"As if anybody is going to enjoy seeing a lot of amateurs making fools of themselves," muttered Elouisa.

The roar of laughter as Freddie and Maddie moonwalked off the stage made a nonsense of this statement, especially as it was followed by a display of very competent tap dancing by the polar bear.

"You were saying?" said Grace as the applause eventually died away.

"Well of course they're going to clap each other, that's the nature of these amateur events. Excuse me." Elouisa stalked off to sit beside her sister, as the hefty snowman got up to join his companions on the stage.

The snowman dance was the least polished of the routines. The three female carnival dancers were all good and Kyle managed very well, doing the dance steps neatly while playing his violin, but the other young male musician clearly found it hard to multi-task. The large man was lighter on his feet than Grace had expected but he was often out of time with the others and, behind his snowman's mask, it was obvious that he was glaring at his fellow dancers, as if implying that the errors were theirs rather than his. However, he gained the loudest laugh of the evening when his much-tried costume split down the back seam, providing the audience with a view of his red-and-blue striped boxers. Freddie and Maddie weaved in and out of the snowmen dancers. He was as sprightly as ever but she seemed to have lost her bounce. Grace was concerned that she was over-doing things and had got too tired.

There followed several singing acts, during which Maddie and Freddie stood at the side of the stage and swayed in time to the music, occasionally taking on the guise of a musical conductor or miming playing various musical instruments. Grace had to admit that

Freddie played a very effective air guitar. Most of the singers were pleasant enough, but the white-haired, elderly lady, who sang 'Que Sera Sera' in a cloyingly whimsical way set Grace's teeth on edge. Fortunately, her suffering was alleviated by Freddie and Maddie pushing on stage an artificial bush adorned with white paper roses and proceeding to pick them, one at a time, and dance around with them.

Relief came when the four college students performed a selection of traditional Christmas tunes. Grace could believe that they were destined to be professionals but her worst fears were fulfilled when an elderly juggler took to the stage. Even when attempting to juggle two balls he often fumbled them. Grace hated to watch anyone look foolish but, just as she felt that she was drowning in embarrassment for the man, the reindeer, polar bear and penguin reappeared. The reindeer and the polar bear stood on either side of the stage behind the juggler and tossed two balls to each other while the short and portly penguin stood in the middle, jumping up and down in a vain attempt to intercept the balls, although her leaps got less and less vigorous and once or twice she almost fell. Grace felt cross with Freddie. Surely he realised that this was too much for Maddie?

Her concerns were confirmed in the finale, when Mrs Mountjoy, magnificent in her guise of leafy green, stood centre-stage and sang 'Oh Christmas Tree', accompanied by soft music from the quartet, while two of the female snowmen, the snow queen, polar bear, reindeer and penguin festooned her with glittering garlands. Then separately or in pairs they did a short final dance. Maddie was last, waltzing with Freddie, and it was evident to Grace that he practically carrying her. Now she felt very worried about her friend.

However, as the rehearsal ended, she switched her fretting back to herself, afraid that she'd be asked to decipher her scrappy notes and relay them to the performers. The thought of explaining and justifying her comments appalled her.

"Thanks everybody," said Maddie, "once we managed to get underway that went very well. I'm sure you all want to get home, or maybe down to the pub. Unless there's anything urgent anyone wants to mention, or Grace has something she really needs to say, I'll run through her observations with her later." She grinned at Grace, who felt a surge of gratitude that Maddie understood how uncomfortable she felt and was letting her off the hook.

"It's usual to hear the feedback straight after a rehearsal," remarked Janetta, "but, of course, one can't expect the same standards from amateurs."

"That's true, of course," agreed Maddie, "that's why we don't keep your little students behind while their parents are waiting so that we can correct all their faults. As we agreed, you can deal with any major problems at their next lesson. I'm sure in professional dance schools they deal with errors straight away, but this is a long way from the White Lodge and it would be a pity to spoil the kids' pleasure in their hobby, not to mention embarrassing you as their teacher."

Janetta looked offended but said nothing more.

"One thing that can't be left until later is sorting out my costume," complained the overweight snowman. "You skimped on the material and now it's given way in several places. It's not right, embarrassing a man when he's trying to do a good deed for the community."

"The costumes are very well made," said the tall, thin man who'd played the polar bear, "much better than a lot of the ones you can hire."

"I agree with that," said Freddie. Grace was afraid he was going to mention his antlers again but instead he said, "Doug, kindly put your costume in the basket for me to wash and, when it's clean, I'll pass it on to Nell to triple reinforce the seams."

"I was thinking quadruple reinforcing would be more appropriate," said Mrs Mountjoy.

"It's still not good enough," grumbled Doug. "I've got my position in the community to consider. Nobody likes being made a fool of."

Grace's irritation overwhelmed her diffidence. "There's one item on my list that seems pertinent to this discussion." She held up her clipboard and read out, "Suggestion: any snowman that is liable to split their seams should make a point of wearing thick, white underpants in order to avoid giving offence to any of the more sensitive members of the audience."

She felt herself blush, overwhelmed by her own temerity, especially when she saw Doug's scowling face turn towards her accusingly.

"Who is this woman anyway?" he demanded.

"This lady is Grace," retorted Freddie, "and she's the latest member of our Entertainment Committee. Now let's get packed up. And please make sure we've done it properly this time, then we can get out of here."

Chapter 11

"Am I really?" asked Grace, as she and Maddie walked slowly back to their cottages.

"Are you really what?" Maddie's mind was on other things. She was tired and her arthritic hip was aching after so much vigorous exercise but she knew she ought to knock on Hatty's door and check she was okay. What had happened to her was odd, even considering Hatty's usual peculiarities, and Maddie hoped it had not been a bad idea to leave her alone. Also, a small doubt kept niggling at her regarding Kyle. Was she right in insisting he wasn't Hatty's attacker?

"Am I really part of the Entertainment Committee?" persisted Grace.

"If you're willing to be. I don't think Freddie was trying to railroad you but he couldn't resist a chance to finish your good work and put Doug firmly in his place." Maddie was sure Grace was trying to avoid being co-opted onto the committee but she wasn't inclined to let her off the hook. She told herself it would be good for Grace to re-establish her interest in the community. If she carried on being an outsider, the chances were high she'd drift away for good.

"I'm not sure I could contribute anything," Maddie could hear near-panic in Grace's voice. "I'm not a performer. I can think of nothing worse than appearing on a stage."

"We've got more than enough performers. What we need are committee members with common-sense, organisational skills and the ability to be part of a united front against Doug, Janetta and Elouisa."

"I can't imagine why they agreed to be part of the entertainment? It doesn't seem their sort of thing at all. Although I suppose Janetta gets a chance to show off her pupils' dancing."

"Yes, she never misses a chance to build up her dance school business, or to cavort around striking romantic poses. And Elouisa will always support her. She runs a ballet school shop alongside Janetta's dance school. Don't let her suspect your knitting skills or she'll start nagging you to make cross-over cardigans for her."

"I've made one for your granddaughter," admitted Grace.

"I'm sure she'll love it. But Elouisa exploits her knitters. I admit I'm biased against her and Janetta. I can't do with their pretentious games. Temp told me that the names on their birth certificates are Janet and Louise but that wasn't fancy enough for them. Temp says that she'll never forgive them for lumbering her with a name like Tempest."

"It is an extraordinary name to give a child." Grace sounded disapproving.

"Apparently Janetta was dancing in the ballet The Tempest when she realised she was pregnant."

"I see. You seem to get on well with Tempest and Kyle."

"I like young people and they're both nice kids as well as being very talented. Poor Temp is sure her mother and aunt are trying to sabotage her relationship with Kyle. There's no dad in the mix and Janetta and Elouisa brought her up between them and they hope to keep their stranglehold on her. They're always telling her how it's her duty to make them proud of her to pay them back for all they've done for her." Maddie hoped that this would make Grace more tolerant of the young musicians; after all, she'd suffered from the demands of smothering parents and had ended up devoting over forty years to the care of her demanding, ungrateful father.

"What about Doug?" asked Grace. "He doesn't seem the type to give up his evenings to caper around dressed as a snowman. And what did he mean about his position in the community?"

"He's an antiques dealer. He's got a posh shop in Southsea. I suspect Janetta told him there may be some plump pickings if he gets on good terms with the older people here."

"That's horrible! Do you have any reason for thinking that? I mean other than him being thoroughly obnoxious? Maybe he's taking part in the show because he fancies Janetta and wants to spend time with her?"

"It's not just me who suspects his motives. A few weeks ago he called on Mrs Mountjoy at a time when he must have known that she'd be alone because Nell was scheduled to be fitting costumes over at the main house. He arrived uninvited and showed a lot of interest in Mrs M.'s collection of jade. He told her there was nothing of any great value but, if she wanted a bit of spending money, perhaps to treat herself and her daughter to a short holiday, he'd be happy to take her little bits and pieces off her hands, and it would be their secret."

"How despicable! What did Mrs Mountjoy do?"

Maddie laughed. "She strung him along and asked how much he'd give her. She told me that, even allowing for fluctuations in the antiques market, the price he offered was derisory, which confirmed her opinion of him. We're pretty sure he'd been told about that time last year when her health problems affected her mental capacity and hadn't realised that the changes in her medication have sorted her out. It worries her that he'll take advantage of other people who are really vulnerable. He's using the show to weasel his way into the community."

"That's terrible! Some of the people in the Nursing Home have things like coin collections and jewellery. They could be easy prey for somebody like him."

"Freddie and I have both warned the Manager but I'm not sure we had much effect. You might have more luck. She thinks we're troublemakers but she listens to you."

"I'll try."

Maddie noted, with satisfaction, that Grace was re-engaging with life on the the estate once again. "Thank you." To her relief, they had reached their row of cottages. She was tired and the distance between the cottages and the large mansion, which housed the nursing home and entertainment facilities, seemed further away every time she trudged it.

"If you come with me to check Hatty's all right we could grab some supper together," she suggested.

"All right. If that head injury is more serious than we thought you might need some help, but I do hope she won't start talking about ghosts again."

"She usually does," admitted Maddie. "Let's get it over with." She limped along Hatty's front path and knocked briskly on the door before Grace could change her mind and find an excuse to abandon her.

"Come in, come in," Hatty swung open the door and greeted them with her usual exuberance. In fact Maddie thought she was even more exhilarated than normal. "It's so kind of you to come and give me the chance to thank you for helping me in my hour of need. I have just boiled the kettle and can have a pot of herbal tea ready within minutes."

"Don't go to any trouble. We don't plan to come in," said Maddie, "we just wanted to check you're okay after you bumped your head."

"I insist ... enter ... enter." Hatty held the door wide open and made a powerful waving motion back and fore, as if they were some sort of exotic essence she wished to waft into her house rather than two elderly and far from insubstantial women.

Chapter 12

"We'll just come in for a minute then." Maddie gave Grace an apologetic look and hissed "Don't drink the tea." "How's your head, Hatty? Have you had any after-effects?"

"Of course not. The blows delivered by a restless spirit are as nothing to a powerful medium. My only concern is for the poor lost soul who strikes out against one who wishes them well and could help them find peace."

Maddie shook her head. "Hatty, it wasn't a spirit that attacked you. It was a person, a housebreaker dressed up as a snowman."

Hatty stared at her. "That sounds most unlikely."

More unlikely than a ghostly snowman? Maddie didn't dare look at Grace. If she did she wouldn't be able to stop herself from giggling. She had to admit, if you believed in the supernatural, Hatty's point of view was entirely reasonable. The only possible way she could convince Hatty that her visitor had been a solid flesh-and-blood person, clothed in synthetic white fleece fabric, was to produce the evidence of the orange nose they'd found in the garden and, at the moment, she'd rather keep the probable involvement of the Carnival Dancers private between Grace and herself.

"Did the person who assaulted you look familiar?" asked Grace. "You couldn't see his face but there may have been something in the way he moved. I know you haven't been here very long but maybe you've seen him around the village or the estate? Perhaps you could tell if he is young or middle-aged?"

She received a reproachful, somewhat pitying look. "No, I've never seen the spectral being before. It's unlikely the poor shy spirit would venture out amongst crowds of unbelievers. It honoured me with contact because I am sensitive to its desperate plight."

"Not much of an honour, contacting you by bashing you over the head with your favourite crystal ball," retorted Maddie.

"You don't understand the turmoil that a lost spirit is suffering. That is why it could never manifest itself to you." Hatty turned back to Grace. "I didn't recognise the spirit that came to me, although I searched for traces that it might be the poor lost soul who lived here before me and died by violence. He is here still. Often I feel his presence close by me, especially in the night."

Maddie suppressed a shudder and, glancing at Grace, spotted a similar look of revulsion on her face. Norman, their late neighbour, had not been a nice man. They hadn't wanted him in close proximity to them when he was alive, and it was even less desirable now he'd been dead for several weeks.

However, one thing did sound plausible. "I have to admit, if Norman did want to make contact beyond the grave, he'd do it in the meanest, most destructive way possible," she said.

"Oh Maddie! No wonder his poor spirit is restless with so much negative feeling centred on the place where he spent his last hours on earth." Hatty sounded reproachful.

"You didn't know him," retorted Grace. "I was brought up not to speak ill of the dead but the truth is Norman was a very unpleasant man. I don't believe his spirit is lingering here but, if it is, it won't be for any good purpose."

"And why come back as a snowman?" added Maddie. "He really wasn't the sort of man who went in for dressing up games."

Hatty looked sulky. "The ways of the Spirit World are not always easy for practitioners to interpret, even a medium as skilled as myself, especially when unbelievers cloud my vision."

There was an awkward silence. Maddie could think of plenty of things to say but it was better not to squabble with neighbours unless it was unavoidable.

It seemed that Grace was thinking the same thing because she switched the subject to an innocuous enquiry. "Are you settling in well, Hatty? It's always a big upheaval, moving to a new place. At least, I found it so when I came down from London. Of course, it must be different if you've got family living close by, like Maddie has?"

"One place is much like another for me. All my loved ones have departed this spectral plane but they are still with me always, watching over me."

"Why did you choose to come to a small village like Clayfield?" asked Grace. "There must be other places with better transport. I wanted to live in the country but wouldn't have considered moving here if I hadn't had my car."

"I came because I was guided to do so."

"Guided?"

Maddie wanted to warn Grace not to push this. It was evident that this conversation was also doomed to head back to the supernatural.

"On the day I received a letter from the local council confirming that my house in Portsmouth was going to be purchased and demolished to make way for a new housing development, I also saw a leaflet advertising the Clayfield Estate. That's why I decided it was meant to be."

Maddie knew that relying on a coincidence didn't really make more sense than allowing a spirit to guide you to choose a future home, but somehow it seemed more pleasantly serendipitous and, from her relieved expression, Grace felt the same.

"I'm sure it was a good choice and you are near enough to Portsmouth to keep up with your old friends."

Hatty smiled. "Yes, I travel into Portsmouth to visit my regular clients. They say they would find it impossible to cope with their loneliness and grief if I was not able to put them in contact with their dear departed loved ones. Once the spirit that lingers in this house has been released, I may invite some clients to visit me. I could not do that in my previous house. It was over a hundred years old and imbued with the aura of all those who had lived there before and have then passed beyond."

"Sounds crowded," snapped Maddie. She was tired of tiptoeing around Hatty's feelings.

"It was," agreed Hatty. "I'm lonely without them."

"Perhaps you should fill the gap with some human contact," suggested Grace. "Have you met any of the people performing in the Christmas show?"

Only one," said Hatty, "and I didn't really like him. "It was that large man who buys antiques. He talked his way in here a few days ago and I thought I was never going to get rid of him."

"Douglas?" said Maddie. "You didn't sell him anything, did you?"

Hatty turned red. Maddie thought she looked flustered. "Of course I didn't sell him anything! Why would you think I'd do anything like that?"

"There's no need to be offended, Hatty. It's just that you're a newcomer here and Douglas seems to have been doing the rounds trying to buy antiques from a lot of the residents. I wouldn't like to think he'd over persuaded you."

Unless they were sure that Doug was up to no good, it was unwise to start lots of gossip about his business practices.

Hatty seemed to relax. "Oh, I see. No, he didn't persuade me into selling him anything. Now, I'm grateful to you for coming to visit me but I really must get on with trying to contact the poor lost spirit that reached out to me earlier. You are both welcome to stay and join me in my efforts."

"No, thanks, we'll pass on that. It's time we went home." Maddie stood up. She noted, with amusement, that Grace had sprung to her feet and was heading towards the door with unladylike alacrity. "Good luck with the reaching out. I hope it doesn't involve bloodshed this time. And, Hatty, no more keening tonight. Grace and I want to have our supper in peace."

Chapter 13

"So what have we found out?" asked Maddie, as she ladled steaming lentil soup into two bowls and slid one of them across the table to Grace.

"I'm not sure." Grace stirred her soup and then raised her spoon and took a tentative sip, wincing as it burned her lips and tongue.

"Blow on it," advised Maddie, suiting her actions to her words.

Grace hesitated. She imagined her aunt's disdain if she had observed anybody doing something as vulgar as blowing on their soup. Aunt Penelope had a code of conduct as rigid as that laid down by Grace's late father, although less interspersed with hell fire Bible quotes.

"I know, 'a lady never huffs and puffs on her soup'." It seemed that Maddie had read her mind. "I promise won't tell anyone."

Grace knew she was being laughed at but she didn't mind. She spooned up another mouthful, gave a delicate puff and put it in her mouth. Delicious! Of course, everything that Maddie cooked was excellent.

"We know that Douglas has talked his way into Hatty's house," said Maddie, "but he didn't buy anything from her."

"At least, that's what she says," amended Grace. "You know her better than I do, but I thought she looked distinctly shifty when you asked her about that."

"I agree. Although I don't really know her very well. I feel like I want to rip aside all those layers of gobbledygook she keeps spouting to see if there's anything genuine underneath."

"I think she does believe that she's really capable of contacting spirits," said Grace. When Maddie sounded so exasperated, she felt willing to be generous. "But, of course, it's a foolish and dangerous thing to do."

"Especially when snowmen spooks start hurling crystal balls at her," agreed Maddie. "Douglas could have checked out the place but there's no way he could have fitted into the missing snowman suit."

"Or squeezed through the kitchen window," said Grace. "He could have set up a robbery with a conspirator who's slimmer and fitter than him." If so, Kyle was the likeliest candidate for second villain but she wasn't going to anger Maddie by saying so.

"If that's the case, whatever he spotted must be worth a significant amount of money. I don't like Douglas and I don't think he'd stop at much to make a big profit, but I can't believe he'd risk being tied into a robbery like that. His style's far more that of a con artist with a touch of the bully boy."

"And there would be the risk that the person he'd employed to do the robbery could turn on him, especially if they got caught. I presume that his respectable reputation is important in his business."

"Not just his business. He's trying to become a local councillor as well."

Grace sighed. "What an appalling thought. I wish I knew more about antique furniture. I wouldn't pay more than a few pounds for anything in Hatty's living room. It's all so ugly and clunky. But that could just be my ignorance."

"And mine," agreed Maddie. "I wonder if Douglas managed to wangle his way upstairs when he invaded Hatty. Perhaps she keeps her good stuff up there."

"If she's got any good stuff. Surely if she had, she wouldn't have bought Norman's old stuff, much less live with it."

"That's the thing I find really odd. When I told you that Hatty had chosen Norman's cottage because she didn't have the money for the newly built ones, I honestly believed it. She's never said she was strapped for cash but I assumed she was because she'd taken over that hideous furniture and she lives very moderately. She never entertains and she goes everywhere on foot or by bus. But if she's just sold a house in Southsea, she should have plenty of money, and surely she'd have some nicer furniture of her own that she'd have brought with her."

"It's not unusual that she doesn't drive or have a car if she's lived in Portsmouth all her life. A lot of people living in cities don't use cars, and not all women of our generation learned to drive. I was only allowed to do so because my father thought it would be useful for me to do parish errands and drive him around. The car was always in his name until he became too confused to handle his financial affairs." Grace felt a fleeting spurt of gratitude for her father's selfishness, which had meant he allowed her that small amount of independence. "But I see what you mean about the furniture. Do you think she's got a secret reason for keeping it?"

"What sort of reason?"

"Well, Norman was a miser. Perhaps he concealed lots of money or gold or something in the furniture."

Maddie chuckled. "Or pirate treasure, with Spanish doubloons and a fortune in rubies and emeralds. I love it when your imagination runs riot, Grace."

"Well you're the one who said this was like a Scooby Doo adventure," retorted Grace. She disliked being laughed at but she knew there was no malice behind Maddie's teasing.

"True. It's certainly weird enough to merit a few Scooby snacks but, failing that, my lemon biscuits will have to do."

Maddie stood up and cleared the table of soup bowls and returned from the kitchen area bearing a tin full of biscuits, which Grace knew from experience would be impossible to resist.

"So you think Hatty has some ulterior motive for keeping Norman's furniture?" she asked.

"I don't know." Maddie bit so viciously into her biscuit that it disintegrated in a shower of crumbs. "Maybe she believes Norman's ghost is more likely to visit her if she keeps his old familiar surroundings, but I think there's something she's hiding."

"I assume you trusted her until tonight if you swapped spare keys with her?" Grace knew there was no point in dwelling on this. After all, she'd been the one who'd left the estate. But her jealousy was like an itching, half-healed wound that she longed to pick at.

"I didn't do a swap. I agreed to take her key when she asked but I told her a friend already had mine ... I'll give it back to you before you leave. If that's okay with you?"

"Of course." Grace tried not to let her pleasure show too obviously. "So you didn't trust her right from the start?"

"Let's say I reserved judgement and I'm still doing so. You know, it might be an idea to ask Freddie if any of Norman's furniture was valuable. Not that it proves a lot unless we can get upstairs to see what Hat's got stashed up there."

"Why Freddie?" demanded Grace.

"He knows a lot about antiques but he's not the sort who boasts about his expertise."

"Like his skill in recognising the difference between stone griffins and concrete replicas?" said Grace sarcastically.

"You know perfectly well that he put that concrete griffin on his wall to tease the snobbier residents. They couldn't work out what to make of him. Anyway, I won't hear a word against that blessed griffin. It helped save my life."

"I know." Impulsively, Grace leaned forward and grasped Maddie's hand, then embarrassed by this unusual show of affection, withdrew again hastily.

"Does Freddie still plan to put up a marble griffin statue on The Green?" she asked.

"He's still hoping to. And I intend to help him get his wish, whatever the Manager says."

"I'll do what I can to help," promised Grace, but in her mind was the unspoken proviso, 'If I'm still here.'

Chapter 14

Grace was up and about early, eager to collect her cat from the cattery. Deep down she was anxious. She'd phoned twice a week to check on Tiggy's welfare but now she wondered if the cattery people had wanted to reassure her and he was miserable, even pining. The guilt she'd battened down during her stay with her aunt had reawakened since her return to the estate and now it was gnawing at her. It had been wrong of her to take herself off for so long, much longer than she'd intended. She shouldn't have abandoned her poor little cat like that, even though the cattery had an excellent reputation. If he didn't love her anymore it would serve her right. She promised herself that, whatever decision she made about her future, she'd keep Tiggy with her from now on.

Collecting Tiggy was daunting in its impersonal efficiency. It wasn't that the staff member who dealt with the discharge was unpleasant. Far from it, she was courteous and friendly as she carried Tiggy in and put him down on the table in front of Grace, so that she could see that he was in good condition, then inserted him into his carrying basket. But Grace had hoped that Tiggy would miaow to greet her, maybe purr, or best of all leap into her arms. But he just sat on the table, looking around, his green eyes narrow slits. He hadn't yowled or struggled when inserted into his basket, just gave a small, plaintive mew. All the way home, Grace wondered if incarceration in an institution had broken Tiggy's spirit. Even though it was advertised as the equivalent of a four star hotel for cats.

Safely home, all doors and windows closed, Grace opened the cat basket. She put down a sachet of Tiggy's favourite salmon-flavoured cat food and a clean litter tray. She wouldn't let Tiggy outside until he'd settled into his home again and, hopefully, forgiven her, if he ever did.

At first he crept out, ginger fur bristling, tail like a bottle brush. He circled the living room, slowly, cautiously, stopping every few steps to sniff the furniture and floor. Grace sat down on the sofa, keeping still and quiet. She resisted the longing to coax him. Even when he moved into the kitchen area she didn't turn round to check whether he was eating. She told herself this was her penance for her selfishness. It was Tiggy's right to choose whether he wished to come to her.

At last he stalked back from the kitchen and she was pleased to see that he was licking his lips and moving with his old confidence. He jumped onto the sofa and sat beside her, elegantly upright, washing his face, then he stepped onto her lap and turned round and round, kneading himself a comfy spot, then curled into a ball and closed his eyes. After a minute, Grace ventured to gently stroke him, he raised his head to allow her to caress his favourite spot under his chin, and when she did so he rewarded her with a steady, resounding purr. She sat there, eyes closed, grateful for the dear familiarity of her home and the warm weight of her cat upon her lap.

The ringing of her phone made her jump and brought Tiggy to bristling wakefulness. She offered him a placatory stroke with her right hand while groping in her cardigan pocket with her left. The caller display showed that it was Maddie, while a glance at the clock told her it was past eleven. She must have been daydreaming for over two hours.

"Maddie, hello," she said. "How are you today?"

"Hi, Grace. I'm fine. I'm sorry to disturb you when you're trying to sort out after your holiday, but I wanted to ask if you'd come round for lunch. I've invited Freddie. I want to talk some sense into him about this crazy show, which is totally out of control, and I'd be grateful if you were there to back me up."

"I'd like to but I've only just got Tiggy back from the cattery and I don't want to leave him until I'm sure he's settled in." Grace felt desperately inadequate; filled with guilt about letting Maddie down but her relief that Tiggy had apparently forgiven her for abandoning him made her determined not to leave him today.

"Of course you've got to get Tigs sorted but I really need your support. Would it upset him if Freddie and I came to you?"

"No, probably not. If he's unhappy, he can always go into my bedroom, like he did when I hosted Book Club. What time were you thinking of?"

Grace had only stopped in the village to pick up fresh milk and a loaf of bread. She'd planned to do a full supermarket shop in the next day or two. Her mind raced frantically over the supplies in her cupboard and freezer, it should be possible to pull together some sort of lunch but, at best, it would be adequate, she was not an inspired cook like Maddie. At least she'd dusted and hoovered yesterday after she'd unpacked. Tiggy disliked the vacuum cleaner and she'd got those chores out of the way before collecting him.

"I was thinking of twelve-thirty. Don't worry about cooking, Freddie offered to order takeaway. We were thinking of Chinese. Does that suit you?"

"Er ... yes ... but it's an imposition to ask Freddie to supply lunch for me as well. Please tell him not to worry about ordering for me." Grace's father had described all foreign food as 'muck'. Since his death, Grace had tried pizza and lasagne and other anglicised versions of Italian dishes but the nearest she'd ventured to Chinese cuisine was a supermarket ready-meal, and even that had seemed extravagant and exotic.

"Nonsense, he's already ordered it, and I told him I needed you in on this meeting. He's ordered a good range, so there's bound to be something that suits all of us. Don't worry, Grace. He's happy to do it. He knows he owes us for getting us involved in his ludicrous show and the food at this restaurant is really good. We had dinner there a couple of weeks ago."

Grace didn't know what to say. Her doubts about trying Chinese food were swept away in astonishment at the idea of Maddie and Freddie going out together for dinner. She knew that Maddie's liveliness and charm made her attractive to men but surely she'd want someone more dynamic than fussy, good-hearted Freddie? Their relationship must certainly be platonic.

"Are you still there?" asked Maddie. "Or have you zoned out? Is it the Chinese food that's worrying you? I'm sorry, I didn't think that you might not like it."

Grace tried to gather together her scattered thoughts. "No, I'm sure it will be delicious. If Freddie is bringing Percy, please ask him to keep him on his lead. I expect Tiggy will be happy to have a play date but he's a bit sensitive at the moment and I don't want him upset."

"Will do. I'll tell Freddie if there's any hint of feline hysterics he must take Percy home."

Grace wasn't sure she liked the term 'feline hysterics', which implied that Tiggy was being over-sensitive. Or maybe Maddie thought it was Tiggy's owner who was overwrought.

"Thank you," she said.

"Thank you for giving up your time on your first day back. You must have tons to do."

"Not really. Apart from getting some shopping in and making a fuss of Tiggy I'm pretty well settled in."

"You're so organised! Give me a shout if there's any food you need before you get to the shops."

"Thank you. Maddie, there's one thing I wanted to check. Did you really mean it when you said you didn't want to be in so many dance scenes?"

"Of course I did. It was never meant to be the Maddie Summer show but it just grew. Trying to do so much dancing as well as all the organising is exhausting. My arthritic hip is painful and we're only in the rehearsal stage. If you can work out a way to cut down my performance time I'll be truly grateful."

"I've got a few ideas. I'll see what I can do."

"In that case, I'll celebrate by doing some sketching. The tree on the footpath behind my cottage has shed its leaves and it looks really dramatic."

"Have fun." Grace considered herself as having no artistic talent, unless you counted her skill at knitting, but she understood that Maddie needed time with her art to balance her equilibrium.

Five minutes later, her phone rang again. "Hi, Maddie, did you forget something?"

"No, I've found something. In the field next to the footpath, just behind Hatty's house. It's a bike. I'm pretty sure it belongs to Kyle. But it makes no sense, I don't understand why anyone would dump it there."

Chapter 15

"Thanks for coming over to help, Grace." Maddie smiled at her friend. "I know you didn't want to leave Tiggy today, but I don't think I could have got it over the fence by myself and I don't want to leave it there in case it goes walkabout again."

"That's fine. It's different slipping out for a few minutes to going out to lunch for over an hour. Where do you want to put the bike?"

"I was thinking my kitchen. That way it can be safely locked up until I can contact Kyle to come and get it."

"The wheels are very muddy."

"I know, but so am I after slithering and sliding in this water-logged field. If I can lift the bike up, can you reach over the style and grab it?" That way there was some hope that Grace wouldn't get as grubby as she was. Her fastidious friend much preferred any adventures she embarked on to be neat and clean.

It was a struggle to hoist the bike high enough to clear the wooden style, but Grace's extra height proved a blessing and she managed to lift it onto the path. Maddie clambered soggily over the style and thought, as she so often had before, how useful it would be to be six inches taller than her five-foot-two.

With Grace hurrying ahead to open her garden gate, she wheeled the bicycle along her garden path and in through her back door, determinedly ignoring Grace's disapproving frown at the state of her kitchen floor.

"There's no snowman outfit," commented Grace. "Unless it's in the field, covered with mud."

"I can't promise I didn't miss it, but I looked around while I was waiting for you to come and help and, unless it's totally buried, I don't think it's there. What I did see was this." Maddie produced a plastic bag and emptied the sludgy contents onto her draining board.

"You found some mud?" queried Grace.

"You see but do not observe, as Sherlock Holmes would say. You shouldn't have left your magnifying glass at home. This is not just ordinary mud, it's a clue." Maddie rummaged in her sketching bag and produced a magnifying glass, which she offered to Grace.

Grace glared at her but accepted the glass and leaned closer to inspect the goo. "I see. I assume those sparkly bits are fragments of broken glass. They could have come from Hatty's shattered crystal ball."

"Yes. I'd guess the person who wore the suit got the bits of glass on them when they attacked Hatty and then brushed them off in the field.

"Or, more likely, shook the suit out when they took it off. They probably wore their clothes underneath the suit but they couldn't have fitted a coat under it so they probably left that with the bike."

"That makes sense." Maddie was delighted that Grace was getting back into the enquiring spirit. "I know there's no proof that Kyle wasn't the person who broke in and attacked Hatty but I really can't believe it was him."

"I agree that it doesn't make sense that he'd abandon his bike right outside Hatty's cottage," said Grace.

Maddie stared at her. Kyle was young and vulnerable, which meant Maddie was instinctively on his side, but she hadn't expected Grace to accept his innocence without an argument.

"You're right," she said. "If Kyle attacked Hatty and wanted to pretend he was elsewhere, it would be stupid to leave his bike there. It would be drawing attention to himself for no reason. And Kyle isn't stupid. If he'd been Hatty's attacker, he'd have ridden his bike away and dumped the snowman costume somewhere or possibly hidden it. Then he could ride back in time for rehearsal. He lives alone so nobody would know for certain he wasn't in his room."

"It seems more likely to be somebody who arrived at the estate unobtrusively, probably using the footpath. I wonder if they were obviously early for rehearsal in order to set up an alibi." Grace frowned. "It all seems ridiculously complicated though."

"I guess that someone who isn't used to committing crimes could make it too elaborate, but I agree there's lots that needs explaining, including how the burglar knew where Kyle would be yesterday afternoon, and how they knew where he'd left his bike," said Maddie. "One thing is certain, whoever did this was deliberately trying to frame Kyle for the attack."

"It seems likely that the person who attacked Hatty would have stayed near the estate, or at least in the village. I know it's a long shot but it would be interesting to know if anybody arrived early at rehearsal yesterday."

"Freddie's usually early."

"You can't think that Freddie would break in to anybody's house and attack them!" Grace sounded scandalised.

"Of course not. He's too short to wear Kyle's costume." Maddie allowed a few seconds for Grace to realise she was teasing then added, "And he's too good-natured. And totally on Kyle's side. I meant that he might remember who else turned up early, especially if they don't usually do so. Of course, the chances are he was too obsessed with his wretched antlers to notice who else was there."

"We can ask him over lunch, but we'll have to be tactful."

Maddie grinned. "You mean we ask him all casual like? Don't worry, Freddie's the most unsuspecting person I've ever known. Lord knows how he became such a successful businessman."

Grace glanced at her watch. "I must get back to Tiggy. Are you still going to do your sketching?"

"No, I think the moment's passed. I'll remove some of the mud and then, if it's okay with you, I'll come over to yours."

"Of course it's all right. I'll lay the table and put some wine in the fridge." Grace looked worried. "Does Pinot Grigio go with Chinese food? I don't want to serve the wrong thing."

Maddie thought how hard Grace made her life, continually worrying about what people thought of her. Of course, if a person had been brought up in an atmosphere of constant criticism and rigid rules it was probably inescapable. She wondered what Grace's aunt wanted that was preying on Grace's mind and hoped it wasn't what she suspected.

"As far as I'm concerned, Pinot Grigio goes very nicely with everything," she said.

Ten minutes later, mud free and clad in jeans and a soft, fluffy, bright pink jumper, Maddie smiled as she confirmed this assertion. Grace's Pinot Grigio was going down very nicely indeed. She congratulated herself on having reformed Grace's Puritan mindset, which had once caused her to believe that drinking alcohol before evening was a social misdemeanour if not an actual sin.

"Here comes Freddie," said Grace, from her position beside the window. "He's carrying an enormous box."

"That will be our lunch." Maddie struggled up from the sofa to join her, thinking ruefully that being upwardly mobile seemed to get harder every day.

"Do you think he's more likely to drop the box? Trip over Percy and fall flat on his face? Or strangle the poor dog by holding his lead too tight?"

Grace didn't answer. She was already hurrying out of her front door and across The Green to assist Freddie.

Maddie didn't follow her. Grace was quite capable of organising Freddie and if she opened the living room door Tiggy might decide it was the optimum awkward moment get out, which would stress his doting mistress. Personally, Maddie thought that Tiggy was a remarkably resilient and sensible animal but when Grace was on one of her regular guilt trips it was better not to attempt to derail her. Especially if it resulted in their lunch getting cold while they played Hunt the Cat.

Freddie bustled in, and nearly fulfilled Maddie's prophecy by tripping over Percy's lead as the excited Pekingese yapped and twirled, greeting his favourite feline friend. Tiggy, showing no signs of abandonment stress, wound himself around Freddie's legs, miaowing his greeting.

"Careful!" exclaimed Maddie, reaching out to steady him. "You break a leg and the show is definitely cancelled. I'm not going to caper across that stage without you."

"Nonsense! A trooper like you would never quit." Freddie regained his balance and kissed her cheek before bending down to release Percy from his lead.

"Don't you believe it."

Maddie's mobile buzzed and she got it out of her pocket. "It's Kyle. He's thanking me again for rescuing his bike and keeping it safe. He'll be round in a little while to collect it."

"His bike?" queried Freddie. "You mean you've found it?"

"Yes, somebody dumped it in the field behind my house. I phoned him to say we'd found it but he wasn't sure when he could get away."

"But he said it went missing in Portsmouth. How did it turn up here? You know, Maddie, I think there's something peculiar going on."

Maddie smiled at his obvious bewilderment. "You know, Freddie, I think you could be right."

Chapter 16

Grace found the Chinese food delicious, especially the dishes with duck and the King Prawns. However, at first she found it hard to concentrate because she kept thinking of something she'd seen out of the corner of her eye. Had Freddie kissed Maddie? Surely not! All the surprise she'd felt when Maddie mentioned they'd had dinner together came flooding back. Grace felt as if she'd been away for six months rather than six weeks.

When they were all full to bursting there was still a lot of the feast left.

"I'm afraid I ordered too much," said Freddie, "but that's better than having too little."

"Everything apart from the rice can be reheated," said Maddie. "If you're happy to store it in your fridge, Grace, you've got a couple of meals to tide you over until you can get to the shops."

"Perhaps I can invite Rose for dinner," said Grace. "It would be good to catch up with her." She always tried to be especially kind to Rose, even when her timid, apologetic manner irritated her. Most of the residents of the Clayfield Estate were reasonably well off, although only Freddie was wealthy, but Rose struggled to make ends meet.

"That's a good idea," approved Freddie. "There are times when I wonder if Rose has enough money to get by. I'd be happy to help her out but I don't like to ask in case it offends her."

Grace remembered Maddie's earlier remark and agreed with her that it was strange that Freddie could have been such a shrewd businessman when, in other ways, he was so naïve.

"I think she might find it embarrassing," she said.

"That's what worries me, but I hate to see her looking down-at-heel. I'm sure those shoes she wears aren't waterproof."

"Well you don't have to worry about that," said Maddie. "When I saw her yesterday she was wearing a nice pair of fur lined boots. They looked brand new."

"You can get some amazing bargains in charity shops. Sometimes wealthy people put in things they've bought on impulse and haven't even worn," said Grace.

"That's true," said Maddie. "Now we've finished eating, let's hear what Grace has got to say about our show."

The moment Grace had been dreading had arrived. "If you're sure you don't mind an outsider making suggestions when I haven't been here all the time you've been putting it together."

"You're not an outsider," said Maddie.

"No, indeed," added Freddie. "You're the backbone of our little community."

For someone designated to be a backbone, Grace felt remarkably spineless. She took a sustaining gulp of wine and took out her notes.

"Overall, I think the show is very good but I have one major concern." She turned more towards Freddie, directing her words principally to him. "I know it's not my place to say so, but I think that dancing the entire show is too much for Maddie. I'm worried that it's too exhausting for her and hurting her arthritic hip."

Freddie looked horrified. "Really?" He leaned across the table and grasped Maddie's hands. "My dear girl, why didn't you say so? I'd rather scrap the whole show than have you suffering."

"Suffering's a bit too melodramatic but my hip does hurt by the time we've finished a full rehearsal and I do get very tired."

"Why didn't you tell me?"

"I didn't realise at first but then my part kept on growing and everyone was so enthusiastic and I didn't want to let you ... let everybody ... down."

"I'm sorry. I think Mrs Mountjoy tried to tell me you were doing too much but I was having so much fun that I didn't listen. But I'm listening now and we'll work out a way to do the show without you."

"No, you won't!" Maddie glared at him.

"I won't let you harm yourself for the sake of a silly show."

"I have no intention of harming myself. I don't think dancing is doing me any actual damage and it's not your decision whether I appear or not."

"But..."

"Would you listen to me, please?" Grace didn't want to get in the middle of this quarrel but she'd started it and she needed to defuse the situation.

"Sorry, Grace," said Maddie. "What do you suggest?"

"I understand that you and Freddie are needed to hold together the whole show and you do it very well. I don't know a great deal about this sort of entertainment, but I wondered if you need to be so energetic in all the numbers ... whether you could let Freddie and some of the others take a bit more of the burden." Grace stumbled to a halt.

Maddie looked puzzled. "How can I do that if the penguin and reindeer are on at every scene?"

"Let's go through in order, act by act."

"But we didn't do the acts in order last night," protested Freddie.

Grace clamped down on her irritation. "Then we'll do it in the order that's in my notes, otherwise I'll get confused. We can always alter things later."

She tried to decipher her notes, wishing that she'd made the effort to transcribe them last night.

"I don't think you should alter the dance with the polar bear, that's brilliant, and so is the final Christmas tree number, but I wondered if you could rework the snowman dance so that Freddie does more of the work ... sort of dance around you a bit more. I'm sorry, that's probably a silly suggestion."

"No, it's not," said Freddie. "It makes perfect sense. I'll talk to the Carnival Dance ladies who choreographed the original dance and see what they suggest. Have you got any other ideas?"

Emboldened, Grace continued, "When you're on stage during the songs, most of the time it isn't too active, but when the lady is singing Que Sera, I wondered if you both had to pick the roses from the bush. Do you think it would work if Maddie stayed in one place and you picked the flowers and brought them to her?"

"I like that idea." Freddie beamed at Maddie. "A beautiful bouquet for a beautiful lady. Very romantic."

Maddie laughed and shook her head. "Really? I don't think a plump little penguin can be classed as beautiful and I'm pretty sure cross-species flirtation is inappropriate for a family show." She caught Grace's disapproving gaze and said, "I know the roses add the final over the top sentimental touch to Miriam's performance. It's not my taste but a lot of people seem to enjoy it and she is one of our residents."

"Is she? I didn't recognise her," said Grace.

"She moved into one of the sheltered housing flats. The show is a pain in a lot of ways but it's brought a lot of people together."

Grace wondered if it meant that people who didn't like performing felt left out. This added an edge to her voice as she said, "And then there's the juggler."

"I know he's useless but he doesn't realise he is. Apparently he used to be really good. He's so keen to be part of the show and none of us have the heart to tell him he's lost it," said Freddie. "That's why we play around in the background to turn it into a comedy routine."

"I understand that, but why does Maddie have to be the Piggy in the Middle? It's much the most strenuous role."

Freddie stared at her. "You're right! We thought it would be funny to have the penguin in the middle because Maddie is so much shorter. Not that I'm very tall but the antlers add to my height, but I'll talk to Stan, he's our polar bear, and we'll sort something out. Thank you, Grace." He looked nervously at Maddie. "If that's all right with you, Maddie?"

"It certainly is. Thanks, Grace. Have you got any more brilliant ideas?"

"Well, there is one thing. There seems to be a lot of organisation and from what you told me it gets trickier all the time. I know it's not physically demanding but it must be stressful and time consuming and it means you have to divide your mind between your own performance and counting costumes and getting everybody to rehearsal at the right time. Couldn't somebody else take on the behind the scenes jobs?" As Grace spoke, she knew she was the logical replacement and was sure she'd sealed her own fate.

"I admit it would be nice to be free of chasing people," admitted Maddie. "A lot of them need to be reminded over and over again what to do with their costumes, not to mention turning up for rehearsals on time. Perhaps Nell would take it on. What do you think, Freddie? After all, she designed and made most of the costumes, so she knows who wears what."

"But would she be able to deal with the awkward ones?" asked Freddie.

"Hopefully she would. After all, she spent a lot of her working life as a doctor's receptionist, so she must have dealt with all sorts of people in her time." Maddie grinned. "And if anyone's too difficult she can get her mother to act as enforcer. I'd put my money on Mrs M. to make even the obnoxious Douglas behave."

Grace knew she should feel relieved that her services weren't required. She hadn't wanted to be involved and it made no sense that she felt snubbed. Of course, she'd known that several of the women on the estate had held down full-time jobs before their retirement but she'd never considered it in context with herself. Maddie had married, brought up two children, had a career as a teacher and continued to work after she was widowed. It was understandable that she'd discounted Grace as a force to be reckoned with. All she'd done with her life was spend over forty years ministering to her father and his various parishes. It made her feel horribly inadequate.

Chapter 17

Maddie thought it was a good thing that Grace had never tried to make a living selling second-hand cars or dodgy real estate. She was hopeless at masking her feelings. Maddie could track the moment when she looked martyred at the prospect of being asked to take on the organisation of the show, and the switch to umbrage when the sacrifice was not required, mixed with a hint of hurt.

It was the grieved bit that dictated her next words. For all of Grace's self-righteous veneer, she knew that she was painfully insecure. "Of course, the best thing would be to have Nell keeping tabs on the costumes and somebody else in overall control of the organisation of the show. Grace, I don't like to ask when you've only just got home but you'd be perfect for the job if you'd consider taking it on."

She was rewarded by the lightening of Grace's expression, without even a trace of martyrdom.

"If you think I could do it? I wouldn't want to let you down."

"You won't. You're good at organisation and people are more likely to listen to you. You've got height and dignity. Nobody ever called me dignified, even before I started running round the place masquerading as a penguin. It can't be any harder than teaching Sunday School to a class of rumbustious kids."

"Well, if it is I can always ask Mrs Mountjoy for help," said Grace with a smile. "By the way, it never occurred to me to ask before, but what work did Mrs Mountjoy do after the war?"

"I think she was a Civil Servant." Maddie spoke with deliberate reserve. Both she and Grace knew that, as a very young woman, Mrs M. had fought an eventful and violent war, but, apart from Nell, nobody else on the Clayfield Estate was aware of this, and Maddie had no intention of betraying the brave old lady's trust.

"Sounds like a perfect job for her," said Freddie. "I bet she set those politicians straight. Sort of like that television programme, 'Yes, Minister'."

"You may well be right," agreed Maddie.

"I must be going," said Freddie. "I need to drop Percy home and then I promised Miriam I'd play the piano for her to rehearse her song. I'm nowhere near as good an accompanist as those clever college musicians but we can't ask them to give up any more time."

"Especially when she's word perfect. Why does she think she needs to practice?"

"She says she doesn't feel that she's got enough emotion into it," explained Freddie. His voice was solemn but Maddie could sense the laughter bubbling underneath.

"Enough emotion! She's already got enough schmalz into that one song to sink a battleship!"

"I know but I didn't have the heart to refuse. She's so anxious to make her daughter and grandchildren proud of her. I'm sure you feel the same about Libbie and her boys."

On the contrary, Maddie had considered offering her son and daughter bribes to take their offspring out of the county, if not the country, for the relevant weekend, to prevent the kids from being traumatised by the sight of their grandmother as a performing penguin. In this she was sure she'd have the full co-operation of her daughter-in-law, who had a firm dislike of anything absurd or vulgar, especially from those who were of an age to know better. The truth was, despite her crazy hair colours and bouncy manner, she wasn't really an extrovert.

The beep of her phone saved her from having to answer. "It's Kyle. He says he's by the tree on The Green chatting to Mrs Mountjoy."

"Just Mrs Mountjoy? Not Nell?" asked Freddie anxiously.

"Nell told me that she was going to buy more material for the new snowman's outfit this afternoon," said Maddie. "It looks like Mrs M. has taken advantage of her absence to pull one of her Colditz stunts."

"That's not good. You shouldn't joke about it, Maddie. You know how Nell worries about her mother going out alone in case she falls."

"Yes, but I also know that Mrs Mountjoy goes stir-crazy when Nell frets about her all the time. Since her medication got sorted, she's totally with it and hates being treated like a child. Anyway, she's not alone. Kyle's with her."

"That's true. He'll look after her."

"More likely she'll be setting his life straight." Maddie stood up. "Grace, thank you for letting us come round and thank you even more for your suggestions for the show and agreeing to take it on. I wish you could come with us to meet Kyle properly but I know you don't want to leave Tiggy."

"I'd like to come but I do need to make sure that Tiggy's settled in."

"Whatever you think best." Maddie looked at the contentedly slumbering cat and suppressed a smile. When Grace had decided something was her duty there was no point arguing with her.

"I'll slip next door later and invite Rose over for an early dinner. That will only take a minute, so I won't have to leave Tiggy for too long. Freddie, thank you for supplying such a delicious lunch." She held out her hand to shake Freddie's.

At the same moment, Freddie chose to bend and fasten Percy's lead to his collar and it looked as though he was bowing in a courtly manner to kiss Grace's hand. Maddie found it hard to conceal her laughter. Grace and Freddie were her closest friends amongst the residents of the estate, but there were times when she felt as if she was taking part in an old-fashioned sitcom.

This feeling didn't abate as she and Freddie walked across The Green and she saw that Kyle and Mrs Mountjoy had been joined by Miriam Davenport.

"Oh dear," said Freddie, "I hope Mrs Mountjoy isn't being unkind to poor Miriam."

"Probably not. Mrs M. usually goes for bigger game than white, fluffy poodles."

Freddie chuckled. "Really, Maddie! You are naughty. I rather like Miriam, she's a very goodhearted person."

"I like her too, apart from when she's singing. The sad thing is, she's got a pleasant voice if only she wouldn't over-egg the pudding." She raised her voice as they drew near, "Good afternoon, everybody."

"It's a really good afternoon now you've found my bike," said Kyle.

"Yes, indeed," agreed Mrs Mountjoy.

"Good afternoon, Maddie." Miriam beamed at them. "I was looking for Freddie. I hope you don't mind me borrowing him for a little while. I need him to run through my song. Practise makes perfect, you know."

Maddie thought that asking to borrow Freddie made him sound like a spare umbrella or a popular paperback book. She wanted to point out that Freddie wasn't her property and therefore not hers to lend, but protesting about a meaningless turn of phrase could give it too much importance. Miriam was a nice lady but, like the majority of the residents, she loved to gossip.

Help came from an unexpected source. "I heard your song last night and it sounded word perfect already," said Kyle. "You must take care not to over-practise and lose the freshness and vitality."

"Sort of like over-egging the pudding," said Freddie mischievously.

"Is that possible?" asked Miriam. Her coat was open at the neck and she reached up to fiddle with the double string of pearls she always wore.

"It can be," said Kyle. "Would it help if I came to the hall, after I've collected my bike from Maddie? We could run through your song a few times at a different pace."

"That sounds like a good plan," said Mrs Mountjoy. "I've always thought that song should be light and airy."

"Do you think so?" Miriam sounded unconvinced and the hand playing with the pearls was twisting more violently.

Maddie disliked Miriam's rendering of the song but she disliked even more the idea of Miriam being manipulated to perform in a way she was uncomfortable with.

"Why don't we all come and listen?" she suggested. "The important thing is that you feel happy with your performance. Nobody wishes to interfere with your artistic integrity." She realised that for three of her audience this was several steps too far but Miriam looked comforted.

"Is that okay with you, Kyle?" asked Maddie. "Your bike is safe enough locked in my kitchen."

"That's fine."

"Maddie, would you text Nell and tell her that I am out and about but quite safe, and you are acting as my parole officer?" requested Mrs Mountjoy. "I'd tell her myself but she's horribly untrusting about such things."

"I wonder why," retorted Maddie as she took out her phone.

Chapter 18

They strolled towards the Main Building. Maddie and Miriam took the lead, while Mrs Mountjoy followed, leaning on Kyle's arm and Freddie hovered beside them, fussing and fretting, clearly conscious of the responsibility of aiding the old rebel lady's escape.

As soon as Maddie and her companion entered the Hall the heat hit her. "Somebody's been hiking up the heating again," said Maddie, pulling off her fluffy jacket. "The Manager's going to go mad when she gets the bill."

"And it's not good to keep going between really hot and really cold," said Miriam, removing her smartly cut woollen coat, folding it neatly and placing it on a chair before going to the full length mirror beside the door to tidy her already immaculate hair.

A quick glance in the mirror told Maddie that her vivid, spiky hair was as neat as it was liable to get. She thought that they were two short, plump, elderly, white, English women who were as unalike as it was possible to get. She had purple hair, a bright sweatshirt in shades of blue and gold and well-worn jeans and flat-heeled, leather boots. Miriam was immaculate in a dove grey, cashmere jumper, pleated skirt in a darker shade of grey, stockings that emphasised her shapely calves and black shoes with a moderate, but flattering heel. Her white hair was perfectly set and she wore a hint of blusher, lipstick and eye makeup. Her double string of pearls looked as elegant with this day outfit as they had with her white, silk, evening dress last night.

Of course, Miriam was in her mid-seventies, about ten years older than Maddie. She considered whether, when she achieved that age, she'd also attain a similar level of sophistication, but it seemed unlikely. Nor, when she considered the effort it involved, did she particularly want to.

"If you keep playing with your necklace you'll break it," she said.

Miriam snatched her hand away from the pearls. "It's a silly habit I've got. I've had it ever since I was a girl."

"There's no harm in it, but it would be a pity to break that lovely necklace."

"Yes, I'm very fond of it, even though it's not nearly as valuable as I thought it was."

"Really? I'd have thought it was very expensive? Not that I know anything about jewels." But Freddie did and, a few weeks ago, he'd remarked to Maddie that he hoped that Miriam had her pearls properly insured because they were the finest he'd ever seen.

Miriam's colour drained, leaving the artificial colour on her cheeks standing out in vivid relief. "I'm afraid not. I'm quite embarrassed about it, but I've decided that I need to tell the truth. When I first moved into my little flat on the estate, a lot of people admired them and I told them how my grandfather had been a prosperous businessman and he bought them for my grandmother. That would have been in Late Victorian times, and she passed them down to my mother and Mama left them to me. I always thought my necklace was worth several thousand pounds, the most expensive single thing that I possess, but when I had them valued recently, I was told that they were worth a few hundred at most. When I heard that I almost sold them there and then, just so that I wouldn't have to see them again, but then I decided against it. After all, they still hold memories of Mama and Grandmother."

"But surely, if they've been in your family so long, they must have been assessed for insurance before now?"

Miriam's eyes filled with tears. "They were! That's what's so awful. They were last assessed just over ten years ago and then they were valuable freshwater South Sea pearls. My husband fretted when I wore them, he wanted me to keep them in the safe. But I had them valued recently and they are only cultured pearls. Even though I wore them all the time, I never noticed the difference. Now I keep thinking I should have realised." She broke off as Mrs Mountjoy, Freddie and Kyle entered the hall and said softly, "I'm sorry! Whatever must you think of me? It's so silly, going on like that. But you're so kind and it's been on my mind."

"It's not a problem. I'm always happy to listen if you want to talk." Maddie suspected that the main cause of Miriam's distress was not the loss in value of her beautiful necklace but the fear that the substitution could only have been done by somebody close to her.

Maddie hadn't intended to stay for the rehearsal. There was only so much Que Seraing that a woman of her temperament could stand. But Miriam begged her to stay and she found herself sitting down next to Mrs Mountjoy to watch the proceedings, ready to intervene if she felt that Miriam was being over-persuaded to take her performance in a way she didn't like. She told herself it was absurd to be so protective when Miriam's rendering of the song made her cringe but if Miriam had the courage to sing in front of a large audience, Maddie felt she had the right to do it the way she wished. After a few minutes, she relaxed, fascinated, not just by Kyle's artistry as a musician but by his skill as a music mentor. Under his gentle direction the song picked up pace and became something quite lively, which, judging by her expression, seemed to both please and puzzle Miriam.

"One more run-through and then, if you're happy, Mrs Davenport, we should call it a day," said Kyle, "we don't want to over-strain your voice."

Miriam beamed at him. "I'm very happy. I don't know how you did it but it sounds quite different now."

"In a good way, I hope? I wouldn't want to interfere with your artistic integrity."

Miriam giggled. "I never thought of myself as having artistic integrity, that sounds much too grand for an amateur like me, but I do like what you've done with my little song. I don't want my daughter and granddaughters to be embarrassed when they hear me."

"They should be very proud of you," said Kyle.

"Hear, hear," agreed Freddie.

"The boy's a genius," Mrs Mountjoy murmured in Maddie's ear. "I didn't think it was possible to transform that poor woman's performance into something that didn't make me shudder. By the way, I've told him to get a proper busker's licence and I'll lend him the money to pay for it. We don't need troublemakers complaining about him and damaging his career before it even gets off the ground."

"That's a brilliant idea." Maddie wished she'd thought of it herself.

"He deserves a helping hand. The way our society treats young people in Care is disgraceful." She raised her voice, "Kyle, would you be kind enough to help me to my feet? These chairs are not easy for someone of my age and build to get up from."

"Of course." Kyle hurried over to assist her. "I'd better walk back with you to your house. It's getting dark and slippery out there."

Aware of Mrs Mountjoy's fiercely independent outlook on life, Maddie expected her to refuse this offer and hoped she'd do so graciously.

To her surprise, Mrs Mountjoy accepted Kyle's proffered arm and said, "Thank you. It might be wise and it will stop my daughter from fretting too much."

"Oh dear! I hadn't realised how icy it had got," said Miriam. "I shouldn't have worn high heels. I'll have to be very careful as I go home."

"I'm sure you'll be fine, those heels aren't that high." Mrs Mountjoy echoed Maddie's thoughts. "But in future I'd suggest a nice pair of solid lace-ups."

Miriam shuddered. "I know you're right, but I do like pretty things. And my late husband always said I had the daintiest feet he'd ever seen."

"Sounds like a foot fetish man," muttered Mrs Mountjoy.

Maddie choked back her laughter and could see that Kyle was similarly struggling.

Fortunately, Miriam did not appear to register what she'd said and Freddie leapt into the breach, "I'll walk round to your building with you, Miriam. Maddie, if you wait here I'll be back for you in a few minutes."

"Thanks, Freddie, but I'm sure I can make it on my own flat feet." She smiled at him, knowing that his offer was kindly meant, but glad to exert her self-sufficiency. "Kyle, come round when you're ready and collect your bike."

She set off briskly. Mrs Mountjoy's cottage was in the same direction as her own but she knew it would fret the old lady if she thought that too many attendants were hovering around her. She felt grateful for her speed when she heard the sound of approaching voices, most of them young and shrill, and realised she'd narrowly avoided Janetta and her little snowflakes on their way to rehearse in the Main Hall. Not that Maddie objected to the children, but encounters with Janetta and her sister were something she preferred to ration to as few as possible.

She skirted around to her side of The Green, congratulating herself on not encountering anybody, when her luck ran out. Hatty's door opened and she hurried towards Maddie, reaching out to grasp her arm. "Maddie, something wonderful has happened!"

"Really?" Maddie had a bad feeling that her definition of wonderful might not match Hatty's. "What?"

Hatty took a deep breath, obviously savouring this special moment. "My spectral visitor has not deserted me! He has returned to communicate with me again."

The thought, 'Here we go again,' echoed around Maddie's mind.

She sighed. "Tell me about it," she said.

Chapter 19

Grace sat in the chair by the front window that she'd sunk into as she'd watched Maddie and Freddie leave her front garden and head towards the large oak tree that dominated The Green. She was thinking that the relationship between Maddie and Freddie had changed during the weeks she'd been away.

As soon as they'd reached the pavement, Freddie had paused, obviously offering the support of his arm to Maddie, and she'd accepted it. Grace told herself there was nothing surprising in that. Freddie had the manners of an old-fashioned gentleman and would extend this courtesy to any lady he was walking with as soon as there was enough room for them to walk two abreast. All the same, Grace couldn't help remembering the kiss she thought she'd seen.

Grace sighed. She wasn't sure if her weariness was due to an excess of food or too much company. While staying with her aunt they had usually lunched on something light, a boiled egg or bowl of clear soup. And, although everybody said how nice it was for her aunt to have Grace's company while the rest of the family were at work, the old lady had slept for several hours throughout the day, while Grace sat reading or knitting.

She wondered if Maddie had guessed about the decision Grace had to make. If she did know, she obviously had no intention of attempting to influence Grace, even though Grace rather wished she would. Part of her knew it would be foolish to give up her long-awaited independence but another deeper instinct made her long to be assured that she was needed once again. And perhaps it was her duty to agree to her aunt's request.

She jerked awake, bemused, then horrified. She'd dozed off! She never slept during the day unless she was ill. She could only be grateful that, with the light off, seated behind her pristine white net curtains, nobody was likely to see her. Maddie loathed net curtains and seemed indifferent to being on show to passers-by, but Grace hated the thought of people looking in.

Movement at the entrance to the estate caught her attention. Grace's next-door neighbour, Rose, was walking slowly, stumbling, along the pavement. She stopped, fumbling ineffectually at her garden gate, succeeded in opening it and trudged down her garden path. Grace was worried. It was not like Rose to walk heavily like that, head down, shoulders slumped. Grace had a horror of being considered a busybody but she hated to think of Rose distressed or ill with nobody to comfort her. It was absurd for a woman in Grace's position to feel that Rose was more alone in the world than anyone else she knew, but Rose always seemed to be so vulnerable.

Hastily, she put on her coat and shoes and hurried round to her neighbour's cottage. Her first gentle knocking met no response, so she tried again more forcefully. She wondered how many of their neighbours were watching. She wasn't the only person to hide behind net curtains. She told herself she didn't care about being observed, squared her shoulders and knocked on the door again.

This time the door opened a crack and Rose peered out. "Grace, I didn't know that you were home."

She opened the door wider and Grace hurried inside. "My dear, what's wrong?" Rose was pale and trembling, her eyes red rimmed and puffy, as if she had been crying for hours.

"I've been so foolish! That wicked, wicked man! I trusted him!"

Grace stared at her in horror. Lurid images of seduction and rape swirled through her mind. Or perhaps it was like those stories that were always appearing in the news about con men who romanced vulnerable women and stole their life savings. Of all the residents on the estate, Rose was the least affluent. Could she have signed over her cottage to a smooth talking Lothario?

She put an arm around Rose and led her into the sitting room. "Sit down and tell me about it."

At first it seemed as if talking was beyond Rose's control. She sat sobbing and shaking, occasionally uttering incoherent broken words. Snowy, her white cat, stalked past and was pounced upon and hugged convulsively.

Grace went to the kitchen for a glass of water and then sat down beside Rose, steadying it as she tried to drink.

"What has happened, Rose?" she asked.

Rose took a deep breath, which turned into a sob, but then she answered, "I needed money ... two weeks ago it was ... I was desperate ... Snowy had a wound and it got infected ... I think another cat must have been bullying her and I had to get her cut treated and even with insurance you have to pay the first hundred pounds."

"Surely the PDSA would have treated her for free?" said Grace, although she knew very little about such things.

"I did wonder about that, but when I was delivering some newly adjusted costumes to the rehearsal, I mentioned I was going to have to take Snowy to be treated and I was told I wouldn't be eligible to go to the PDSA because I owned my own house and lived in a nice village."

"I'm not sure that's right." Grace wondered who'd told Rose that. There were several busybodies on the estate who always thought they knew best. But even if their advice was rubbish, it was too late to do anything about it now.

"They made me feel like I wasn't fit to have Snowy if I couldn't look after her. I was afraid they'd call the RSPCA and have my darling girl taken away."

"What did you do?" asked Grace.

Rose sniffled, then controlled herself again. "I sold Guinevere Henriette," she said.

Chapter 20

"Guinevere Henriette?" repeated Grace. "I'm sorry, Rose, I don't understand."

Rose made an obvious effort to speak coherently, even though tears were torrenting down her face. "I had two dolls, they belonged to my great-grandmother and were passed down in the family. I was the only girl in my generation and so for my twenty-first birthday my mother gave me her doll, Jemima Jane, and later when my aunt passed away she left me Guinevere Henriette. They are both so beautiful and I love them so much. They were one of the few things of any value that I managed to keep when my husband ... when things went wrong with his business ventures and he had to go away."

"I see."

However tactfully Rose phrased it, Grace knew that Rose's errant husband had not merely been guilty of bad management and bad luck. He had speculated with his employees' pension fund and had then fled abroad, disappearing into a country with no extradition and leaving Rose to face the ignominy and hatred of those who had been robbed. The police had investigated her role in the fraud and concluded she was innocent of complicity in the crime. Nevertheless she'd had to liquidate the business and sell their mansion in Cheshire and the luxury flat in London, plus all their other possessions of any value, in a vain attempt to meet an insurmountable mountain of debt.

"You never told me how you came to live here after your losses?" Grace had often wondered how Rose could afford this estate. As soon as she asked this, she felt guilty about indulging her curiosity when Rose was so vulnerable. "I'm sorry! It's none of my business. I didn't mean to intrude."

"I don't mind telling you, Grace. You've always been so kind." Rose scrubbed at her eyes with a soggy tissue and sat up straighter. "Everything I could bear to part with had gone to pay our debts. I even sold my jewellery and the diamond set I'd inherited from my mother. I had nowhere to live and I didn't know what to do. I was so afraid. So I gathered up my courage and wrote to my only remaining relative, George. He's my second cousin and near the same age as me, so we were quite friendly when we were young. I told him I had nowhere to live and asked if I could stay with him, at least until I could get some help from Social Services. He didn't like that idea but he did offer to buy me a small retirement place, as long as it was nowhere near him."

"I see." Grace realised that her voice sounded more acerbic than she'd intended.

Rose gave her a tremulous smile. "I know what you're thinking. It's true that George didn't want to be associated with me after all the things that were said in the news. He's a business man with lots of friends in the Government. But he wasn't unkind. My greatest fear was that I'd have to re-home Snowy. Sheltered accommodation often doesn't allow cats. But George found out that there was this cottage available and it wasn't too expensive because the firm responsible for building them had to allocate a certain percentage of the cottages for housing the less well off. Not that the cost would matter to George, he's a very wealthy man, but, as he said, I wouldn't want to be too beholden to him when he'd been so kind."

"I see." Grace thought it would have been even kinder if he'd arranged an allowance to help Rose to meet the mandatory tenant contributions for the upkeep of her cottage and the grounds.

"I'm grateful to him," said Rose. "He didn't want our relationship mentioned, which is why I've never told anyone how I came to be here, but I know I can trust you not to talk about it. Of course he made me make a will that left the cottage to him when I die."

Grace had heard enough about Rose's cousin. "What happened with your dolls that upset you so much?" she asked.

Rose's face crumpled but she managed to hold back her tears. "A few days ago I was so desperate. When this man came knocking on my door it seemed like an answer to my prayers."

"What man?"

"Mr Bartlett, although he told me to call him Douglas. He said he was going round the estate enquiring if anybody had old furniture or paintings or jewellery or other antiques they might be willing to dispose of for a cash sum." Rose pressed her disintegrating tissue to her lips and Grace rummaged in her handbag and withdrew a new pack of tissues to offer her friend.

"Thank you." Rose struggled to control her emotions. "At first I said no, but he was so confident and jolly. He reminded me of the days when I had someone to turn to. And he was kind. He told me that I shouldn't be embarrassed, lots of people had exchanged things they no longer needed for the money to buy things for themselves or their families. He made it seem like quite an ordinary thing to do and I was so desperate to get the treatment for Snowy."

"Did you tell him what you wanted the money for?"

"I think I must have. He seemed to know about it. Somehow, without actually saying it, he made me feel that it would be selfish and cruel of me to let Snowy suffer. At first he was disappointed that I didn't have any valuable furniture but then he asked if he could go upstairs and, as soon as he entered my bedroom, he saw Guinevere Henriette and Jemima Jane. He said bisque dolls were out of fashion nowadays and pointed out a tiny crack on Jemima Jane's neck, but in the end he offered me £500 for Guinevere Henriette and £300 for Jemima Jane."

Grace knew little about the antiques market and was surprised that the dealer was willing to pay so much for antique dolls but she could see why Rose had been tempted. She was certain that Rose would always value Snowy above any toy. "You sold Guinevere Henriette?" she said gently.

Rose nodded. "I couldn't bear to sell both of them," she whispered, "but it was very hard to choose between them."

"Are you upset because Snowy didn't need the veterinary treatment after all?" asked Grace.

"No, she did need antibiotics to help clear up her infection. She's getting better now and I'm so glad I got her treatment in time. I told myself it was all for the best and I've saved the rest of the money for a rainy day. Although I did treat myself to a pair of warm, second-hand, winter boots that were just my size at the Church Bring and Buy."

"That sounds very sensible."

"I know. I do try to make the best of things." To Grace's dismay, Rose's tears started to pour down her face again. "But I miss Guinevere Henriette so much, and Jemima Jane looks so lonely sitting on my bed without her friend."

"I wish I'd been here. I could have helped out with Snowy's treatment."

Rose shook her head. "I wouldn't have borrowed money from you, not when I couldn't pay it back. Like

I said, I try to be grateful for what I've got, but I couldn't get Guinevere Henriette out of my mind, so today I used my bus pass and went down to that man's shop. I just wanted to see her one more time."

"Did you see her? Was that what upset you? Or had she been sold?" Grace wasn't sure which Rose would find worse: to see her beloved doll in a shop and have to abandon her there again, or to discover she was missing and never know where she'd gone."

"At first I couldn't see her. I thought that she'd gone forever. But after I'd watched for a while I was sure that man, Mr Bartlett, wasn't there, so I went inside. Then I saw her. She was in a special, secure cabinet, with tinted glass. I asked the lady in the shop why that was and she said it was to keep her from the light because she's so valuable. She looked so sad, and reproachful, as if she knew I'd betrayed her."

Rose's voice ascended to a wail. "And there was a price tag beside her. He gave me £500 but he's charging £4000 for my Guinevere Henriette."

Chapter 21

"I've got news!" Maddie had been watching out for Grace and intercepted her as she walked the short distance between Rose's cottage and her own.

"So have I. It's really important. Come in and I'll tell you about it."

Maddie followed Grace into her living room, took off her jacket and sat down on the sofa next to Tiggy, who opened his eyes, regarded her sleepily, climbed onto her lap, turned round twice and curled up.

"I've got something odd to tell you," she said as Grace sat down opposite her.

"My story is really important," repeated Grace.

"How do you know mine isn't?" Despite her protest, Maddie saw the stubborn look on Grace's face and knew she was determined to have her say first. It occurred to her that she'd missed many things about Grace but not her bossiness.

"It's about Rose and that dreadful antique dealer man. He bought one of her dolls for £500 and is trying to sell it for £4000. Surely that must be fraud or something like that?"

"It sounds like sharp practice but that's probably different to downright fraud. Let's have a few more details. Not that I'm an expert about antiques or the law. The person we want for that is Freddie."

"Rose has given me permission to share her story with anyone I want. She's very upset but she's angry too."

"Then let's call Freddie, and maybe Mrs Mountjoy and Nell. I remember Mrs M. saying that Douglas had waited until he knew she was alone to call on her and he'd offered her a ludicrously small amount for her jade figures. I'll see if they're free." Maddie got out her phone. She resigned herself to putting the story she'd heard from Hatty on the back burner until Grace was satisfied they'd fully discussed Rose's latest crisis.

Twenty minutes later they were all assembled in the Mountjoys' cosy sitting room. Nell had been happy to meet with them but insistent that her mother should not go out again in the cold. Grace told the story of Rose's need for money and the hard decision to sell Guinevere Henriette. As expected, they were all indignant and Freddie was particularly horrified.

"Why didn't she tell me that she needed money for Snowy's vet's bill?" he demanded. "Surely she knows I would have happily helped her out?"

"I'm sure she does know." Maddie patted his arm. "But I imagine that when you're the only person who desperately needs money, living amongst a lot of people who are reasonably well off, it must feel important to keep up appearances."

"Especially considering, until a few years ago, she lived in a mansion and had enough money to buy anything she wanted," said Nell. "I think she's been very brave to face things the way she has."

"Well said," applauded her mother. "I agree she's been good about picking up the pieces of her life but I suspect her downfall will always be in the men she decides to trust. I wonder if her ex-husband was a big, blustering, bully-boy, like Douglas Bartlett."

"I think he may have been. She described Douglas as confident and jolly," said Grace.

"How sure are we that he's been going round the estate trying to buy up antiques at a low price and lying about the objects' value?" asked Freddie. "I mean, how widespread are his games? He hasn't called on me."

Maddie smiled at him. "That's not surprising. Around this estate, you're acknowledged as an expert on antiques."

"And that's despite your games with the concrete griffin, pretending you thought it was a valuable stone carving," chuckled Mrs Mountjoy. "And, as well as being an expert, you are also known to be wealthy enough not to need to sell off any antiques."

"A couple of weeks ago, he came round to my cottage and started a long spiel about how I must want some extra money to treat my grandchildren at Christmas, but I kept him standing on the doorstep and didn't let him in," said Maddie.

"Well done you," said Freddie.

She shrugged. "I was painting. Anyway, I never liked the man."

"You shouldn't have let him into our house, Mother. Not while I was out," said Nell. "It's not as if you like the man any more than Maddie does."

"True. But there are very few people I do like. Present company excepted." Mrs Mountjoy surveyed her guests with mischief in her eyes. "I was bored and I wanted to find out what game he was playing. It was interesting to see his technique. For a couple of the less valuable pieces he was spot on, even generous in his estimates. Then he came to the jade and it was interesting to see the difference in his body language and his tone. His voice changed from jolly to carefully casual. The estimate he gave of their value was pathetic but I could see the covetousness in his eyes and there was a small muscle beside his mouth that started to twitch."

Maddie thought that Mrs Mountjoy's smile was that of a predator about to spring. She wondered whether Douglas had the wit to realise he'd met his match in this indomitable old lady.

"Oh Mother, I wish you wouldn't take such risks!" exclaimed Nell. "If he was tempted to steal your jade, he could have hurt you and run off with them."

"Very unlikely," retorted her mother. "He's a conman, not the sort to resort to physical violence in his professional life, unless he's cornered and I made sure I didn't do that. In fact, I made sure I didn't take my eyes off him all the time he was here, and he knew it. I admit there was one point when I thought he was weighing up my little white jade horse and I wondered if he was tempted to slip it in his pocket. That's when I told him that all my antiques had been appraised and recorded for insurance purposes. His shifty look turned to embarrassed and he put it back on the shelf. He left rather hastily after that."

Maddie admired Mrs Mountjoy more than anyone else she knew but she felt constrained to say, "I wish you'd told me before. It would have added weight to my arguments when I told the Manager that I was sure Doug was trying to con people into selling their antiques for a lot less than their value. The wretched woman never listened to me, she just bleated 'I can't believe that. Such a charming man and so public spirited, giving up his valuable time to appear in our little show.' She refused to take any action."

"I apologise for that, Maddie. If I'd realised it would be helpful I'd have told you. I did email her expressing my concerns. I prefer to do that, rather than in person or phoning, because it leaves a record. A person like our Manager is prone to deny receiving information whenever it suits her."

Maddie thought that Mrs M. was truly magnificent. She could only hope, if she lived into her nineties, she could be half as full of vigour and willingness to embrace change.

"What can we do about what that man did to Rose?" demanded Grace. "Can we prove he conned her?"

"I doubt it," said Freddie. "It's obvious he was less than honest with her but, as far as the law goes, she agreed to sell the doll for £500 and I'm sure he got a receipt. Rose may be naïve but nobody could claim she's incapable of running her own life. If he tries to sell the doll on for a substantial profit it just proves he's a sharp businessman."

"So there's nothing we can do?" Grace sounded profoundly dissatisfied.

"There's one thing I can do, and will do first thing tomorrow. That's go down to his shop and buy back Rose's doll," said Freddie.

"I know Rose is upset about her doll but she'll feel humiliated if she thinks you've bought it back," objected Grace.

"Not to mention it means the slime-ball has got away with making three and a half thousand pounds profit out of your money," protested Maddie. "Just the thought of that makes me want to do something violent."

Chapter 22

"I'm sorry." Freddie looked apologetic and stubborn, both at the same time. "I agree with both of you but I feel it's urgent to secure the doll as soon as possible. I suspect Rose won't have been able to conceal her distress when she was in the shop and if the shop assistant mentions it to Doug he could decide that it's better to ship the doll off to an auction to avoid any fuss Rose might make. Once we've got the doll, we can think about how to get it back to Rose without hurting her feelings."

"We could tell her that Doug had a Road to Damascus moment and saw the light," suggested Maddie, mischievously revelling in Grace's outraged expression at the idea of her comparing the blustering antiques dealer to St Paul.

"I'm not sure either of us could get her to believe that," said Freddie. "It would take more than a miracle to turn Doug into a decent human being." A sly wink confirmed that he shared Maddie's amusement.

"I'll drive you down to the shop tomorrow," she offered. Despite his wealth, Freddie did not own a car. When he was a young man, a serious accident had traumatised him so severely that he'd never again got behind the wheel.

"Hopefully we won't encounter Doug in the shop," said Freddie.

"I'd be happy to never see him again," agreed Maddie. "I hate the way he's using our show to wheedle his way into the estate. It's given him access to people he'd never have met in the ordinary way of things and helped to win their trust."

"I assume it's too late to ban him from the show?" asked Nell.

"As far as the performance is concerned, I'd rather have his space than his company," said Maddie, "even if Janetta withdrew her little snowflakes in a huff."

"She wouldn't. She likes the limelight far too much. And she wouldn't want to upset all the parents. That would be bad for business," said Freddie.

Maddie pulled a rueful face. "I don't think it would make things better as far as getting him out of the estate goes. He's too well established and, believe it or not, some people find him charming."

"Do we know how many more people have sold things to him?" asked Grace.

There was a blank silence.

"That's the wretched man's strength," said Mrs Mountjoy. "Very few people are willing to admit they've sold off their heirlooms."

"I think maybe Ron and Amy could have done so, or, at least, Amy," suggested Maddie. "I've got no proof, but I noticed she'd been updating her aviary and there were a couple of very nice new plants in her garden, expensive ones, and you know how tight-fisted Ron is when it comes to anything he doesn't want for himself."

"I could invite Amy over for a cup of tea tomorrow," offered Grace, "although I don't know if she'll tell me anything."

"She might as long as she's sure you're not going to tell Ron," said Maddie. "The only other person I can think of is Miriam. She didn't sell anything to Doug but he did look at her pearls and told her they weren't nearly as good as she thought they were. She was very upset because she thought it meant somebody in her family had lied about their value or possibly stolen them but she's carried on wearing them anyway. Freddie, do you know of somebody who's an expert in pearls and totally trustworthy?"

"I can certainly find someone."

"In that case, I'll see if I can convince Miriam to have them reappraised. It may be tricky because I suspect she rather liked Doug but if I suggest that nobody can be expert in everything and she owes it to her daughter and granddaughters, I'm pretty sure she'll agree."

"When I get back from Portsmouth, I'll see if Joel wants to go for a drink, and maybe drop in on our newcomers, Frank and Isabel, and have a chat and try to lead it round to antiques," said Freddie. "I'll have to tread carefully, I don't want them to realise what we suspect."

"I'll come with you to see Frank and Isabel," offered Maddie, "and I'll see if I can catch Kate and Essie in-between their Scrabble games."

"I think I'll attend the coffee morning in the sheltered accommodation tomorrow and see what the residents there have got to say," said Mrs Mountjoy.

"I'll go with you," said her daughter.

"Honestly, Nell! I don't need a minder! Surely you don't think any harm will come to me in the Residents Lounge?"

Nell laughed. "No, I'm thinking of protecting the other residents, some of the quieter ones are scared of you."

"I suppose that's true." Mrs Mountjoy sounded remarkably complacent as she considered this idea. "So many Baby Boomers lack fortitude. Very well, you may to come along and pacify the wimps."

Maddie's gaze met Freddie's and saw her amusement mirrored in his eyes. Mrs M. had insulted all four people present in her sitting room, all of whom had been born in the relevant time period, but only Grace looked offended. Maddie wondered if it was being called by the slang name for their generation or the suggestion that she might lack courage that had vexed her.

"We've all got our assignments for tomorrow. Is there anything else we can do?" asked Mrs Mountjoy.

"I wonder..." Freddie hesitated.

"Wonder what?" Maddie tried to encourage him.

"We've got a good description of his technique from Mrs Mountjoy and some idea of what he does from what Rose told Grace, but would it be helpful to witness what he gets up to for ourselves? Maybe film him with a hidden camera? At the moment, we haven't got anything we can use against him other than undervaluing certain articles. That's immoral and underhand but not illegal. If Mrs Mountjoy's right and he was going to pocket one of her jade figures, perhaps we could catch him in the act of stealing. What do you think?"

"It could be useful," agreed Mrs Mountjoy. "As long as we've got someone who can carry it through. He's tried his games on me and come off worst, and I don't think he'd believe that Nell would go behind my back to sell our treasures. You're known to have an expertise in antiques, Freddie, as well as being wealthy enough to not need to sell your things. That leaves Maddie or Grace."

"I'll give it a go, if you like," offered Maddie. "It won't be easy. I'll have to be nice to him."

Freddie chuckled. "He's despicable but he's not a fool. If you start being all sweetness and light to him he'll suspect something. Especially when you slammed the door in his face a few days ago."

"You may have a point, although I wasn't thinking of sweetness and light so much as being moderately polite. I'd have to tell him I'd thought it over and decided I could do with a bit of extra cash. I can probably pull it off. I managed to keep up a civilised facade throughout my teaching career. Even when I was considering ways and means of covering the headmaster in concrete and adding him to the foundations of the new school annexe. I never found a feasible way of doing it, though," she added, contemplating one of the on-going disappointments of her working life.

"Most senior managers, whether in education or elsewhere, are encased in a shell of arrogance," said Mrs Mountjoy. "A con artist like Douglas may have a more sensitive antennae for those who are trying to trap him. We need another alternative."

Maddie saw Grace brace herself. At last she spoke, her reluctance obvious, "I suppose I'm the logical person to do this, although I don't have any antiques that are likely to tempt somebody like Douglas. But I'll do it if you think it's necessary."

"Don't worry," said Freddie, "I can supply the antiques. As long as you're happy to do it."

Judging by Grace's expression, Maddie thought she'd much prefer to juggle with red hot coals.

Chapter 23

Grace was silent as she left the Mountjoys' cottage, accompanied by Maddie and Freddie. She was cross with her companions, who, she felt, had pushed her into being the bait to trap Douglas. Of course, they hadn't actually asked her to do it but the silent pressure had been relentless.

She should have stood firm. She was a hopeless actress and she didn't believe she could fool a smooth operator like Douglas, however well Freddie coached her about the antiques she was supposed to own. What was worse, she'd have to lie, and lying was a sin.

She felt hurt that Maddie hadn't come to her rescue. She knew how much Grace hated putting herself on the line and yet she hadn't said a word to help her. Even now, instead of offering reassurance, she was chatting to Freddie about what was likely to be the best strategy to recover Rose's doll, and what to do if Doug was in the shop when they arrived.

"I suppose it could be a problem," said Freddie. "Do you think he'd be suspicious?"

"Like Mrs Mountjoy said, I think somebody who spends their life scamming people will definitely be suspicious. Especially if the woman who works for him has told him about Rose turning up at the shop and how upset she was."

"So how do we play it?" asked Freddie.

"I'll have to sacrifice myself and pretend that I've always coveted Rose's antique dolls and, when I heard she'd sold one, I insisted we hurried into town and you bought it for me."

Freddie chuckled. "You're not the sort of woman I've ever thought of as passionate for dolls but I'm sure you can pull it off."

115

"I think I can get away with it," agreed Maddie. "I'll have to draw on my inner desire for Barbies."

"You had an inner desire for Barbies? Who'd have thought it?"

Maddie screwed up her nose and stuck out her tongue at him. "I'm a woman of remarkable and exceedingly murky depths, but I agree the desire for Barbies is going too far. I'll try to channel pink and frilly thoughts."

"I can see them already, like a sparkling tinsel halo around your head."

Grace was feeling increasingly irritated by this banter. They were almost at Maddie's cottage and she decided it was time to bring the pair of them back to a more sensible discussion. "Even if you can convince Douglas that you want an antique doll, how are you going to make him believe that Freddie would buy it for you? Or that you'd accept such an expensive gift?"

Maddie and Freddie looked at each other and smiled.

"Toy boy?" suggested Maddie.

"Sugar daddy?" Freddie spoke at the same moment.

Grace stared at them and felt hot colour rushing up her neck to heat her face. "You mean you'd pretend to be in a relationship?" she stammered.

"I think we could carry that off," said Maddie.

"It's a lot easier to believe that I have an overwhelming passion for you than that you have one for dolls," agreed Freddie. "Of course, you'll have to pose as a bit of a gold-digger, nobody's going to believe that a lively lady like you would would fall for an old bore like me if I didn't have money."

"Whatever else you are, you're not boring," protested Maddie. "Weird, maybe, but never dull. But it would be fun to play the role of a gold-digger. I'll have to size up any diamond necklaces that Doug's got for sale as well as Rose's doll."

"But if you do that, Douglas will gossip about it and it will be all over the estate within hours!" Grace was horrified.

"With any luck he won't be in the shop tomorrow and the shop assistant won't know who we are," said Freddie.

"Anyway, the Manager didn't think to sneak a morality clause into our residents' agreement," said Maddie. "Freddie, I'll see you tomorrow at nine for our trip to Portsmouth. I've got to go and see Hatty now."

They were beside Hatty's gate and she had opened her front door and was waving to them.

Grace felt annoyed, it seemed as though she'd never get Maddie to herself.

"Good afternoon, Clayfield's answer to Mystic Meg," called Freddie, waving back to her.

"How many times have I got to tell you I'm a medium not an astrologer?" she retorted, but she didn't look upset by his teasing.

He laughed and turned away to cut across the ice-rimed grass of The Green towards his own cottage.

"Maddie, do please come in," said Hatty. "I'd expected you ages ago. I'd almost given you up."

"Sorry about that." Maddie hurried down the path to join her. "I hadn't forgotten but Grace had something she wanted me to do that she considered a priority and I got sidetracked."

"That's quite all right. Not everybody can understand the importance of spiritual experience."

Hatty smiled at them. She may have meant to convey forgiveness but Grace thought she looked patronising. How dare this eccentric woman with her bizarre beliefs imply that Grace, a constant churchgoer, was not a spiritual person? She stood, halfway down the path, and glared at Hatty.

Maddie reached the front door and turned around, matching Grace's glare with her own. "Come on, Grace! Don't stand there dithering. If you're interested in what has happened, come inside. You didn't give me a chance to tell you about it before."

Stricken with shame, Grace realised this was true. Maddie had told her she'd got news but she'd been so preoccupied with the wrong done to Rose that she'd brushed it aside. She longed to withdraw, to go home and close the curtains and bolt the door, but she knew that would be a cowardly thing to do. Worse, her friendship with Maddie was at risk. One more withdrawal and she could lose her friend for good.

"Sorry," she said, hurrying the rest of the distance along the path and into Hatty's cottage. "I was so preoccupied with that other business we were discussing that I forgot to ask about your news."

To her relief, Maddie smiled at her. "That's okay. I had planned to tell you what Hatty told me but now she can tell you herself."

They followed their hostess into her sitting room and refused offers of refreshment on the grounds that they'd only just left the Mountjoys' cottage.

"Tell Grace what happened," commanded Maddie.

Obediently, Hatty directed her attention at Grace and lowered her voice to a melodramatic whisper. "I was sitting at this table, just where you are now, when suddenly I sensed something behind me." She paused for effect.

Grace was not quite able to suppress a shudder but she did succeed in quelling her instinct to look over her shoulder. "Was there anyone there?" she asked, although she was sure the answer would be 'yes'.

Surely even Hatty would not waste such an emotional build up on a non-event?

"He was there. My spectral snowman. The same but different. His voice was low and hoarse. He said he'd come to warn me."

There was another dramatic pause. Grace knew Hatty was waiting for her to ask what she had been warned about, but she felt it was time to introduce some reason into this discussion. She knew what Hatty had seen yesterday was almost certainly a real person dressed up but this second sighting must be the product of a disordered imagination. She tried for a soothing, reasonable tone, "I'm sure your nerves are still upset from what happened yesterday. If you were looking into your crystal ball, I think..."

Hatty interrupted her. "I wasn't trying to summon the spectre. I wasn't thinking about it. I was sitting here, reading a magazine and eating a late lunch, sausages and baked beans."

Chapter 24

Grace heard Maddie give a snort of barely controlled laughter. For a moment she felt offended, then the humour of Hatty's down-to-earth reply struck her. She avoided looking at Maddie. One shared glance and they'd both be giggling and she suspected that Hatty would be offended, which wasn't a good idea when there were still a lot of questions they needed the answers to. It seemed that her first theory had been wrong and Hatty had been revisited by the person who'd assaulted her.

Grace risked a quick look at Maddie who smiled at her. "I know," she said. "If only she'd been eating something less mundane than sausages and baked beans."

"I happen to like sausages and baked beans. Not everybody goes for fancy food, like, like, steak tartare, or stuff like that." It was evident that Hatty was offended.

"I'm sorry, I didn't mean..." Grace stopped speaking. She didn't know what to say. How could she assure Hatty that she wasn't sneering at her menu choices when she'd been brought up to believe such food wasn't what people of refinement ate?

"Sausage and beans are really tasty, as long as they're good quality, not like the stuff they served up for school meals," said Maddie. "Grace and I weren't commenting on your choice of lunch but we thought it wasn't the sort of meal we expected a ghost to turn up for."

Grace had to admit that was a good save of a tricky situation. Certainly Hatty was looking pleased.

"The spirits will appear when the time is right for them," she announced, in what Grace considered an affected, die-away voice. "Even a medium of my experience and power cannot predict when they will make themselves visible."

"I must say I'm glad I haven't got any powers that way," said Maddie. "I can think of nothing worse than having spooky visitors materialise without a moment's notice. With my luck it would be just when I jumped in the shower. Or do spirits not like the damp? It could make their auras soggy."

"Now you're being silly and teasing me," said Hatty.

She sounded perfectly good humoured about it and Grace wondered why Maddie could get away with such silliness, while her own sensible, well-meaning comments caused offence.

"Tell me about the snowman. Where did it come from? What did it say?" She was determined to keep this investigation on track.

"I didn't see him materialise. That's the way of spirits, they simply appear out of the ether."

"So you didn't notice it come through the door?" persisted Grace.

This earned her a pained look. "The spirits do not need to come through doors."

Maddie intervened. "You said the snowman looked different. In what way?"

"I'm not sure, there was something about the face. I know! It was the nose. It looked flatter and rounder. I fear I must have harmed him when I tried to push it away, but that's very strange, I would not have thought that any human force, even that of a medium, could physically harm a spirit."

Grace exchanged a fleeting glance of triumph with Maddie. "I agree, it doesn't seem likely. Did it speak to you? What did it say?"

"He warned me! He said, Hatshepsut you must depart from this place! Be gone! If you do not leave here you will die!"

This time, the look that passed between Grace and Maddie was far more serious. It was Maddie who spoke first. "Hatty, you called it a warning. It sounds to me like a threat."

Grace thought that, for a moment, Hatty looked afraid. If so, the expression swiftly vanished and was replaced by extreme stubbornness.

"It was not a threat. It was a warning. The spirits of the departed would never harm me."

"What even though you whacked it on the nose?" asked Maddie.

Grace had been about to deliver a reasoned, theologically sound explanation of why Hatty's statement made no sense, but she had to admit that Maddie's argument packed far more punch, literally and metaphorically. Thinking of which, "Hatty, when you hit the snowman, what did it feel like?"

"Soft and squi..." Hatty pulled herself up mid-word then continued, "ethereal, my hand just went through." She covered her face with her hands and muttered, "I won't talk about such shameful behaviour. To dwell on it will weaken my psychic powers."

Grace was sure that Hatty's initial response had been more factual and more truthful. What she didn't know was whether Hatty was attempting to fool her questioners or herself.

"You said you didn't see the snowman arrive but how did it depart?" she asked. "Did it go through the front door or the back?"

"Spirits do not need to use doors. My spectre was absorbed into the ether," retorted Hatty.

"Hatty, just for a minute, consider the possibility that the snowman that keeps visiting you is not a ghost but a person dressed up, who's trying to scare you away. This person is willing to hurt you. You could be in real danger." Maddie sounded calm and measured but Grace knew her well enough to sense the underlying exasperation in her voice.

"That's nonsense! Why should anyone want to hurt me or scare me away from here?"

"Perhaps it's nothing to do with you personally. Maybe they want something from this house."

"There's nothing here that anyone could possibly want," insisted Hatty.

"Are you sure of that? Perhaps there's something amongst the things you bought from Norman? Were there any papers or letters left behind? It was Norman's poking and prying into other people's business that got him killed."

Hatty was frowning, then her expression lightened and she began to smile. "You're right, of course, that makes perfect sense."

"Hallelujah!" muttered Maddie.

"Of course my spectre is a manifestation of your friend, Norman. I should have realised that before. He is trying to make contact but he finds it hard. I must work harder to keep the channels open to let him explain what he needs to be freed from his mortal bonds." Hatty shook her head. "If only he could tell me his reasons to return as a snowman. I've never heard or read of anything like that. It's very strange."

Chapter 25

"Strange!" exploded Maddie. "I'll tell you what's strange and that's that anybody could believe such rubbish!"

She considered resisting Grace's efforts to usher her down the path and away from Hatty's cottage. She wanted to go back and tell her foolish neighbour how wrong-headed she was being and that she was placing herself in danger, but deep down she knew that was likely to do more harm than good.

"I don't think she does believe it, at least not wholeheartedly, but she's trying to convince herself she does" said Grace. "She desperately wants it to be a ghost she saw and she's rejecting anything that might indicate otherwise. Do you want to come back to my cottage to talk things over? I've already left Tiggy alone for longer than I wanted on his first day home."

"Yes, okay. We've certainly got a lot to talk about, what with Hatty and her spectral snowman and Doug trying to con people out of their valuables. I wonder if we've got two mysteries to solve or if they're connected?"

"I don't see how they can be." Grace opened her front door and they both took off their coats and made their way to the comfortable sitting room, where Tiggy greeted them with loud demands for food.

"I'll just see to him and put the kettle on," said Grace, hurrying to draw her curtains.

Maddie smiled. Some things didn't change, and Grace being uncomfortable sitting in a lit room with open curtains once it was dark outside was one of those things. As an artist, Maddie appreciated the light provided by the large modern windows but she suspected Grace would prefer the heavily leaded apertures of an earlier age.

At last, sitting comfortably with their mugs of tea, Grace returned to Maddie's question. "There doesn't seem to be any obvious connections between Douglas' deplorable schemes and Hatty's intruder. Not unless he knows of some item of furniture of such immense value that he thinks it's worthwhile to frighten Hatty out of her house, and that would mean employing somebody else to dress as a snowman. We know he wouldn't fit in either the missing snowman suit or through Hatty's kitchen window."

"I suppose it's possible, but it doesn't seem likely that either Norman or Hatty would have anything so valuable that it would be worth that sort of risk," said Maddie.

"Although if she had a big house in Southsea, she must be quite well off."

Maddie nodded. "True. And I did find out that Doug had got upstairs when he came to try and size up any antiques that Hatty had lying about. I asked her about it when I went round the first time today, after she'd told me about her latest snowman visitation. She said that when Doug was at her house somebody knocked at her back door and, by the time she'd got rid of them, Doug had sneaked upstairs. She said she had to be very firm with him to get him downstairs and out of the house."

"So there might be something upstairs that Douglas recognised as valuable." Grace sighed. "Not that we're going to get a chance to find out. She's so cross that we don't believe in her phantom that she's probably not talking to us."

Maddie appreciated that Grace was willing to share the blame, especially when she'd been so good about curbing her own tongue.

"From what I know of Hatty, she'll get over it, as long as I don't offend again. She's pretty good-natured. Besides, I think she's lonely. As far as I can see, she hasn't made many friends since she moved here. It's strange, I don't think she's shy but if she doesn't want to mix or join any clubs why move to a place like this?"

"It's not always as easy to join in as you think. I wouldn't have found it easy to settle if you hadn't come round to visit me the first day I moved here and made me so welcome." Grace looked embarrassed, the way she often did when talking about anything personal. She changed the subject. "As far as Hatty's strange visitor is concerned, we're no further forward, are we?"

"Maybe not." Maddie thought of one area of progress and grinned at her friend. "Except I'm glad to say there's one suspect we can definitely cross off our list for today's snowman charade, and that's Kyle. He was with us all afternoon when Maddie had her visitation."

To her relief, Grace returned her smile. "That is good. It's much more conclusive than our thoughts about his bike. And, Maddie, I'm sorry I didn't listen when you said you'd got news too. I was so wrapped up in what Rose had told me and how distressed she was that I didn't consider anything else."

"That's okay. I was annoyed at the time but it was a good thing we got Mrs M. and Nell and Freddie involved before it was too late to get together and make a plan for tomorrow. The question is, do we want to tell them about Hatty and her strange visitor or visions or whatever they are?"

"I'm not sure that's a good idea, not until we can work out what's going on. The trouble is that Hatty is so..."

"Odd?" suggested Maddie. "I agree."

"And her story is so unbelievable."

"You think we'd look like idiots if we repeated it? Again, I agree. Added to which, if we're going to make this Christmas show work, I don't want to add any more tension into the mix than we can help and tales of ghostly snowmen could be the final straw. Especially as everybody knows that Kyle's costume is missing and some people won't want to listen when I say he's got an alibi for the second snowman appearance. As Freddie keeps saying, 'The show must go on', though I've never worked out why."

"Yes, I think it's better if it's just the two of us," agreed Grace. "Maybe we can talk to Hatty again tomorrow when we've all calmed down."

"You mean when I've got control of my temper and don't tell her again that it's all in in her imagination? We can try but I'm not sure it will do any good. She wants to believe in her spook and she's rewritten the narrative, so now she's convinced that his nose dissolved into vapour when she hit it and that he wafted through the walls instead of walking in and out of the doors. I don't know how she can believe it but she does." There again, as an agnostic, Maddie had never understood how Grace could be so convinced of the things she believed in, but this wasn't the time to say so.

"She does seem very invested in her beliefs," said Grace. "I wonder if she officially changed her name to that strange Egyptian one."

That made Maddie laugh. "If she did, I'd love to know what the official who dealt with it made of it: 'And how exactly do you spell Hatshepsut, Madam?'" The import of what she had said hit her. "Hatshepsut!" she repeated. "Now that's interesting."

"In what way?" demanded Grace.

"When Hatty arrived at Clayfield, I went round to welcome her, the way I always try to do with newcomers, and while we were talking she told me her real name was Hatshepsut because she was the reincarnation of an Egyptian queen. I suggested to her it might be better not to mention that to anybody else, not until she was properly settled in. I explained how a lot of people around here were very conservative in their views and she promised not to mention it and to stick to Hatty."

"But how many people did you tell? After all, you told me before I'd been back an hour."

Maddie was tempted to explain that she'd told Grace because she knew it would wind her up but decided to go with the option that was less likely to cause Grace to explode. "That's because I knew I could trust you not to tell anyone."

Grace looked gratified. "Of course I wouldn't. But, assuming Hatty did do what you suggested and didn't tell anybody else, that means you and I are the only people in Clayfield who know about Hatty calling herself Hatshepsut."

"I've got my alibi for the time of the snowman appearance this afternoon. How about you?" Maddie knew it was wicked to tease Grace but the temptation was irresistible.

"Don't be silly, Maddie. Either Hatty was imagining it, or making it up, or she didn't take your advice and told somebody else, or, if none of those options, it must mean the snowman is somebody who knows her outside of the village and the estate."

Maddie sighed. "I agree, and if it's a stranger, it's going to make it even harder to sort out."

Chapter 26

"I'd heard it was posh but it's a lot bigger than I expected." Maddie surveyed the lavish window display of the shop situated in a quiet Southsea street.

"Yes, it's pretty obvious that Douglas is doing very well for himself." Freddie scowled and she knew he was thinking that Doug's affluence was coming from ripping off people like Rose.

"Stop looking so grumpy and focus on channelling your sugar daddy persona. I didn't get dressed up like this for you to blow it by glaring at Doug or whichever of his minions he's left in charge of his shop."

She glanced down at the dark red, suede boots she was wearing, with their tall, slender heels, It was at least five years since she'd last worn them and she thought longingly of the comfortable, flat shoes she'd used for driving and had changed out of when they parked. She was glad she'd found a parking place in a side road quite near the shop. There had been a nasty couple of minutes when she doubted whether she could balance in these boots at all. One thing was certain, she'd have no problem playing the clinging woman, draped over her escort. It was a good thing Freddie was stronger than he looked.

"What are you thinking?" asked Freddie.

"That I look ridiculous in these clothes. Talk about mutton dressed up as lamb." She thought the dark blue, knee length dress was reasonable enough, although Grace had barely concealed her horror when she she saw the plunge neckline, which revealed more of Maddie's ample bosom than she regarded as seemly. But teamed with a tight-fitting, red leather jacket, another refugee reclaimed from the back of her wardrobe, the whole ensemble screamed past-the-sell-by-date tart.

"You look scrumptious," said Freddie.

She was tempted to point out that describing her in such a lavish way merely demonstrated his fondness for collecting antiques, but she knew he hated it when she put herself down.

With great restraint, she said, "Are you ready to get this show on the road?" And pushed open the door.

Her confidence took a nasty knock when they walked into the shop and were confronted by Elouisa Briar, who emerged from the back premises as soon as the bell above the shop door pealed out its warning.

"Elouisa, this is a surprise. Whatever are you doing here?" She decided it was better to move into the attack than show any sign of guilt.

"Douglas is at an auction and his assistant had an emergency dental appointment, so I stepped into the breach."

"How good of you. Have you got any experience with antiques?" The longer Maddie could keep her talking, the more time she had to work out a reason for her own over the top appearance.

Elouisa shrugged. "I used to help in the shop quite frequently and Douglas said he'll make it worth my while. What are you doing here?" Her gaze raked over Maddie from her purple dyed hair to her high-heeled boots. "I've never seen you dressed up like a ... like that. You're usually so casual in what you wear. Are you going to some sort of fancy dress parade?"

"Sort of," said Maddie, struggling for inspiration. "We're going to a Seventies themed dance."

"At nine-thirty in the morning?" Elouisa didn't bother to hide her scorn.

"It doesn't start until eleven. It's a lunchtime dance." Maddie felt as if she was digging herself in deeper with every word.

"Really? How unusual. Where is it held? I've not heard about it or seen any adverts for it."

"It's not likely you would have," said Freddie, his curt voice a contrast to his usual pleasantness.

"I can't think why not! Janetta hears about most of the local dance events. She's often asked to perform at them."

"But not at this one. This is for people in a certain income bracket and of a certain class, and I'm afraid that neither small-time dance school teachers nor shop assistants meet the required criteria."

Maddie clenched her lips tightly together as she attempted to hide her amusement. It didn't surprise her that Freddie had risen up in her defence. He was usually the most mild mannered of men but the ruthless, successful businessman still lurked beneath the surface.

Elouisa's face flushed bright red and then drained leaving her very white. Her eyes glistened dangerously. "Indeed? You don't seem to have made as much effort to dress up in Seventies clothes as Maddie has."

"Maddie always goes for everything wholeheartedly. It's why so many people admire her so much. I'm afraid I spent most of my youth in rather a dull, conventional way."

Enjoyable though it was to listen to Freddie snubbing Elouisa, Maddie thought it was time to get their mission back on track. At least she'd thought of a good reason for wishing to buy an antique doll. Or if not good, it was more believable than trying to pretend she was the sort of woman who hankered after antique dolls.

"We were looking at the antique shops because Freddie wanted to buy a special gift for my little granddaughter," she said.

"I didn't know you'd got a granddaughter. I thought you'd got two grandsons."

"My daughter's got two sons, my son has one of each." That was true and if Elouisa asked anybody who knew Maddie well they'd confirm it.

"I see." Elouisa gave them a bright, salesperson's smile. "We've got some nice silver bracelets. How much were you thinking of spending?"

"Oh, probably not more than five thousand." Freddie made the handsome sum sound quite usual. "I was thinking of something that could form the start of a collection, perhaps a teddy bear or doll."

"That's very generous." Elouisa was looking at Freddie with new respect.

"Well a godparent has certain duties, don't they?" Freddie beamed at Maddie and she returned his smile, admiring the way he'd made his extravagance sound quite acceptable. Now they had to hope that Guinevere Henriette was still here and that Douglas hadn't heard about Rose's visit yesterday and taken her with him to enter her in the auction he was attending.

Chapter 27

Their suspense did not last long. Fortunately, Douglas' stock of expensive bears and dolls was moderate and Freddie had done his homework by asking Grace to procure a description of Rose's lost darling. Within a few minutes, Guinevere Henriette was theirs, and at eight hundred pounds cheaper than the original asking price, after Freddie had insisted Elouisa checked whether Douglas had left instructions about a 'best price' and whether there was a reduction for cash.

Maddie thought that Elouisa looked rather sullen as she agreed the price and wondered whether, if Freddie hadn't haggled, she'd have skimmed her 'commission' off the total paid. She knew if she shared her thoughts with Grace, she'd shake her head and sigh, ostentatiously mourning Maddie's cynicism, but the fact remained that cynics were often right.

At this point, with Guinevere Henriette safely in Freddie's arms, Maddie would have cut and run, or cut and hobbled, crippled by her boots, but Freddie put the doll down on the counter and seemed determined to check out the rest of Douglas' stock. As he pored over the locked showcases of jewellery, she hoped he wasn't planning to buy anything as a gift for her. There were some beautiful pieces on display but she'd always wonder if they had been acquired by underhand or illegal means.

To her relief, Freddie turned away and indicated a locked cupboard that was protected by fine wire mesh, which made it hard to see the contents. "May I look at these?"

"I'm not really supposed to open that cupboard and I certainly can't sell them," protested Elouisa, "they're items that will go for auction when Douglas finds the right one and they're not priced."

"No harm in letting me take a peek," insisted Freddie, "after all, I may wish to attend the auction and bid." He smiled at her. "If I do acquire something you've shown me, I'll make sure you get your commission."

"Very well, but you must both promise you won't tell anybody I let you look."

"I promise," said Freddie.

"Me too," said Maddie, although she made mental exceptions in the case of Grace, Mrs Mountjoy and Nell.

"I know where Douglas keeps the key, I'll get it for you." It was evident that Elouisa had forgiven Freddie's previous snubs, dazzled by his wealth and his offer of commission.

She disappeared into the back premises and returned a few seconds later. She looked nervous, shifty and yet curiously triumphant. Maddie wondered about her relationship with Doug, it didn't seem to be as simple as being on friendly terms with her sister's lover.

She wandered across to look as Freddie examined the contents of the showcase. Some of the vases and small statues looked quite attractive but none of them seemed to her to warrant the appreciation that Freddie was displaying. Admittedly, only a few of Mrs Mountjoy's valuable jade ornaments appealed to her.

"Now this really is a treasure!" exclaimed Freddie, indicating a pale blue vase that she assumed was Chinese.

"Is it? I don't know how you can tell," said Maddie.

"The same way that you judge things, experience and instinct. Believe me, this is very valuable."

"How much is it worth?" She was fascinated by Freddie's transformation into an authoritative antiques expert.

"It's hard to say for certain in an auction situation but, assuming it's the right auction, and Doug seems to know what he's doing that way, and if the provenance is sound, I'd estimate it could raise several hundred thousand."

"More than a hundred thousand?" Elouisa's voice sounded strangled. For a moment she remained motionless, as if paralysed. Regaining movement, she took the vase from Freddie with hands that shook so violently that Maddie thought she was in danger of dropping it.

Apparently Freddie shared her fear because he reached out and rescued the vase and replaced it on the shelf. "I'd have thought so but it would need authenticating by suitable experts. I'm surprised Douglas doesn't keep it in a safe but I suppose he may think it's better to conceal it amongst other less valuable items. Hiding a tree in a forest sort of thing." He looked concerned, "Are you all right?"

Good question! Elouisa was hyperventilating and her face was sickly white.

"Yes, of course. I don't want Doug to know that I'd opened a cupboard when he'd told me not to." Elouisa's hands were trembling as she shut the cupboard door, realised she'd left the key on one of the shelves, opened it again, snatched up the key and turned it in the lock.

"You'd better go now." She picked up the wrapped doll from the counter, thrust it into Maddie's arms and hustled them towards the door. Once they were on the doorstep, she took a deep breath and said in a determinedly jolly voice, "Enjoy your dance. Mind you don't turn your ankle in those boots."

"I will." Maddie was glad that dancing wasn't really on the menu. She'd settle for staggering back to the car without damaging herself.

The shop door clanged shut behind them with a force that was just short of a slam.

Outside, on the pavement, they stared at each other.

"What do you make of that?" said Freddie. "She seemed really scared that Douglas would find out she'd opened that cupboard for us."

Maddie shook her head. "I don't know. I didn't get the feeling she was frightened but she was certainly upset. Maybe she was worried that Doug wouldn't pay her if he found out she'd disobeyed his instructions." But as she thought back to the frozen look she'd glimpsed on Elouisa's face, she found it hard to believe it had been produced by something so trivial.

Chapter 28

"That's better!" Maddie came downstairs and grinned at Grace and Freddie, who were waiting for her in her living room. "It's official, I'm never going to wear those boots again."

"I told you that dressing up in those unsuitable clothes was a bad idea." Grace made no attempt to keep the smugness out of her voice. She'd been scandalised when she'd seen Maddie's outfit earlier today and she very much enjoyed being proved right. Not that she totally approved of Maddie's current choice of jeans, trainers and a multi-coloured sweatshirt. For women of their age, a tailored pair of trousers, low-heeled leather shoes and a good quality jumper in a subdued shade was more appropriate.

"I rather liked the dressing up," said Freddie. "It made it more of an adventure. Of course, we didn't know that Elouisa Briar would be there, eager to spread gossip about us all around the village."

"It's not just the gossip." Maddie got a bottle out of the fridge and poured three glasses of white wine. "If Elouisa tells Doug we're onto him, he could go off to victimise another set of vulnerable people."

"I don't want to sound defeatist but don't you think that might be the best option?" said Grace.

She accepted the glass that Maddie was offering her, even though she knew she ought to refuse. It was only just after eleven in the morning, much too early for alcohol whatever Maddie said to the contrary.

"What do you mean?" asked Maddie.

"Do you really think we can get evidence against a man as crafty as Douglas? He knows all the tricks and how to manipulate people. Perhaps the best thing we can do is to scare him away. At least that way we can

137

protect our own people." In the back of her mind there was the hope her co-conspirators might abandon the plan for her to sell some carefully chosen antiques to a man who was bound to see right through her.

"Do you really think it's right not to try?" said Maddie. "You're the one who's always claiming the moral high ground. I thought you didn't approve of NIMBYism."

Grace tried to conceal her embarrassment by taking an extra large gulp of wine. She hated it when her happy-go-lucky friend challenged her on a point of principal.

"I don't want him to get away with it but I don't see what we can do. It seems he covers his back very well. It's only a few things he buys for a long way beneath the price he sells them for so we can't prove he's consistently cheating people, and if we catch him stealing something and challenge him, he just has to apologise and say it was an oversight. The police don't like prosecuting prominent, respectable businessmen unless they're sure they're going to get a conviction."

"I understand what you're saying but I think the only thing we can do is keep poking and prying until we find his weak spot," said Freddie.

"Well said, Freddie!" Maddie beamed at him.

Grace felt excluded, which she didn't like. It gave her a certain, gloomy pleasure to pour cold water on their hazy plan of action. "I spoke to Amy while you were out."

"And?" demanded Maddie.

"This is strictly between ourselves. She doesn't want it to get back to Ron, but she did sell Douglas some stamps she'd inherited from her late brother. Ron didn't know about them. She wanted to make some improvements to her aviary and garden."

"I thought she had," said Maddie. "It's amazing how she can get these things past Ron. I suppose she spins him a story and it never occurs to him that she'd lie to him."

"Yes," said Grace. She didn't approve of lying but Ron Bunyan was a tight-fisted, controlling man.

"And did Doug cheat her?" demanded Freddie.

"No." Somehow, bursting their bubble didn't feel as satisfying as Grace had expected.

"You're sure?" asked Freddie.

"Amy was sure. When she heard that Douglas was buying antiques, she wrote to three dealers who specialise in stamps describing what she had to sell. They all sent her similar estimates and she told Douglas she wouldn't sell for less and he agreed to her price."

"I bet he loved that," said Maddie.

Grace smiled. "Amy said she was afraid she'd offended him because he looked quite cross but she couldn't help that."

"Just when you think you know somebody they totally surprise you," said Maddie. "Who would have thought Amy could be so shrewd?"

"She certainly didn't have any Chinese vases to sell," said Grace. "I checked specifically after Freddie texted from the car while you were coming back."

"Nor did anyone else that Nell and Mrs Mountjoy spoke to today," said Maddie, who'd been checking the messages on her phone. "Freddie contacted them straight after he texted you and Nell has just come back to say they found a few people who had sold things to Doug but none of them said that they felt cheated. I guess Nell had to work very hard to stop her mother disillusioning them about what a lovely man Douglas was."

"I can imagine." Freddie chuckled. "Nothing if not forthright, that's our Mrs M."

"Nell said Mrs Carruthers, who's in the nursing home, was saying something about her ruby and diamond pendant that her husband had given her but they couldn't make sense of what she said."

"She loves that pendant," said Grace. "Surely she would never have sold that?"

"No, Nell said she was still wearing it, like she always does, but she said something about not feeling the love in it was the same any more."

"Poor lady. Dementia is such a cruel condition." Grace sighed. "What do we do now?"

"I was thinking of doing the same as Nell and Mrs M. are doing, resting and relaxing in preparation for the rehearsal tonight. It's got the potential to be a battle." Maddie grinned at Grace. "This is where you start thinking wistfully about how peaceful it is at your aunt's house."

Grace tried to return her smile, wondering how Maddie had read her thoughts.

Outside of Maddie's house she said goodbye to Freddie, who started back across The Green at his fastest pace, mindful that his elderly dog had been left alone for longer than usual. She strolled back towards her cottage, still pondering Maddie's last, rather pointed, remark.

A scream jerked her back to the present. She looked all around she could not see anyone in trouble. She heard a girl sobbing, "Stop! You're hurting me" and a man's voice shouting, "Give it to me you little tart!"

This was followed by burst of profanity that made Grace long to clasp her hands to her ears to shut it out. She mastered this cowardly impulse and followed the sound to one of the small alleyways that separated each pair of cottages.

Heart thumping, she ran to investigate. A man was there, a large and burly man, who at a second look she recognised as the subject of their investigations, Douglas Bartlett. He was twisting the arm of a tall, slender, brown-haired girl and reaching into her coat pocket.

"Stop that!" Grace shouted. She felt horribly afraid. A man who could assault a young woman could attack an old one.

He turned to face her and she stopped, frozen by the bestial rage in his face.

"Let go of her!" A young man brushed past her and squared up to the older, bulkier man.

"Mind your own bloody business!" Douglas snarled the words. He spun the girl round and thrust her at the boy. He caught her, but this put him off balance, unable to defend himself as Douglas attacked, punching him around the face and head. "I'll teach you to interfere in my business!"

The boy got one punch in but that seemed to enrage his bull-like assailant even more.

Grace watched in horror. She had to summon help. She knew she should add her screams to those of the girl, who was screeching for somebody to come as she clung to Douglas' arm, trying to minimise the viciousness of the blows. Grace tried to call out but all her years of training acted against her, stifling her voice. 'A lady should never shout or scream or behave in a way that draws attention to herself,' her mother's reproof echoed in her memory.

The boy staggered and went down. He curled into a ball as Douglas stood poised to stamp down on him. The girl renewed her efforts, kicking at Douglas and putting him off balance. He turned back to her and restrained her with one hand while, with the other, he again fumbled in her coat pocket.

As he did so, Grace remembered something she'd never expected to use. She rummaged in her own pocket and produced a small plastic cylinder. Maddie's daughter had bought it at the same time as she got one for her mum, after the trouble they'd had on the estate a few months ago. She'd begged them to remember to keep them with them at all times.

With trembling fingers, Grace pressed the button and the shrill wail of the personal alarm echoed around the estate.

Chapter 29

The screech of the alarm caused Douglas to pause. He turned and stared at Grace. For a moment, she feared he was going to snatch the alarm from her hand, probably to stamp on it. In a childish gesture of defiance, she put her hand behind her back. He scowled at her but made no attempt to approach, instead he made a final attempt to wrench the object he was seeking from the girl's pocket, then turned and lumbered off towards the footpath that ran between the cottages and the farmer's fields. As he did so, a spray of small white beads pattered to the ground.

Grace found that she was shaking. She managed to gasp out, "Are you all right?"

"Yes, thanks to you," croaked the boy as he struggled to get up.

The girl rushed to help him. "Kyle, I'm so sorry," she gasped.

Kyle! Now she'd heard the name, Grace identified him the young man she'd met at the rehearsal. The boy she persisted in thinking of as 'Maddie's protege'. And she was pretty sure the girl was Tempest Briar, Janetta's daughter.

By now the first respondents to her alarm had arrived. Maddie and Freddie were there amongst them, which was good, but she was less happy to see Joel, who lived on the opposite side of The Green. Joel was a decent man and Grace liked him well enough but he had an authoritative manner and always seemed to feel he should take charge of any situation. There were questions he was bound to ask that she didn't wish to answer until she'd consulted Maddie. Worse, hobbling after him, came Ron, so eager to see what was happening that he was still struggling into his coat, even though he was a chill-obsessed hypochondriac. Joel tended to be bossy but Ron was the biggest gossip on the estate, and if he couldn't be sure of the facts he'd make them up.

"What happened?" demanded Joel.

"A man was trying to mug this young lady and the young man came to her aid. I pressed my alarm to get help." Grace's voice was as shaky as she felt but she was encouraged by the approving look she received from Maddie, which she interpreted as commending her brevity.

"Let's get the young people to my cottage out of the cold, and you too, Grace," said Maddie. She started to usher Kyle and the girl towards the footpath behind the cottages.

Freddie stooped down and picked up the scattered beads. "I see you've broken your pretty necklace, Temp. I'll see how many of these I can find. Joel, will you give me a hand please?"

Thwarted from taking control, Joel didn't look happy, especially at being ordered around by Freddie but he was too polite to refuse. Their bent forms, as they scrabbled on the rutted frozen ground, created a suitable barrier that prevented Ron from getting through. He stood there, gasping for breath and leaning on his stick, as he stared around him. He peered at Grace and edged towards her. To avoid Ron's inquisition, she backed away and went down the front path, heading towards Maddie's cottage by an alternative route.

When she reached the cottage, she hesitated, then skirted round the side of the cottages and approached from the rear. Maddie was in her kitchen, filling a bowl with warm water. She saw Grace coming down the garden path and smiled and hurried to open the door.

"Thank goodness! I was afraid you were so upset that you'd gone home."

"I was trying to avoid Ron and Joel." Grace tried to sound brisk but she realised she was trembling again.

"Good strategy. I only hope Freddie shows as much sense. He knows he ought to lose the nosy neighbours but a lot of the time he's too good-natured to do anything ruthless. I'll just take this water and some cloth through to Temp to mop up Kyle's face, then I'll make tea or coffee, whichever people want."

She did as she said, then returned to the kitchen, where Grace was still standing. She was trying to push the unpleasant experience out of her mind, although she knew Maddie would insist upon discussing it some time soon.

Maddie took one look at her and gave her a swift, fierce hug. "Well done, you. It was quick thinking, using that alarm. Are you okay? Douglas didn't hurt you did he?"

"No, he didn't touch me." Grace heard her voice quaver. "But I was so afraid!"

"I'm not surprised you were scared. I'd have been terrified. But you kept your head, and Temp said you stopped Kyle from being beaten up far worse than he was."

"Really?" Grace still felt shaken but now it was eased by a faint tinge of pride.

"Definitely. Do you mind telling me quickly what happened? I know we'll have to go over it again when Freddie gets here."

"But shouldn't we call the police before we do anything else? And does Kyle need medical treatment?"

"He says he's not too badly hurt. I'm not sure there's much we can do apart from keep an eye on him. You know what the waiting times are like at A&E."

"But the police should be told."

Maddie shrugged. "The kids both say they don't want to call the police."

"But why?"

"I'm not sure about Temp's reason but I know what Kyle's thinking. He doesn't trust the police, or social workers or anybody in authority. In his experience, if it's a choice between him and someone like Douglas, they'll believe Douglas every time."

"But I saw Douglas attack him. I can tell the police." Grace knew her duty and was determined do it.

"We can tell Kyle that but I'm not going to call the police without his agreement. Think what idiots we'd look if we call the police and tell them Kyle was attacked and he and Temp deny it."

Grace had opened her mouth to object but now she shut it again. After a few moment's thought, she said, "What are we going to do then?" Even to her own ears, she sounded pettish.

"I assume we'll run through the whole story now that Freddie's on his way." She nodded towards the back window and laughed at the sight of Freddie scuttling along the garden path as though the hounds of hell were at his heels.

"What good does he think that will do him? Joel and Ron will know where he's going anyway?" said Grace grumpily.

"I'm sure he knows that but he also knows I'll be a lot more ruthless in my methods of getting rid of anyone who comes snooping around. And Ron and Joel know it too." Maddie opened the door. "Go on through to the sitting room, Freddie." She loaded a tray with mugs full of coffee and a sumptuous looking chocolate cake. "Come on, Grace. Let's go and see the kids."

Grace obeyed, wondering when Maddie had found the time to bake on top of everything else.

Kyle looked much better now that the blood had been washed off his face, although his lip was swollen and his eye puffy. Maddie took out her phone and took a few photos of the damage.

"Why are you doing that?" protested Kyle. "I already told you, no police."

"I know, but I'm still going to record the evidence." She presented him with a plate and knife to cut up his cake and asked, "Do you want a straw to drink your coffee? Or would you prefer something cool to drink?"

"No, that's fine, thanks. I'll just wait for the coffee to cool down."

"You told me you didn't lose consciousness, but did he hit you in the body too?"

Grace guessed that Maddie was worrying about fractured ribs or a ruptured spleen.

"No, just my face," said Kyle.

Grace thought how odd that was. She didn't know much about physical violence but surely a man beating an opponent would hit out at any vulnerable place he could?

"I see," said Maddie.

"See what?" demanded Freddie. "I don't understand."

"Douglas has his own agenda."

"That's very cryptic," he complained.

"I suspect he thinks a battered face will stop Kyle appearing in our show."

"It's more than that," said Tempest, "he's often threatened to rearrange Kyle's 'pretty face'. I know a lot of people on this estate like him, especially some of the older women, but he's a dishonest, lying thug who won't keep his hands to himself."

147

"Don't hold back," said Maddie. "Tell it like it is. We all agree with you."

Tempest smiled at her. "Thank you." She turned to Grace. "And thank you for sounding that alarm. It's a great idea. I'm going to get one for myself as soon as I can."

"You're welcome," said Grace, but her mind was on the implications of what Tempest had just said. "When you said that Douglas didn't know how to keep his hands to himself, did you mean he'd tried to molest you?" She felt herself blush at the very idea.

"Not if you mean forcing me to have sex with him, although sometimes he's threatened 'to show me what a real man can do'. But he's always physically bullying me when no-one else is around. It's usually pushing me against walls, or grabbing my hair to pull my head back, or twisting my arms, but a few times he's put his hands around my throat and squeezed. It's worse when he's drunk."

"But have you told your mother?" Grace was shocked.

"I tried, but he told her I was trying to make trouble because I was jealous of their relationship and she believed him. She likes having him around. He takes her to posh places and buys her lots of expensive stuff." Tempest grabbed her coffee mug and raised it to her lips, concealing half her face. Her hands were trembling.

"I'm sorry, Temp, you deserve better than that," said Maddie. "But what happened this afternoon? Why did he risk attacking you and Kyle on an estate full of old people? Surely he knows what a nosey lot we are."

"When he loses his temper he doesn't care about anything like that. He always thinks people will believe his version of things," said Tempest, still half-hidden behind her mug.

148

"But what made him so angry?" persisted Maddie.

"It was my fault. I didn't do what I was told, not totally. You see, I opened the box?"

"What box?" demanded Maddie.

"The box with the pearl necklace in it."

"Pearl necklace!" exclaimed Freddie, leaning forward eagerly. "I see! Now it's beginning to make sense."

Chapter 30

"Now who's being cryptic? It may make sense to you but it doesn't to me," said Maddie.

She looked at Grace, Kyle and Tempest who all shook their heads. "And apparently it doesn't make sense to anybody else. Kindly explain and stop looking so smug or I'll confiscate your chocolate cake."

Freddie tightened his grip on his plate. "You're a hard woman, Maddie. I will tell you what I'm thinking, but first could Temp tell us where she got the necklace from and who told her not to look inside the box?"

"It was my mother," said Tempest. "She told me I must teach her ballroom dancing class this morning because she was going out and Aunt Lou was busy. But I refused. Kyle keeps telling me that I should stand up to Mum and Aunt Lou, so I tried. I hate the ballroom class, they're all at least twice my age and they patronise me. Mum was so angry. She told me it was really vital that she did an important errand and when I still refused she threatened to throw me out of the house. She said if I was so ungrateful I could find a new place to live and support myself." She scrubbed at the tears that were welling up in her eyes. "I know I'm really lucky and I owe her a lot and I nearly gave in, but I was angry at the way she's always bossing me around, so I kept saying 'no' and in the end she said she'd take the class but I had to do her errand for her. She said she'd pay my bus fare and I didn't really mind going into Portsmouth, so I said I'd do it. She gave me the address and told me what to ask for and so I went and collected the box."

"Where did you collect it from?"

"A little, second-hand jewellery shop, in a back street in Fratton. It was pretty run down."

150

"The bus was late and I'd promised to meet Kyle after he'd had his fitting for his new snowman costume with Miss Mountjoy, and I knew I'd miss him if I went in to the village to give the box to Mum. So I thought I'd come here first and tell him where I was going and I'd meet him at the bus stop to go into college together."

Tempest looked down, clearly embarrassed. "Mum told me to bring the box straight back without opening it. But you know how it is. Or perhaps you don't, perhaps it's just me. The more I thought about not being allowed to see inside that box, the more I wanted to. Walking along the footpath behind the cottages, I couldn't resist any longer. The box wasn't sealed so I opened it and saw the necklace. I'd just taken it out and was looking at it when I saw Kyle coming down the footpath and waited to show it to him. The next thing I knew, Douglas was roaring towards me, calling me all sorts of nasty names. I suppose he must have followed me from the bus stop. I panicked. I shoved the necklace back in my pocket but he grabbed me and hurt me and tried to snatch it away. So I screamed. Then Kyle got there and tried to stop him and he started hitting Kyle, swearing and saying he was going to spoil his face. Then this lady sounded her alarm and Douglas ran away."

She covered her face with her hands. "I didn't mean to make all this trouble."

"You didn't make it alone," said Maddie. "Now, Freddie, it's time to tell us what you're thinking." She smiled as she saw he'd polished off his slice of cake in record time.

"I may be completely wrong." He stood up and went into the hall where his winter coat was hanging. Maddie leaned forward and craned her neck so that she could watch him and saw him remove an envelope from his coat pocket. He returned to the sitting room. "Have you got a clean tray I can use, Maddie?"

"Of course." She guessed what he wanted to do and fetched one from the kitchen that had a deep rim and put it on the coffee table in front of him.

"Thank you." He tilted the envelope and poured out a stream of beads, milky white and shimmering like moonlight, followed by a frayed piece of thread. "Do these remind you of anything?"

Glancing around, Maddie saw that Grace and Tempest looked puzzled but in Kyle's face she could see a glimmer of the same understanding she herself felt.

Tempest spoke first. "I don't know what you mean. It doesn't remind me of anything but it's the necklace I collected from Portsmouth, at least most of it."

"Undoubtedly," said Freddie. "You can see the frayed bit of thread where it got caught in your pocket zip when Douglas wrenched at it. Anything else?"

He beamed at Maddie and she knew he was teasing her.

Before she could answer, Kyle cut in. "It looks like the necklace that old lady always wears. You know, the Que Sera woman, Miriam."

"There's certainly a strong resemblance," agreed Freddie.

"But that doesn't make sense," protested Kyle. "She was wearing it yesterday. How could it have got to a shop in Portsmouth? And why would Temp's mum have sent her to collect it?"

"Never mind that!" exclaimed Tempest. "If they're real pearls they must be valuable. Are all of them still there? I'm going to be so much trouble anyway and if I've lost some Douglas will say I've stolen them, or blame Kyle and say he's done it."

"I'm not certain if we've got all of them, but I really wouldn't worry about that," said Freddie.

"But..." Tempest's voice trailed away. "I don't understand."

"I think I do," said Maddie. "Miriam told me that she felt very disappointed because she'd just had her pearls valued by an expert and they weren't nearly as valuable as she'd been told they were. She felt hurt because she assumed somebody in her family had lied to her and upset because she'd looked forward to handing them on to her daughter and granddaughters."

"That fits in with what I'm thinking!" said Freddie. "Is she thinking of getting rid of them?"

"She said not. She said she loved them even if they weren't the valuable freshwater pearls she'd been told."

"When she said they're not valuable, does that mean they're glass or paste? Something I can manage to replace," asked Tempest.

"I'm no great expert on jewellery, I've always been more interested in ceramics, but I'd think the ones we've got here are reasonably nice cultured pearls, worth about five hundred pounds," said Freddie.

"I see. I'll try to get the money but it won't be easy." Tempest slumped back in her chair.

In contrast, Grace looked eager. "Was Douglas the expert who valued Miriam's pearls?" she asked.

"Give the clever lady a balloon and bunch of flowers. He was indeed," answered Maddie.

"So do you think he was up to his old tricks?"

"Not exactly, Grace. I think this may be a new version of the trick he played on Rose. You see, Miriam doesn't want to sell her pearls. She doesn't need the money and she's still got a sentimental attachment to them. I think Douglas planned a trick that was riskier to pull off because it's illegal." Maddie glanced at Freddie who nodded encouragement. "I think Miriam's original pearls are every bit as valuable as she's always thought and when Douglas was valuing them he took the chance to get a good look at them. He probably weighed and measured them. Maybe he even took photos of them. I'd guess that Miriam isn't a suspicious sort of woman, and not very observant."

"I'd agree with that," said Freddie. "She's a bit like me. When she's chatting away, she doesn't notice much."

Maddie ignored this interruption and continued to explain her theory. "I think Douglas had a replica necklace made up. I wouldn't mind betting that he knows lots of dodgy jewellers and other forgers and it's worth spending a few hundred if you're going to make thousands on the deal. I guess he planned to do a swap whenever he got a chance and Miriam would have carried on wearing them not knowing that she'd been robbed."

"There's a full dress rehearsal this evening. That would be a good opportunity for him. Perhaps that's why he was so eager to get the cultured pearls today," said Grace.

Maddie thought it was strange that Grace, who had such high moral standards, should accept Douglas' guilt so readily. She said, "You're probably right."

"It's horrible! Stealing things from old people who can't protect themselves," said Tempest. "Especially when it's things they care about. And my mum sent me to get the fake necklace. Do you think she knows?"

"She probably doesn't, or she wouldn't have involved you," said Freddie. "It's likely that Douglas fooled her as well. It seems he's good at fooling lots of people and I'm sure he's shown Janetta his most charming side."

Maddie spotted a look of deep scepticism on Grace's face. She also had her her doubts about Janetta's innocence but she approved of Freddie's kindness in trying to let Tempest down easily.

"What am I going to do? I can't go home." Tempest was shaking. "It was bad enough if I had to tell mum I'd disobeyed her and the necklace had been broken, but I can't face her now."

"You can stay with me," said Kyle.

"But mum and Douglas know where you live. They'll come and drag me home. He could hurt you even more than he did before." Tempest rubbed her sore wrist.

Maddie knew she had no choice. "You're eighteen, aren't you Temp?"

"Yes."

"I just wanted to check that you're an adult. Your mum may hold the purse strings but she can't force you to live anywhere you don't want. You can stay in my spare room, at least for a few days, if you'd like to."

She resigned herself to spending a vigorous half hour clearing the spare room of all the Christmas presents she'd got stored there, but at least it would make her remember to carry her little cockatiel back downstairs as soon as all the visitors had dispersed.

"Thank you but..." Temp was looking at Kyle.

Maddie guessed what she was thinking. If Douglas knew where Kyle lived he'd be vulnerable to attack.

"And, Kyle, it would be a good idea if you stayed here as well."

Grace cleared her throat. "I'm sorry, but I don't think that's a good idea."

155

Chapter 31

Grace's protest took Maddie by surprise. She knew her friend was prudish but she'd always thought her goodhearted. Maddie hated the idea that she'd send Kyle into potential danger rather than let him share a room with his girlfriend. Angry words bubbled up in her thoughts. She felt like a volcano about to erupt and spill hot lava all over the room.

"I'm not being prudish, at least, I don't think I am," said Grace, as if she'd plucked the word from Maddie's mind. "It's just I was thinking about what you said a little while ago, Maddie. There may not be a clause in our tenancy agreement that says unmarried people can't sleep together but people do gossip and if Tempest's mother starts telling everybody that Kyle has corrupted her daughter, it could turn the whole estate against him just when he needs people on his side."

"That's true," said Maddie. "Janetta could even twist it so that it looked like Douglas had hit Kyle to protect Temp." She felt guilty that she'd misjudged Grace and glad she hadn't actually said the things she'd been thinking.

"She's right, the Filth would love that story. I'd be in a cell before I could blink. No way they'd believe I was rescuing Temp from him, they wouldn't want to believe it," agreed Kyle.

"They might change their tune when they encountered the solicitor I'd employ to represent you," said Freddie grimly, and for once it was easy to see him as the tough, successful businessman he had been. "However, it might be wise to keep public opinion on our side, at least within the estate. I'd be happy if you stayed in my spare room until this is sorted out, Kyle."

"Thank you but I don't want to cause you grief with your friends." Maddie thought that Kyle couldn't believe that anybody would offer him kindness when it could cause them trouble.

"Anyone who's a friend of Douglas isn't a friend of mine," said Freddie.

"If I were you, I'd say yes," intervened Maddie. "I'll bet that Freddie's spare room is far more luxurious than mine and you won't have any excuse for being late for rehearsals if it's only five minutes walk away."

"You still want me? I thought after all the aggro..."

"You're not the one I'm going to recommend to the committee is removed from the show," said Freddie. "I'd planned to email the committee to let them know we've enlisted Grace's help but I think we'll need a full meeting to dislodge Douglas."

"I agree that he's the one who should go but what will happen if Janetta removes her dance school children? Won't it leave you, I mean us, with a gap in our programme?" asked Grace.

"Mum may have a tantrum but I don't think she'll withdraw the kids," said Tempest, "it's bad for business, especially when the parents have paid her a fortune for the costumes and dragged out in the rain and ice to take them to rehearsals."

"Paid her a fortune for the costumes?" queried Maddie. "I thought the parents were making them? And the material shouldn't have cost much because Nell sourced it at a bulk discount and passed on all the savings."

Tempest looked embarrassed. "I didn't know that but I do know that mum and Aunt Lou and me made all the kids' dresses and charged for doing it. Mum said they had to have consistency and some of the

157

parents would be so useless at sewing that the dresses would fall apart."

"And it didn't matter to her that kids whose parents couldn't afford to buy a Janetta Briar dance dress would miss out on taking part in the show," said Kyle savagely, which mirrored Maddie's thoughts.

"I'm sorry," said Tempest.

"It's not your fault," said Maddie. "But we need to contact Joel and Nell and warn them that the committee needs to show a united front."

"I thought that Joel didn't want to take part in the show?" said Grace.

Maddie grinned. "He doesn't, but he loves being part of a committee and he's good at sweet-talking the manager. So we linked his one man reading to our burlesque. Not that he allows us to interfere with one word of his show."

"Before we do anything else, we ought to collect what Kyle needs from his bedsit," said Freddie.

"I'm afraid I can't give you a lift, I've got to fit in an extra rehearsal with Stan," said Maddie.

"I can take you," offered Grace, although she didn't sound enthusiastic.

"I'll get the bus," said Kyle.

"No need for that," said Freddie, "and no need for you to spend your afternoon chauffeuring us about, Grace. Just because I don't drive doesn't mean all my friends have to give me lifts. Kyle and I can take a taxi down, as soon as I've taken Percy for a quick walk. The poor old fellow's been left alone too long."

"Bring him over to me. He and Tiggy can play together," said Grace.

Maddie smiled. It was evident that Grace found this a more appealing option than driving to the rougher parts of Portsmouth and visiting Kyle's bedsit.

Ten minutes and two phone calls later and the Emergency Christmas Show Committee meeting had been set up to take place at the Mountjoy's cottage early that evening. Maddie's sitting room was gloriously, if temporarily, empty of visitors. Grace had gone home and Tempest had decided to accompany Freddie and Kyle to Portsmouth, both to avoid her mother, aunt and Doug and to buy a few cheap necessities for her refuge at Maddie's house.

Feeling rather jaded, Maddie went to meet Stan in the Main House. She hoped his expectations regarding her performance weren't very high.

"I'm sorry, Maddie. I'm wasting your time. I'm finding it hard to concentrate."

Stan sounded so apologetic that Maddie couldn't stay cross with him, even though it was the fourth time he'd mucked up their Polar Bear and Penguin routine.

"Aren't you feeling well? Do you want to call it a day?" she asked.

"No, I'm not ill. Just worried."

"Is there anything I can do to help?" Maddie had the unworthy thought that now wasn't the time to ask if he could fill Douglas' place as a snowman if the committee voted to exclude Douglas from the show.

"Thank you, but I don't think there's anything anyone can do to help." Stan sighed. "I've been visiting Antonia, my sister, in the nursing home."

"Is she worse?" Maddie thought there could be nothing crueller than to see someone you cared for slip away from you like that.

"Some days are better than others but she does seem to be deteriorating. I've never seen her so agitated before. Usually, she loves to look at old photos, sometimes it helps to call her back, but today,

159

when I showed her one, she grabbed it from my hand and tried to tear it up."

He picked up his jacket from the back of a chair and took a small photograph album out of the pocket. "You can see there's nothing in it to upset her. It was taken when she was godmother to my son. Her husband died young and she never had children. She and my wife were dear friends and she's been like a second mother to my boys. She's seen this picture hundreds of time before, it's always been one of her favourites. I don't know why it should upset her now but that's dementia for you."

He held out a crumpled photo of a smiling, dark-haired woman holding a small child. The little boy was reaching out towards the beautiful ruby and diamond pendant the woman was wearing.

"She won't wear her pendant any more and yet she's always loved it." He shook his head.

"I'm so sorry."

"Please, don't repeat this to anyone, but she's started to be nasty to the nurses. She lashed out at one of them the other day and scratched her face. All the poor woman was doing was getting her dressed. She started to put the pendant round Toni's neck but she just tore it off and threw it across the room. I've got an appointment with the Manager tomorrow. I'm sure she'd going to tell me that I'll have to find somewhere else to care for Toni. I understand why but it's going to send her even further into her own, strange, troubled world."

Maddie could think of nothing to say that would comfort him. She stared at the photo and something in her memory stirred. She thought she might know why Antonia wouldn't wear her pendant. The greed that would destroy a woman's last hold on reality made her feel sick.

"Excuse me, Stan. I need to do something. I'll be back in a minute."

She left the Hall and got out her mobile. "Hi Freddie. I know this is a funny question, but have you done anything with those photos you took of the jewellery in Douglas' shop?"

"No, I haven't had time to transfer them onto my computer yet. Why are you asking?"

"I'll explain later. Are you back yet?"

"No, we're just getting back into the taxi but Temp wants us to stop off at a supermarket so she can buy a few things. If you want those photos, I'll send them through to you when we stop talking. I'm not as clever as the youngsters, I need to stop and think things through when I'm using technology."

"As long as you don't delete them by mistake."

He chuckled. "I won't. I'll ask Ryan or Temp to supervise."

"Thanks. I'll see you later."

"Count on it. I'll call round to walk you to the committee meeting. I want to know what you're up to."

He rang off and Maddie waited for the photos to arrive. With part of her mind, she hoped she was mistaken but deep down she felt certain she was right. A ting from her phone announced the arrival of a message. She opened it and scrolled through the images. The one she remembered was there. It was just as she thought.

She had to go back into the Hall to tell Stan about her suspicions and show him her evidence. If he was seeing the Manager tomorrow there was no time to lose. She had no idea how he'd take it. He might reject her idea totally but if he believed her, she was worried about what he'd do. He'd always appeared to be a gentle, quiet man but it was obvious he loved his sister very much.

Maddie prided herself on her independence but she didn't want to face talking to Stan about this, especially not alone.

Her phone rang. It made her jump. She looked down at the caller ID. and felt a surge of relief. "Hi, Grace."

"Maddie, what's going on?" Grace's voice was urgent. "Freddie phoned me. He said you were up to something and could I make sure you were safe and he'd get back as soon as he can."

A little of the burden lifted from Maddie's heart. She didn't have to do this alone. She took a deep breath to make sure her voice was not as shaky as she felt and said, "I'm perfectly safe but please can you come to the Main Hall straight away. I really need your support."

Chapter 32

Grace hurried to put on her shoes, coat and scarf, then grabbed her handbag and added keys and mobile to its contents. She considered for a moment: Tiggy was regarding her with the calm disdain habitual in cats but Percy was snuffling around her feet. She thought she could discern the destructive look of a dog who will make people pay if he's left alone. She only hesitated for a moment, then bent and clipped on his lead, glad that she hadn't removed the coat Freddie insisted his Pekingese wore in the winter. Grace felt rather conspicuous towing along a small fluff ball dressed in a bright coloured tartan coat but it was better than risking Freddie's beloved dog getting ill.

She took a shortcut across The Green, tutting to herself when Percy fussed about being forced to walk across the icy grass. After a few steps, she gave in and picked him up. She could cope with being accompanied by a dog clad in a coat but not one wearing striped booties, not to mention the time she'd waste trying to get them on Percy's feet. Maddie had sounded anxious, but perhaps that was normal with so much going on.

"Are you all right?" she demanded breathlessly as she met Maddie outside the Main Hall.

"Yes, well sort of. I've got to tell Stan something and I don't know how he'll take it. Thank you for coming, Grace."

"Do you want to tell me what's going on? Otherwise, I won't know how to help."

"I may be completely wrong..." Maddie broke off and started again. "You know how we thought that Douglas wanted the cultured pearls so he could replace Miriam's necklace with one less valuable? Well, I suspect he may have already done the same thing to Stan's sister, Toni."

"Antonia who's in the Nursing Home? I know her, I visit her sometimes and read her poetry. If you're right, I can't imagine a more wicked thing that anyone could do."

"Have you seen the pendant she likes to wear? Does it look like this?" Maddie pulled up the photo on her phone and held it in front of Grace.

"It's hard to be certain but yes, I think it's the same. When she was having a lucid day, she told me that her husband gave it to her on their first wedding anniversary. He died a few weeks later." Grace's tone was bleak.

"Stan's waiting for me in the Hall. He'll wonder where I've got to. Should I tell him what we suspect?"

"I think we've got to." Grace pushed the door open and walked into the Main Hall, forgetful of the small dog who was still tucked under her arm.

"Are you okay, Maddie? I was getting worried about you," said Stan.

"I needed to check something out. I need to tell you something but, please, remember I could be completely wrong." She held out her phone. "This necklace, is it like the one your sister wears?"

Stan stared at the picture then took the phone from her to look closer. "It's the image of it. But the design of Toni's is unique, my brother-in-law created it and had it made for her." He frowned. "Where did you take this picture? It looks like it's in a display case?"

"It was. In a display case at Douglas Bartlett's antique shop. Freddie and I were there today. Freddie took lots of photos of the contents. At the time, I didn't know why."

164

"Do you know now?" The sharpness in his voice made Grace wince.

"I'm not sure," said Maddie. "I don't even know if Freddie had a reason or if he was acting from instinct. It's just when you showed me that photo of your sister wearing the pendant, I was sure I'd seen it before."

Stan stared at her, clearly trying to think this through. "You mean somebody stole Toni's pendant and replaced it with a cheap replica?"

"It's possible. It explains why your sister rejected the pendant so violently, even though she didn't have the words to explain it properly."

"And I didn't listen properly to what she was trying to say. Presumably, this person who stole it sold it to the antiques dealer?" Grace could hear Stan's anger rising with every word.

"Maybe," said Maddie.

"What do you mean 'maybe'? She's in a nursing home with round the clock care. Nobody can just walk in there and help themselves. It must be someone who works there, a carer or cleaner, somebody who has access to the patients and wouldn't be noticed if they took something."

"Or a volunteer," said Grace. She didn't want to get involved in this increasingly heated debate but her conscience wouldn't allow her to keep quiet.

Stan frowned at her. "The volunteers are closely monitored, I've been assured of that."

"I'm a volunteer and there have been many times when I've signed myself in and gone to patients' rooms without supervision, including that of your sister. She's always been very proud of her ruby pendant and has taken it off to show it to me. Because she doesn't always remember that she has done so, she'll do it again and again. I'd have had ample opportunities to steal her necklace but I assure you I did not." Grace felt herself grow pink and flustered as she realised the implications of what she'd said.

"I didn't think that!" Stan looked as embarrassed as Grace felt. "I didn't realise you visited my sister? I'm sorry if we've met before but I don't remember you."

"I've been away for a few weeks but before that I visited her regularly. I used to read poetry with her. My name's Grace Winton." Grace tossed the information at him, still feeling discomposed.

"Grace?" a smile creased the edges of Stan's mouth. "Ah yes! Amazing!"

"What's amazing about it?" demanded Maddie.

Grace felt ready to sink through the floor with embarrassment.

"Not what, who. Amazing Grace," replied Stan. "Toni says her poetry lady is called Amazing. I didn't think that could be her name but Toni's logic isn't always clear and I never realised where the name came from until now."

"Despite her dementia, Toni is obviously a lady of great discernment," said Maddie solemnly.

"Oh do stop it, both of you!" exclaimed Grace. "What I'm trying to say is that most of the volunteers are totally reliable, like Nell Mountjoy and her mother. But, because of this, some of the others may have been allowed more access than is desirable."

"I see," said Stan.

"It's a difficult balancing act. It's good for the people in the nursing home to have new visitors. It stimulates them. But not all the volunteers are necessarily reliable." Grace was doing her best to be fair even though the thought of those in charge allowing unbridled access to people who'd prey on the vulnerable made her very angry.

"A few weeks ago, Janetta Briar gave a talk about her dancing career and Douglas did a talk about antiques, a sort of mini Antiques Roadshow," said Maddie, "it was quite interesting."

Grace thought it was also an ideal opportunity for him to spy out any valuables but she didn't say so. It was obvious that her companions were thinking the same thing.

"I know that Toni would never willingly have parted with her pendant. Do you think Douglas Bartlett stole it by having a cheap look-alike made and swapped them?"

"We know he has tricked people by undervaluing their antiques but that's immoral not illegal," said Maddie. "Would you know the difference between your sister's pendant and a copy?"

"Now that I know what I'm looking for, I'm pretty sure I would."

"Then go and check it out as soon as you can. If nothing else, it will give you a weapon to use against the Manager when you meet her tomorrow if she threatens to throw Toni out."

Grace had always been taught that blackmail was wrong and it shocked her how wholeheartedly she approved of Maddie's suggestion.

"I'll go up to see Toni now." Stan looked anxious. "Would you come with me? Both of you. I'd appreciate the moral support."

Grace knew that might make them late for the Committee Meeting but she didn't hesitate. "I'll have to wait outside. They don't allow dogs in the Nursing Home."

"You don't think they'd accept Perce as an Assistance Dog?" joked Maddie. "I guess I can see your point. We'll both wait outside the Nursing Home, Stan. It's probably better if we don't look like a deputation."

They walked through the covered walkway to the Nursing Home, Grace carrying Percy in the hope that

167

it would be a lesser breach of rules than if he was on his own four fluffy feet.

They reached the entrance to the Nursing Home and Grace and Maddie sent Stan in, assuring him that they were on his side. Maddie got out her phone and sent off texts to tell Freddie where they, and his dog, were lurking and to apologise to Nell and Mrs Mountjoy if they were late for the meeting. Grace concentrated on restraining the increasingly petulant peke.

It was only ten minutes later that Stan returned. One look at his face told them their suspicions regarding the pendant were justified.

"You looked at the pendant?" asked Maddie.

"Yes!" Stan snarled the word. "It's an obvious fake. A different weight to Toni's real one. No wonder she rejected it like that."

"I know you're angry. I don't even know Toni and I'm furious. But at least you've got some ammunition to confront the Manager."

"I'll do more than confront her! I'll put in an official complaint about the quality of care. This place is paid to keep my sister safe."

Grace understood how he felt but now wasn't the time to encourage him in seeking retribution. Antonia had to come first. "Please be careful you don't make things more difficult for your sister. She's always seemed happy here." She amended mentally that Antonia was as happy in the Clayfield Nursing Home as she could be anywhere. "The care staff have always seemed to be very kind to her," she added.

"And you're afraid they might be less kind if I stir things up? And Toni hasn't got the capacity to tell me if anybody was cruel or neglectful? You're right, of course."

"Maybe, if she gets her real pendant back, she may settle down again." Grace wasn't sure she believed this but it seemed important to calm Stan and give him some hope to hang on to.

"I'll get her pendant back, but I'm afraid the damage may be permanent."

Stan's hands were clenched. Stan was twenty years older than Douglas but Grace feared that he could still cause him serious damage with those fists.

"One thing I swear, when I catch up with Douglas Bartlett, he'll wish he'd never come near my sister. Give me five minutes alone with him and I'll make sure he never victimises anyone again."

Chapter 33

To Maddie's relief, the Committee Meeting was surprisingly harmonious. Soothed by the delicious cakes and sandwiches that Nell provided, everybody was in agreement that Douglas should be asked to withdraw from the show because they felt he was a disruptive influence.

"What if he objects?" asked Grace. "I suppose I'll have to say what I saw when he attacked Kyle and Tempest?"

"That may be necessary," said Joel. "You may find it unpleasant but I know you will do your duty. But before we discuss the violence you witnessed, we can prioritise telling him about our concerns about his business practices. It will be better if we don't mention our speculations about his intention to steal Miriam's pearls or what we think happened with the other poor lady's pendant. After all, we have no proof of his intentions in the first case and, in the latter, he could claim that she agreed to sell it. It's possible he tricked her into signing a receipt."

Maddie sighed. She appreciated Joel's good points but she really hated his pomposity.

"He'd come unstuck if he claimed that," said Mrs Mountjoy. "Her brother's got a Power of Attorney, had it for several years." She smiled at her daughter. "Nell told me she consulted him when I was losing my marbles but fortunately they got the chemicals in my brain balanced again so we never had to take it any further."

"We're all glad that your marbles are definitely in place," said Maddie, suppressing a grin at Joel's shocked expression. One of the things she loved about Mrs M. was her determination to tell it as it was.

"But I agree with Joel that we reserve our suspicions of Douglas' jewel-thieving until Stan has done whatever he needs to do to recover his sister's pendant. We have enough other good reasons to get rid of him," said Mrs Mountjoy. "The snowman dance won't be quite as funny without him thumping around always out of step but the whole atmosphere will be more congenial without him."

Maddie thought how funny it was that Mrs Mountjoy was not an official part of the committee and yet not even Joel, the stickler for protocol, objected when she laid down the law.

"I suppose I'd better be the one to tell Doug he's out of the show," said Freddie. "Prepare for fireworks."

"I'll support you if you like." Joel sounded reluctant but Maddie had to give him credit for making the offer. "After all, it's a man's job to stand up to a nasty piece of work like Douglas."

On second thoughts, perhaps he didn't deserve too much credit for nobility, although he got full marks in the male sexism category.

She said, "That's okay, Joel, although you're part of this committee, you aren't part of the main show. Freddie and I let Douglas join us and it's up to us to throw him out." She took out her mobile. "I've got all the performers phone numbers saved, I'll text Douglas and ask him to turn up at the Main Hall thirty minutes early for rehearsal. With any luck we can get this sorted before most people get there."

"Thank you, Maddie, I appreciate your support" said Freddie.

"You're welcome." She trusted Freddie to stand his ground even if Douglas bullied and blustered. Joel was far more likely to crumble at the first hint of a threat.

Freddie also got out his phone. "Kyle and Temp are hanging out at my house, eating pizza and chips, I'll let them know to stay there until I tell them otherwise. We don't want another encounter between Kyle and Douglas today."

"I'll come too in case we have to discuss the assault. I was the one who saw Douglas attack Kyle," said Grace, which Maddie considered truly noble.

"And you'll need Nell too. Don't worry about leaving me to get ready alone, I'm quite happy to accompany you and stay for the rehearsal," said Mrs Mountjoy.

"There's no need for Nell and you to come. Douglas could be unpleasant when he's challenged," protested Freddie.

"Exactly! I may not be an official part of this committee but I have no intention of missing all the fun," said the old lady in a tone that allowed no argument.

She turned towards Maddie and gave a conspiratorial wink and, despite the fact she wasn't anticipating the next few hours to be any sort of fun, Maddie couldn't resist smiling back.

Chapter 34

"What the hell do you mean you don't want me in your stupid bloody show?" Douglas Bartlett's voice reverberated around the little side room off the Main Hall as, already in costume, he towered over Maddie and Freddie, glaring down at them. Maddie wrinkled her nose in disgust at the mixed odours of his heavy aftershave and his whisky sodden breath.

"It would be wise to stop shouting, unless you want the entire estate to hear why we've chosen to exclude you from the show," said Freddie.

"I don't give a damn what your stupid, bloody estate hears or what they think." Douglas continued to bellow.

"That's just as well," said Maddie, "you haven't got much chance of keeping it quiet anyway. It was typical that, driven by their inherent instinct for gossip, Ron and Amy Bunyan had turned up early for the first time in the history of the show and were lurking in the Main Hall.

"One reason for our decision is that we have good reason to believe you have been swindling some of the more vulnerable residents by offering to buy their antiques at a fraction of their true value and then marking them up by three or four hundred per cent to sell in your shop," said Freddie.

Mrs Mountjoy was seated at the rear of the room, flanked on either side by her daughter and Grace. Maddie heard the old lady snort with disapproval and thought she'd have chosen to start the accusations with the assault on Tempest and Kyle. That would certainly have been Maddie's choice but she suspected that Freddie had held back because Janetta had insisted on accompanying Douglas into the small room and he felt uncomfortable talking about the attack on her daughter.

"It's standard business practice," asserted Douglas. "You pay less than you sell for. It's not my fault if a few old bit ... biddies want to go back on the deal as soon as they've got the money in their greedy little claws."

"We have evidence to prove that you constantly undervalued articles for people who trusted you," insisted Freddie.

"Doug wouldn't do a thing like that!" protested Janetta, clutching Douglas' white fleecy arm with her two sparkling hands.

Maddie wished that Doug and Janetta had not changed into costume before this meeting with the committee. It added a note of farce to try to reason with a bellicose snowman and an indignant Snow Queen. She was glad that she'd insisted on Freddie and herself remaining in ordinary clothes.

"You valued an antique doll at £500 and within two days you had it on sale for £4,000. It broke the owner's heart to part with it but she needed the money to get veterinary treatment for her injured cat." Maddie tried to keep her voice calm and the language formal. She preferred to not give Douglas any excuse to 'kick off'. As well as Ron and Amy, other performers were arriving in the Main Hall and it was inevitable that a lot of them were near the doorway, listening in.

"That's not true!" bellowed Douglas. "Don't forget I'm a reputable businessman. You needn't think I'd be afraid to take you to court, there are serious penalties for slander."

"It's only slander if it's not true. We have the original payment receipt for the doll, a photograph of it in your shop with the price tag clearly visible, and the receipt for the amount that the person serving in your shop sold it for, after the customer asked what was the Best Price you'd sell for." Maddie had never been much of a card player but she guessed this was how it felt to hold a winning hand.

"Nonsense! If anything like that has happened it must be a mistake. My assistant has obviously mislabelled it. I can understand why you might get the wrong impression but you'd be wise not to spread these lies any further."

"You see, it was just a stupid mistake on the part of one of Doug's subordinates," said Janetta. "You should be grateful to him for appearing in your amateurish little show. The snowflakes are waiting so can we please get on with..."

"No, it wasn't a mistake." A voice cut across Janetta's demand that rehearsals should commence.

All eyes turned to focus on Elouisa, who was framed in the doorway. Dressed in black trousers and jumper, she was like a dark shadow compared to her sister's sparkling, sequinned daintiness. She stepped inside the room and closed the door behind her. "I was working in Douglas' shop today and I got in early to check with him about his new stock. I like to appear knowledgeable about the items that are for sale and find out what price he's willing to accept if a customer wants to haggle. He was very pleased with himself about the doll. He said he'd got it for a song, considering how rare it was."

"She's lying!" roared Douglas. He turned and strode towards Elouisa, arm raised, fist clenched. The heavy gold rings on his fingers glinted like an ornate knuckleduster. "You jealous, vindictive bitch! You're trying to make trouble because I preferred your sister to you. Face it, you'll always be the ugly sister."

Maddie saw Elouisa wince, but she didn't retreat. She stood with her back to the closed door, glaring at

Douglas, her dark eyes twin pools of hatred in her white face.

Freddie stepped between Douglas and Elouisa. "That's enough, Bartlett!"

A noble gesture but foolish. Freddie was six inches shorter than his opponent and at least seven stone lighter, as well as twenty years older. Maddie hurried forward, reaching up to latch onto the upraised arm. She felt his muscles tense as he prepared to throw her off.

"Stop!" a voice like a whiplash froze them all in their tracks.

Chapter 35

Mrs Mountjoy rose to her feet, slowly and with the aid of her daughter, but with great dignity. "Thank you, Nell, I can manage now with my stick."

Steady as a rock, she used it to point at Douglas and then at a chair against the wall. "You, Mr Bartlett, will sit there. You will not assault anyone else today."

Douglas looked astonished but he crossed the room and sat down.

Mrs Mountjoy then indicated to her right. "Miss Briar, kindly take a seat over there. Not directly opposite to Mr Bartlett, direct eye contact may lead to confrontation. Thank you. Now, Sugar Plum Fairy, kindly decide whether you wish to support your family or your lover and take a seat."

"How dare you!" Janetta tried to meet Mrs Mountjoy's steady gaze but failed. Encountering a hostile look from her sister, she flounced over to a seat beside Douglas.

Maddie grabbed Freddie's arm and towed him to the back of the room so that they could both sit next to Nell. She didn't delude herself that Mrs Mountjoy couldn't tell exactly what was going on behind her back but, if she could avoid it, she wasn't going to risk receiving a rebuke.

Mrs Mountjoy looked around the room and nodded, clearly satisfied with their cowed obedience. Her gaze settled on Douglas and she spoke in measured tones. "Mr Bartlett, you may save all your bluster and denials for when those you've defrauded take legal action against you. I know you think you've been very clever and I agree you've demonstrated a measure of low cunning but when you battened onto the vulnerable you crossed a line. Right-thinking people despise those who prey on those who are desperate for money and even more they hate people who deceive those whose mental powers are failing."

"I don't know what you mean." Compared to his usual bombast, Douglas' protest sounded weak.

"Doubtless you will find out in good time. But, for the present, it is sufficient for you to accept that the committee of the Christmas show have decided you are not the sort of person they wish to have associated with it. I understand this is in relation not merely to your dubious business dealings but because of the violence you offered two young people on our premises. If you require further explanation, Mrs Summer will doubtless provide it."

Maddie had been listening with awe to the magnificent manner in which Mrs Mountjoy had quelled Douglas and staved off the danger of physical violence. Unfortunately, Mrs M. had handed the baton back to her and she realised the situation could escalate again.

"Light the blue touch paper and run like buggery," she whispered to Freddie, then stood up and moved beside Mrs Mountjoy in order to confront Douglas. "You may be able to lie your way out of your despicable treatment of some of our residents but you can't deny that you attacked two young people on our premises today."

"Of course I deny it! You old women are all alike. You'll take the word of that young scumbag against that of a decent businessman." Douglas surged to his feet.

"Sit!" snapped Mrs Mountjoy and he subsided again.

"I'll take the word of a respected resident of this estate who witnessed your assault," retorted Maddie.

"Some senile old bat who can't see beyond the end of her nose!"

Grace stood up. She was trembling but her voice was firm. "I'd be careful, Mr Bartlett, legal action for slander can work both ways."

"If you saw Doug disagreeing with that horrible boy, I'm sure it was to protect my daughter," said Janetta.

"Do you call swearing at her and twisting her arm until she screamed with pain, protecting her?" demanded Maddie. "As well as beating up Kyle when he tried to prevent the assault on her."

"You're lying! Doug wouldn't do that!"

Maddie accessed the photos she had taken on her phone and held them up for Janetta to see, keeping far enough away that Douglas could not grab her phone.

"These are the pictures I took of Temp's arm after the assault. You can see the injuries caused by those rings he wears quite clearly. She tells me it's not the first time your boyfriend has manhandled her and you always accept his word rather than hers."

Janetta shook her head. "No!" she whimpered. "Doug, tell me it's not true."

"I hardly touched her. They've smeared paint or something on it to make it look worse than it is. She's always been a jealous little madam, trying to break us up."

"You can believe what you want, Janetta," said Maddie. "Perhaps you'd better hang on to what you've got. It's probably too late to save your relationship with your daughter anyway. She's decided to find somewhere else to stay because she doesn't feel safe at home." She scrolled onwards. "I doubt if this will concern you, but this is what your boyfriend did to Kyle when he tried to protect Tempest. If the resident who saw what was happening hadn't sounded her panic alarm it would have been much worse."

Janetta's eyes turned from the images of Kyle's battered face to stare at Douglas. "You didn't do that? Tell me you didn't," she implored him.

Douglas' already florid colour darkened even more. "Don't you dare judge me, woman! That boy's a waste of space. A parasite who expects taxpayers to pay for him. As for your precious little princess, I hardly touched her. Just taught her to stay out of my business and do what she's told. The same as you should learn."

"You hurt my Tempest!" Janetta sprang up and went for him. Her nails raked down his face.

He thrust her away so violently that she went sprawling. "You bloody bitch!"

"I'll kill you!" she screeched.

She scrambled to her feet, shedding sequins with every movement.

Douglas fended her off. His vindictive stare alighted on each of them in turn as he glared around the room. "You can keep your bloody show! I wouldn't appear in it if you begged me to." His voice dropped to a vindictive, vicious hiss. "And remember, I know things about you and what you've done and I've no reason to keep quiet. I'll make you sorry you crossed me." He backed towards the door, pulled it open and slammed out of the room.

Everybody stared after him.

"Quite a Shakespearean exit." Mrs Mountjoy broke the silence. "If we supplied him with yellow stockings and cross garters he'd make a very tolerable Malvolio."

Chapter 36

Everybody turned to stare at Mrs Mountjoy. Most people seemed shocked by the malevolence of Doug's departure and it seemed to Maddie that she was the only one who shared the old lady's amusement.

"You are very bad," she said, smiling at her, "and totally magnificent. Thank you for dealing with that objectionable man."

Mrs Mountjoy smiled. "My pleasure. I said that it would be fun and it was."

"It had its moments." Maddie glared at Freddie. "What do you think you were doing, going all macho and taking on a thug twice your size?"

"You don't see it as heroic? You're probably right. But what were you doing leaping in to protect me?"

"Call it a gesture towards equality. I always was a bit of a feminist." Maddie hugged Grace. "And you were very brave, standing up to him like that."

"Not as brave as you. You should be more careful. That man is dangerous." Grace, usually so undemonstrative, returned the embrace.

"Where's my daughter? I want to see her." Janetta broke across the mutual congratulations.

"She's an adult and it's her choice whether she sees you," said Maddie, "but I'll certainly warn her not to break cover until Douglas has had time to get changed and leave the estate."

"That could prove difficult. He said he didn't trust the people here so he locked his outdoor clothes, wallet and keys in the boot of my car." Elouisa sounded grimly triumphant.

"He's not going to get far on foot wearing a snowman costume. Do you want someone to go with you while you open your car for him?" offered

Maddie. Or possibly several people. If Douglas was still on the rampage, she didn't want anybody placed in harm's way, but she did want the wretched man as far away from the estate as soon as possible.

"He can wait, unless he wants to come and ask me. My sister needs my help with the snowflake dance. That man has caused enough trouble already."

"You were the one who introduced him to me," snapped Janetta. "I don't care about the dance children, it's my own child I need to see."

"I know I introduced you but you were the one who decided you wanted him as soon as you found out how rich he is. I tried to warn you he wasn't to be trusted but you wouldn't listen," retorted Elouisa. "You heard what Maddie said, Tempest is quite safe but you've upset her and she doesn't want to see you until she's had time to calm down. We can't lose this opportunity for the dance school just because of that man. I've got your cosmetic bag. It's time you cleaned your face and put some fresh make-up on. We can't let the children and their parents see you in such a state."

Elouisa advanced determinedly upon her sister, and removed a large, bejewelled make-up bag from her formidable black handbag.

"Let me know when you're ready to rehearse your dance," said Maddie. "Elouisa's right, it's not fair to drag those little girls out in the cold and then not do your job. I'll talk to the other performers and explain a bit of what's happened, at least as far as Douglas not being part of the show any more."

"I'm sure you two ladies will agree that there's no need to go into details about the problems we've had," said Mrs Mountjoy to the Briar sisters. "It will not enhance the reputation of your dance school to reveal our suspicions regarding Mr Bartlett. The Committee will take the necessary steps to deal with the matter."

"Of course we won't say anything." Elouisa glanced up from where she was holding a mirror for her sister to wipe off the smeared make-up and repaint her face.

The entertainment committee filed out of the small room into the Main Hall to deal with the performers and helpers, all of whom were trying to pretend they hadn't been crowded round the door, listening to everything that had been going on.

"Allow me," murmured Freddie, and led the way to the stage, the committee and the other performers trailing after him.

Once he'd achieved the height that allowed him to command the crowd, he said, "Quiet, please!" and allowed everybody time to settle down. "Thank you. As some of you may have gathered, there has been a disagreement between Douglas Bartlett and the Show Committee, with the result that he has agreed to withdraw from the show. This decision is backed unanimously by the committee. We will discuss with the Carnival Dance choreographers how to replace him. Are you here?"

Two hands were raised and waved. "Here, Freddie."

"Excellent. I know it's late notice but we were wondering about some other tweaks to the choreography. I apologise for the extra work but it has been brought to our attention that one performer may be finding the demands upon her a little too strenuous."

"No problem. I was thinking the same thing myself the last time we rehearsed but I didn't want to upset anyone."

Maddie wasn't feeling upset but she was embarrassed that her weakness had been obvious and yet nobody had dared to mention it. "Please, never hold back for fear of upsetting me. A lame penguin isn't a good look for a happy Christmas show."

183

"Sorry. It wasn't that your performance wasn't good. It's just that I'm a physiotherapist. It's my job to notice when people are in pain, but that's more reason I should have said something."

"No problem. Fortunately, we have a new committee member who knows me well enough to tell it like it is." Maddie joined Freddie on the stage where she had a better view. "Many of you will know Grace Winton, who's a resident in one of our cottages. Grace has agreed to take over the general organisation of the show."

"Stage Manager," said Freddie helpfully.

"And Nell Mountjoy will be in over-all charge of costumes," continued Maddie, ignoring the interruption.

"Wardrobe Mistress," chipped in Freddie.

"And I'll take on keeping track of other props," announced an assertive voice from the audience. "Them balls need lots of maintenance you know."

"Okay. Thank you, Ron."

"What do you call that job, Freddie?" demanded Ron.

"Prop Master," said Freddie with a lot less enthusiasm.

Maddie shared an apologetic look between Grace and Nell, who'd have to deal with Ron. With any luck, he only wanted the grandeur of the job title and would get bored at the first hint of work. When that happened he'd pass the chores over to Amy.

She was aware of an escalating rowdiness from the far end of the hall. "We must allow the Snowflakes to get on with their rehearsal." She smiled across at the children and their parents. "Thank you for waiting so patiently." She turned back to the older performers. "One final point, I'm afraid we're several adult dancers and musicians short and can only do a limited rehearsal but we can discuss the choreography and possibly rehearse some of the songs."

She was not surprised that Kyle and Temp were absent. They were obeying Freddie's instructions to stay safely in his house behind locked doors. But Stan's absence worried her. She hoped he hadn't been provoked into acting unwisely. And, at the back of her mind, she kept wondering who Douglas had been aiming his words at when he said he knew things about someone. It had sounded like a very direct threat and she feared the trouble he'd made was far from over.

Chapter 37

"I think it's a shame. Dear Doug is such a charming man. That committee are so bossy but, mark my words, they'll regret not begging him to stay in the show." The woman in the group around the stage had lowered her voice but Grace, standing just in front of her, could hear every word.

"I know what you mean," replied the woman standing next to the first one. "It was always a pleasure to do business with him. He was so polite and knowledgeable. He was really pleasant when he called a few minutes ago to collect the things I'm selling him. He caught me just as I was coming down to rehearsal. He said he was sorry to hold me up but I told him there's no sense in people like us leaving our flats early, they never start on time and always keep the choir hanging round till last."

As soon as she'd heard Douglas' name mentioned, Grace had sidled sideways and then backwards, keeping close to the two women as she manoeuvred into a position where she could see them as well as hear.

"You missed all the excitement," said the first woman. "I was standing outside the door when the committee were talking to him and I've never heard Freddie Fell sound so severe. And Maddie was positively fierce. And that Mrs Mountjoy! It sent shivers down my back when she rapped out her commands. So rude! And that dance school woman turning on him like that. It's not surprising poor Doug got upset and shouted back at them. I wanted to catch him and tell him how most of us didn't believe a word against him but he left too fast for me to speak to him."

"I thought he seemed upset when I saw him. Not as chatty as he usually is, if you know what I mean. You saying about the unpleasantness explains it. At the time I thought he was embarrassed because he hadn't got the money on him to pay for the things he'd bought from me. He said he'd locked his wallet in someone's car and didn't want to hang around until rehearsal was over but he'd put a cheque in the post tomorrow morning."

"I'm surprised you were selling anything to him. I thought you collected things."

"I am a collector! Proper collectors sell in order to buy and upgrade their collection. Doug understood that. He's a real professional and knows how to treat a fellow professional."

Grace liked to think of herself as a morally upright person and she was shocked to realise that the woman's supercilious tone had awoken the hope that Douglas had been playing his tricks on her. She thought that Maddie would want to hear about this possible new victim of Douglas' sharp practices but she didn't know how to identify the women. The only person nearby that she knew well enough to ask was Ron Bunyan and he'd want to know why she was asking. She tried to memorise both women's appearances. The collector was tall and thin, with sharp features and a mass of improbably dark hair tied in a bun. Her companion was grey-haired and plump. Grace didn't recognise either of them, which meant that they were probably in the new sheltered housing.

"I'm surprised you let him take your things without paying you," said the grey-haired woman. "I mean what with you being so experienced at buying and selling things. I don't believe, for one moment, there's any truth in what Freddie and Maddie said about Doug not being straight, but you never know, do you? But I'm sure you know best."

The collector frowned. "You may have a point. I've got his invoice promising to pay but it's going to be inconvenient if he doesn't pay up straight away. There's some things I've got my eye on in an auction next week. Now I think of it, even if Doug found it uncomfortable to come back to the estate, the way he told me, I could have met him elsewhere and given him my artefacts when he'd got the money on him to pay for them."

"Neither a borrower or a lender be, that's what I always say," said her friend. She sounded pleased with the profundity of this great thought.

"I think I'll go and see if I can catch him. Get my things back until he's got the means to pay. I may come back and sing in the choir at the end but I don't fancy hanging round watching those kids prancing, you'd think they'd know what they're doing by now."

She stepped clear of the people who'd attended the impromptu meeting and pushed through the crowd of parents who were urging their little snowflakes up onto the stage under the direction of Elouisa and Janetta. Grace thought the Snow Queen seemed to have regained control of her emotions, although her voice was shriller than usual and her movements were jerky.

A few of the older residents sat down to watch the rehearsal, while others were bustling round trying to avoid Ron, who obviously believed his new Prop Master role gave him the authority to boss everyone around.

"I need someone with a good eye for detail to count them snowballs and see if any of them need repairing," he announced and Grace knew he was staring straight at her.

She looked around the hall, trying desperately to avoid making eye contact with Ron. She saw Maddie waving at her and hurried across the hall to join the rest of the committee who were filing back into the little side room.

Chapter 38

Grace had anticipated some resentment that she'd come onto the committee at such a late hour and been given such an important role but, to her relief, nobody objected to her suggested changes. Indeed, the young women who choreographed the dances seemed happy to make the alterations, and even happier that Douglas was no longer one of their number.

While they were discussing the alterations, there was a soft knock on the door and the other young male musician sidled in.

"Hi Sam, what can we do for you?" asked Maddie.

"I wondered, as you're changing the snowman dance routine anyway, would it be okay if I just played and didn't try to dance? I know Kyle can do both together but I keep falling over my feet."

"That's fine," said the chief choreographer, smiling at him. "As long as you're happy with it. I thought you wanted to dance as well."

The boy blushed. "I did. I thought anything Kyle could do, I could do as well. But now I know I can't. To be honest, the only reason I kept on trying was because Mr Bartlett kept sneering at me and calling me useless. I didn't want to quit because I knew he'd go on about young men today never sticking with anything. He's friendly with my father and he'd start nagging me as well."

Maddie groaned. "I'm sorry. I didn't know he was doing that but I should have guessed. Once a bully, always a bully. But you don't have to worry about it now."

"It's okay. You wouldn't have been able to stop him anyway."

"Don't count on it. I was already considering asking Nell to sew up the mouth opening on his costume so he couldn't talk."

Sam smiled. "Thank you. I'm really looking forward to the concert now I don't have to dance." He left as quietly as he'd entered.

"There goes another fully paid up member of the Douglas Bartlett fan club," commented Maddie and everybody laughed.

"I did encounter two people who were Douglas fans," said Grace to Maddie as the meeting ended and they were leaving the room.

"There are a few deluded people who fall for his game," said Maddie, "who were these two?"

"I don't know their names. I thought they might live in the sheltered flats. The one who'd sold something to Douglas was tall and thin and had dyed black hair tied in a bun. The other one had grey hair and was … thicker set than her friend."

Maddie's smile indicated that she'd noticed this clumsy attempt to avoid saying 'plump' or 'fat' about a woman who was close to her own size. "The one who looks like a wicked witch who's escaped from Halloween is Jean Battle. It's an apt name. She's so bad-tempered that most people back down rather than stand up to her. I understand from Nell that she gave a talk to the WI about her collection and bored them all stiff."

"What does she collect?" asked Grace.

"I don't know. I think I was told but I can't remember. I'd be surprised if even Douglas could put anything over on her."

"I think he may have done. She let him take some artefacts without paying for them. He told her that his wallet was locked in somebody's car, which I admit we

191

know is true. The other woman said how surprised she was that she'd let him take them and the Jean woman had second thoughts and said she was going to look for him."

"The other one will be Lucy something-or-other. She's quite pleasant when she's not hanging round with Jean." She slipped her hand through Grace's arm. "It's good to have you back, Grace. Are you staying round to hear the singers do their stuff or do you want to get back to your Tiggy cat?"

Grace was tempted to grab that excuse and flee but Maddie's pleasure in her return made her feel warm and obliging. "I'll do whatever you want me to."

"Why don't you both head home?" suggested Freddie. "I'll stay on here and make sure everything's put away to your standards. Nell hopes to take Mrs Mountjoy home soon. She's gone to get her wheelchair. Mrs M. insisted on walking here but Nell thinks her mother has had enough excitement already today."

"You mean created enough excitement," commented Maddie. "If you're sure you don't mind, Freddie, I'll take you up on your kind offer."

Her mobile rang. She took it out and frowned. "It's Hatty. It doesn't look as if I'll be allowed to relax just yet."

"If you have to go and see her, I'll come too," offered Grace, glorying in her own nobility.

"Thank you." Maddie waited until they were clear of the hall before she accepted the call. As she listened her casual attitude vanished. "Hatty? What's wrong? Are you ill?"

She pressed the hands-free button and Grace heard Hatty's hysterical sobbing. She thought she could distinguish the words, "The snowman."

"I'm coming over," said Maddie and headed off at top speed.

"We're coming over," said Grace and hurried after her.

There was thick cloud cover which made the garden murky and damply cold. The only sound was a rhythmic creak as Nell pushed her mother's wheelchair from their cottage to the Main Hall. Then Grace saw a stream of light pouring from Hatty's open front door.

Maddie quickened her steps and Grace matched her pace.

There was something lying in the doorway. It looked like a huddled hump of white fleece. Grace's trembling hand found Maddie's and clung on tight. Together they crept along Hatty's garden path.

The hump was Douglas Bartlett, still in his snowman costume. Lying face down in Hatty's hall. Even before Grace reached him she was certain he was beyond her First Aid skills. All the same, she crouched down and pushed up the fleecy sleeve to feel for the pulse in his wrist. There was nothing.

"Help me turn him over," she said, although she knew the chances of CPR succeeding were remote.

"Wait a moment." Maddie took out her phone and took several photos of the body. "We need to record the position he was in before we move him."

Grace found the idea of photographing the dead or dying repulsive but she knew it made sense.

"He's probably had a heart attack or stroke. A natural death."

The photos were swiftly taken and Maddie came to Grace's assistance. Working together, they managed to turn the heavy, inert body onto his back, no easy task in the narrow passageway. Douglas' eyes were open and staring blankly and his mouth was slack.

"Or maybe not so natural," said Maddie.

Grace gazed down at him, her shocked mind recording what she couldn't bear to process. The neck of his white costume was saturated with the sticky red of blood and, underneath where he'd been lying was a spike, coated with blood, at the top of which gleamed an oval jewel, iridescent green and blue like a peacock's feather.

"What's that?" she whispered.

"The answer to your earlier question," replied Maddie, her nonchalant words belied by the tremble in her voice. "I've just remembered what Jean Battle collects. It's antique hat pins."

Chapter 39

Maddie forced herself to look away from Douglas' corpse to Hatty. She was curled in a ball on the fourth stair up, shaking and whimpering, her hands pressed to her face. Through her tense fingers she kept opening her eyes to peer at the body, then she'd close them again and give a little moan.

"Grace, can you phone the police please? I'll see if Hatty's okay."

"Yes, and I'll call the paramedics too."

Maddie thought it was rather too late for medics to be any use to Douglas but she didn't say so. Grace didn't like what she called 'inappropriate flippancy' and paramedics would be useful if Hatty was as deeply shocked as she appeared. Maddie stood up and edged her way around the recumbent form, grateful to Grace who raised a hand to steady her.

She reached the stairs and crouched in front of Hatty. She'd have preferred to sit beside her but the stairs weren't wide and the thought of their two substantial bottoms getting wedged there was too embarrassing. She wondered if other people allowed their minds to wander along such ludicrous byways. She was sure Grace kept her thoughts firmly under control.

She put her hands on Hatty's forearms and tried to gently draw her hands away from her face.

"Hatty, it's okay. We're here. You're safe now. Please open your eyes and look at me." In the background she could hear Grace providing information to the 999 operator.

At last, Hatty opened her eyes but Maddie saw she was looking past her, focusing on Douglas' body. She asked, "What happened, Hatty?"

"That snowman. He's not..." Her voice was harsh and rasping.

"Not what, Hatty?"

"Not a spirit."

"Oh, I don't know. He's a lot nearer being a ghost than he was an hour ago." The words were out before Maddie could stop herself.

Grace glared at her as she ended her call.

Hatty looked bewildered. "You don't understand. This was never a spirit, just a man dressed up."

"Yes, I do understand that," replied Maddie. "What happened here tonight? Did you see who stabbed Douglas Bartlett?"

In the silence that followed this question, Maddie thought the tension was so thick you could cut it with a knife. It occurred to her that if Hatty was the killer, she could only hope she hadn't got any more hat pins on her that she could weaponize.

"I opened the door and he, the snowman, fell inside." The answer, when it came, was a distinct anticlimax.

"Why did you open the door? Were you expecting him?"

"No. I don't know what he wanted." Hatty shook her head and, having started, seemed like she couldn't stop.

"So he knocked on the door and you went and answered it?" persisted Maddie.

"No, I mean I didn't when he first knocked."

"Why not?"

Hatty shrugged. "I was comfortable, watching TV and I'd treated myself to a pack of jam doughnuts and I didn't want to be bothered."

"Why did you answer, then?" Maddie felt like she was having to dig for every scrap of information.

"He knocked again and again. It worried me. Then I thought it might be you, so I opened it."

"Why me?" She wondered if she was the most annoyingly persistent person of Hatty's acquaintance.

"You're the only person who calls on me. The only one who's been kind."

"Oh! I didn't realise." Maddie hadn't seen that coming.

"What happened when you opened the door?" asked Grace. She stood up and came to join them by the stairs.

"He fell in. On top of me. The weight nearly knocked me over." She shuddered.

"What did you do then? Did you try to help him?"

"I couldn't! There was blood!" She looked down at her navy and emerald cardigan. Maddie thought she could see a sticky smear down the front of it. "I phoned Maddie."

Hatty shivered. "It's so cold. Can't we shut the door? And go somewhere else?"

"We can't shut the door, Douglas' body is in the way, and we shouldn't move anything until the police come," snapped Grace. "That may be them now."

"I don't think so." Maddie had also heard the sound of footsteps on the path. "I know there's been cutbacks, and they may be short of sirens and blue lights, but I don't believe the cops would come here on foot." She stood up and shouted, "Who's there?"

"Only us," replied a familiar voice, "Kyle and me. We saw the door open and the light on and wanted to check there was nothing wrong?"

"Freddie, send Kyle straight back to your house. Kyle, don't come any nearer and don't touch anything." Maddie knew, as soon as the police found out about the fight this afternoon, Kyle would be their Prime Suspect. He was an easy target and, even if

Tempest said they'd been together all evening, they'd dismiss her evidence because she was his girlfriend. Maddie had no intention of giving them the present of forensic evidence that Kyle had been at the crime scene.

She heard Freddie and Kyle debating the matter on the garden path and hoped Kyle would get clear before the police arrived.

"Maddie, are you all right?" called Kyle.

"We're fine. Just do what I told you."

"Okay. If you say so. Phone if there's anything Temp or I can do."

"May I come nearer?" asked Freddie meekly.

Maddie considered. Like Grace and herself, Freddie had an alibi for the period between their last sight of Douglas alive and discovering him dead.

"Yes, but come in carefully. Don't tread on the body or walk in the blood."

"Body? Blood?" Freddie bustled down the path and stopped. He stared at Douglas' body. "My dear girl, whatever have you been doing?"

"It wasn't me, Guv." Maddie encountered Grace's steely gaze. "Sorry. I think it must be the shock."

"I'm not surprised. Are you all right, my dear?"

"I'm fine. It's Hatty who has first dibs on finding this body. Grace and I came in on the second act." She saw a blue light on the road behind Freddie and the sound of a car drawing up. "The police are here. With the waiting times for ambulances, it will probably be hours before that comes."

"Well I can't see there's much hurry," said Freddie, "it's not like they can bring him back to life."

Maddie saw Grace's glare laser past her and fasten on Freddie. She felt glad she wasn't the only person who said things that Grace designated as inappropriate, insensitive and incorrect.

Chapter 40

"Are you all right, Maddie? Yesterday was really difficult." Grace carried a tray from the kitchen side of her cottage into her sitting room and sighed as she surveyed the two mugs of instant coffee and plate of neatly arranged custard cream biscuits it bore. "I'm sorry, I still haven't had a chance to go shopping."

"It's fine. I love custard creams. And describing yesterday as difficult is remarkably moderate. But, yes, I am okay. Surprisingly so. I guess the first dead body you find is the hardest, even though there was a lot more blood this time."

"You're doing it again! You shouldn't make a joke out of something as serious as violent death."

"Sorry if you don't like it, but it's the way I cope with things. You say a prayer or two and think religious thoughts. I make bad jokes."

"I see. I'm sorry if I'm being over-sensitive. I couldn't sleep last night, but that's not surprising when the police kept us there so long.

Maddie decided it would be insensitive to say that she'd slept as soon as her head touched her pillow and positively provocative to mention the really weird dream she'd had about Hatty, dressed as a Snow Queen, pointing a hairdryer at Douglas, dressed as a snowman, until he started to melt.

Instead she asked, "How are you coping? It's been quite some welcome home."

"I think I'm managing. Thank you for arranging that Hatty could have a guest room at the nursing home. I was afraid I'd have to invite her to use my spare room until the police say she can go back home."

"No problem. She may be a totally innocent victim in all this but, until we're sure about it, I wouldn't invite her into either of our homes."

"And yet you still let Tempest use your spare room?"

"Temp may be a little idiot but I don't believe she's dangerous. At worst, if Temp killed Douglas, which I don't believe she did, it was personal, aimed just at him. She wouldn't hurt me. If Hatty attacked Douglas, it's probably part of a more serious mental health problem and I'd rather play it safe. Have you heard of chionoandrophobia?"

"No." Grace managed to fit a large amount of suspicion into the single syllable word.

"It really is a thing. It's a fear of snowmen. If Hatty suffers from it, I'd rather keep a distance. She may turn her fear onto penguins next."

"That's not funny!"

"Did I say it was?"

Ignoring Grace's look of disapproval, Maddie dunked a custard cream in her coffee, ate it and then drained her mug. She got out a notebook and pen and said, "Right, let's get started."

"Started with what?"

"Listing our suspects, of course. Our investigation has to begin somewhere."

Grace stared at her. "You can't be serious! Last time, when we interfered in something that was none of our business, it almost got you killed."

Maddie remembered that only too well but she was certain that living with uncertainty would be worse. "I know, but the only way we can get on with our lives is to find out the truth."

Grace shook her head. "The police are investigating, they won't like it if we get in their way."

"We won't." Maddie felt tired of Grace's faffing. "Don't you get it? Libby and the boys are due back from their holiday in a couple of days. I can't have my grandkids here if there's a killer running loose." She opened her bag to put the notebook back. "It's okay, I understand how you feel. I'll go and see Freddie, and maybe Mrs Mountjoy, I'm sure they'll be willing to help investigate."

"No, there's no need for that. Of course I'll help if I can."

Maddie took her writing stuff out again and opened her notebook. "Thank you." She was glad Grace hadn't realised that she'd been played. "Now where do we start?"

"With Hatty, although I'm sure the police are looking at her."

Maddie giggled. "They didn't know what to make of her. Especially after she told them her full name was Hatshepsut Josephine Coggs."

"I still can't believe they let you stay with her while they were questioning her."

"Yes, that surprised me too. I guess they decided it was better than her having the screaming ab-dabs if they made me leave."

After Maddie had given her statement, the harassed young detective constable had allowed her to stay to support an incoherent and increasingly hysterical Hatty, who'd gone to pieces as soon as the police arrived. Maddie wondered if her panic-attack was coincidence or an indication of guilt or merely that Hat wasn't good with authority.

"I'm not sure that Hatty's got much of a motive," she said, "but she claims to have been harassed by a different snowman, who we think is a fraud and she claims to think is a spectre. And she says she has a long-term fear of snowmen."

"And she had excellent opportunity," said Grace. "Douglas died on her doorstep, although she claims she doesn't know what he was doing there. I suppose, if Douglas was killed by a hat pin that he acquired from Jean Battle, he must have brought it with him. Do you think Hatty pulled it out of the wound?"

"I think it's more likely he did that himself. It would probably be instinctive."

"If Douglas was wielding the weapon, do you think Hatty might have taken it from him and stabbed him in self-defence?" asked Grace.

Maddie wasn't sure you could wield a hatpin, even though it had proved fatal, and she couldn't imagine short, plump Hatty overpowering a man as large as Douglas. But she didn't want to discourage Grace now she was getting involved. "I suppose it's possible, but if it was an accident why didn't she phone for help instead of backing away and sitting there quivering?"

"That's a question that needs answering even if she's telling the truth when she says she opened the door and he fell in on her."

"I suppose what she said about being scared of snowmen could explain her panic," said Maddie.

"Or explain why she'd panic and lash out, or even take her hatred of snowmen out on the one standing on her doorstep," retorted Grace.

"That's true. There's one thing that might help clear her though." Maddie considered. "How tall are you, Grace?"

"About five foot nine. Why?"

Maddie stood up. "Can you come over here and stand on this little stool." She waited until Grace did as she was bid. "Now hold these big, fat cushions around your middle and chest."

"Seriously, Maddie, what do you think you're doing?" Grace clutched the cushions as she'd been instructed but she looked flustered and cross.

"A reconstruction of the crime if Hatty is the perp." Maddie held out her pen, having made sure the top was firmly on. "Hatty is no more than five foot and I'm five foot two. When you're standing on that stool you're about the same height as Douglas and the cushions make you bulky, though not quite as big as him." She reached up with the pen. "What do you think Grace?"

"It's not impossible that she managed to stab him in the neck but it would have been very difficult," admitted Grace. "I suppose she could have jumped up and thrust."

"But does Hatty strike you as the athletic type? Even by my standards of jumping I'd say that was improbable. And I've never known her to wear high heels or platform shoes." She thought the matter through. "Of course, that doesn't prove anything. He could have bent forward for some reason when he was struck."

"No," said Grace decisively.

"You sound very sure about that?"

"When you were with Hatty in her sitting room, I was sitting in the hall."

"I wasn't sure how you managed that. I thought they'd send you home."

Grace looked triumphant. "They insisted Freddie went home but they sent an officer with him to take his statement, which left them short handed, and I looked frail and shocked and kept insisting I couldn't leave until I was sure you were all right. So they let me sit quietly in the hallway, and I could hear what the forensic people were saying as they cordoned off the area."

"You're brilliant! What did they say?"

"There was blood on the door and door frame and it was the same height as Douglas' neck."

"You mean when he was standing upright?"

Grace shuddered. "Yes, as if it had spurted from the wound."

"Was it on the outside or the inside of the door?"

"The outside, I think."

"That makes it even less likely that Hatty did it. Surely she wouldn't step outside and shut the door if she was talking to him?"

"She might do if he insisted on talking to her and she didn't want him in her house, but I admit it's unlikely. I suppose it depends on whether they find any incriminating bloodstains on her clothes."

"Maybe it would show something if they discover incriminating stains on her right sleeve, but it doesn't really prove much, anybody who tried to help him could have smears on their clothes and hands, ourselves included. Hatty seemed to be remarkable non-proactive in caring for the wounded. We'd both got more blood on us than her."

"Yes. I never thought I'd be forced to undress in front of a policewoman and have my clothes taken away for analysis. As if I was a common criminal. I dread to think what people will say."

Maddie had already heard all about Grace's outrage at what she regarded as an infringement of her rights as an innocent bystander to the crime. She knew it was useless to point out that the police had been considerate enough to escort them home and allow them to change into their own clothes. Time for a change of subject. "Did you overhear anything else in your role as an undercover agent? It was quick thinking of you to manage to stay."

Miraculously, it worked. Grace's expression changed from indignant to smug. "I did hear one thing. They rigged up some powerful lights in Hatty's garden and they found some sequins glittering just beside the path."

Maddie stared at her. "Really?" She wrote down Janetta's name. "That puts our Snow Queen firmly in the frame. Case closed!"

Chapter 41

This time Grace was sure Maddie was joking. "That's wishful thinking," she said. "I know she's got a motive and she was angry with Douglas, but the sequins may not be significant. She was shedding them everywhere and, before she got in a temper with him, she was holding onto his arm. They could have stuck to his costume and fallen off when he was attacked."

"True. All the same, we need to find out if she's got an alibi after she stopped rehearsing her dance children last night," retorted Maddie.

She gave Grace a searching look. "Until I insisted I was going to investigate, you weren't going to mention what you'd overheard about the blood smear and sequins, were you?"

"I don't know. I wasn't sure it was a good idea. I suppose I was hoping you'd leave it alone. After all, the police are looking into it and it's nothing to do with us."

"I guess you've got no great passion for justice?" The sarcasm in Maddie's voice made Grace flinch.

"You're only worried because of your family visiting," she said defensively.

"It's true I need to know what happened for my own sake, but I also need to make sure the police don't go for the easiest target. Hatty hasn't fitted in here very well and it's going to make things worse if she's arrested for a crime she didn't commit. Even if she isn't charged, she'll have everybody gossiping about her and making her life miserable. And Kyle's a soft target, they could easily try to railroad him, or they would if Freddie hadn't sworn to engage the best defence lawyers available for him. But, even so, when people start talking they'll soon claim there's 'no smoke without fire', especially when it's about a kid brought up in Care."

"Hasn't Kyle got an alibi?"

"Freddie tells me that Kyle and Temp say they were together at his house, but you can imagine how much credit the cops will place on that. And the motive is clear for either or both of them." She wrote their names with strokes so savage they scored the paper.

Grace felt ashamed of her selfish desire to step clear. "I'm sorry," she muttered,

"Then there's Stan," Maddie continued. "He's a nice guy but he's angry about what happened to his sister and he wasn't at the rehearsal. If he encountered Douglas he could have lost control and he's tall and strong enough to have done it easily." The name went down on her list.

"Wouldn't Hatty have heard if they'd been quarrelling on her doorstep?" asked Grace, "I can imagine Stan losing his temper but I don't think he'd creep up silently and stab Doug."

"Good point, but Hatty tends to have her television on quite loud. I often had to phone and ask her to turn it down. She usually remembers nowadays, but if she knew I was out she could easily put it up to full volume again."

"What about Elouisa Briar? She didn't seem to like Douglas very much."

"If Janetta's split with him, I don't see why she'd want to kill him. Like Janetta, we need to find out if she has an alibi after the kids finished rehearsing. It's annoying that we don't know exactly when Doug was stabbed."

"Yes, if Hatty had phoned for help we'd have a more accurate time frame," agreed Grace. "Then there's Jean Battle. The hatpin belonged to her and I

207

heard her say she was going to try and catch Douglas and ask for payment. I think she's tall enough and you said she's quarrelsome."

She realised she was racking her brains for suspects that Maddie felt less protective of than Kyle and Tempest.

"I suppose she's a possibility but I'm not sure she's likely. She's a professional dealer, even if she's small-time. I bet she knows the going price for all her pins and wouldn't accept an undervaluation and I don't think she's got an emotional attachment to her collection. I'm sure she got an invoice and she's more likely to take Douglas to the small claims court than attack him if he tried to cheat her."

"I suppose so." Grace felt disappointed. She hadn't taken to the sharp featured, razor tongued woman.

"I don't think Miriam Davenport felt any dislike for Douglas," said Maddie. "She believed what he'd told her about her pearls and, thanks to Temp's nosiness, he won't have had a chance to swap them. Plus I think she's too short. And I'll check with Freddie, but I'm pretty sure she was at the rehearsal during the time period when Doug was stabbed. And I know it's type-casting, but can you imagine a woman who sings a 1950s song in that soapy manner creeping up in the dark and stabbing a tall, strong man?"

Grace had to smile at that. "It always turns out to be the least likely person," she said. "The problem is there are probably lots of other victims of his swindles that we don't know about."

"That's true. And there's one more we do know about. Rose," said Maddie.

"Not Rose!" protested Grace.

"It's not so comfortable when it's somebody you're fond of, is it?" said Maddie. "Not the same as when it's a woman who keeps blithering about spectres or a kid with a dodgy past."

"I didn't mean that," protested Grace, miserably aware that's exactly what she'd meant. "Rose is so timid. She's scared of everything. She'd never attack a big man like Douglas."

"She's not so timid that she'll stop wandering around the estate in the dark looking for her cat," retorted Maddie. "And you must admit she's passionately attached to those dolls of hers. They're part of the happy, safe childhood she's lost. And, with all that's happened, we haven't found time to tell her Freddie bought the doll back for her. In her mind, Douglas cheated her and still owns something she cares about. I can see that festering. And she's tall enough, even though she's thin."

"I hate this!" exclaimed Grace. "You care about Kyle because he's young and damaged and vulnerable and I care about Rose for much the same reasons. I mean the damaged and vulnerable bit. Oh Maddie, why do these horrible things keep happening in our estate?"

Maddie shrugged. "Ley lines? Poltergeists? Ancient magic from the start of time? What are you complaining about? I'm the one who lives next door to the cottage of doom."

"That's ridiculous. You have castles of doom, or towers, or possibly a house of doom, but cottage of doom sounds..."

"Too downmarket?" Maddie finished for her. "You may be right. I presume all this has made you decide to cut and run and go to live permanently with your aunt?"

Grace stared at her. "How did you know I was thinking of it?" she asked.

"I know you quite well. You've been gearing up to try and tell me since you got back. Will she let you take Tiggy?"

"Yes, as long as I keep him in my suite of rooms."

She expected Maddie to joke about the opulence of her being offered a suite of rooms but she made no comment.

"I haven't decided yet. I won't while everything here is such a mess."

Maddie smiled at her. "That's good to know. Thank you. That's all the suspects I can think of, apart from..."

"Apart from what?"

"When Douglas was having that tantrum before he left the committee meeting, he said something about knowing somebody's secrets and making them sorry. I'm not sure who he was looking at. It felt like he was looking at me but I haven't got any secrets worth killing for and, anyway, you're my alibi."

"And you're too short," said Grace.

"Harsh but true. Who was sitting behind me?"

"I was, but I didn't do it and you're my alibi, even if I am tall enough."

"Pity, that would have made a good Agatha Christie twist ending. Who was sitting next to you?"

"Mrs Mountjoy." Grace stared at her friend. "You don't think? I mean, she's over ninety and not that steady on her feet. Surely it's not possible?"

"With Mrs Mountjoy anything's possible, but no, I don't think she killed Douglas." Maddie was seated facing the front window and now she stood up and moved the nets aside to look out. "But she's coming up your path, so this is your chance to ask her for yourself."

Chapter 42

Maddie listened as Grace opened her front door and ushered her visitor in, all the time assuring her that of course she wasn't intruding and it was a pleasure to see her. Her embarrassment made her greeting sound false and fulsome and Maddie didn't think Mrs Mountjoy would be fooled.

"Good morning," she said, as Mrs Mountjoy entered the room, followed by a visibly flustered Grace. "Are you absconding or does Nell know you're out?"

"Nell knows that I refuse to be treated like I'm nine years old instead of ninety." Mrs Mountjoy accepted the tall, solid chair that Grace had pulled forward for her. "However, I know she worries about me and I have no wish to make her life more difficult than it need be, so I've allowed her to activate a tracking app on my phone. And if I go for a walk alone, I text her to say I've arrived safely." She matched the action to her words.

Maddie knew that Mrs M. was fond of midnight wanderings around the estate when her daughter was fast asleep, and wondered what she did about being tracked on those forays.

It seemed that Mrs Mountjoy had read her mind. She smiled sweetly and added, "Of course, being a foolish old lady, I sometimes forget to keep my phone with me, and I find the alarm Nell wants me to wear so very restricting."

"I can see that," agreed Maddie. She saw a look of horror flit across Grace's face as if all her darkest suspicions about the old lady were being confirmed.

"I hope you don't mind me calling like this, Grace," said Mrs Mountjoy. "When Maddie was not at home, I guessed she'd be with you. I told Nell that I wanted to check how you both were after the ordeal of falling over another body last night."

"That's kind of you. Thank you. Of course you're always welcome." Grace seemed relieved at this civilised reason for the old lady's visit.

"I also wanted to know how far you'd got with investigating the murder. Have you decided how to tackle it?"

"Investigate?" stammered Grace. "I don't understand."

"Don't tell me Maddie hasn't been running through the pros and cons of all the suspects?"

Maddie saw how helpless Grace looked and decided to intervene. "We have been discussing it. We were just trying to decide who Douglas was looking at when he had his Malvolio moment and threatened to tell what he knew about someone. Do you have any thoughts on that?"

Mrs Mountjoy paused a few moments, apparently looking back through her impressions. "He appeared to be looking towards the centre of the room, towards us in fact."

"That's what we thought," said Maddie.

A look of satisfaction crossed Mrs Mountjoy's face. "As you two can alibi each other that must make me your Prime Suspect. I was home alone at the time."

The deep red that suffused Grace's normally sallow face made it clear that was exactly what she feared.

"We did discuss the matter but I said I didn't think it was you." That was about as tactful as Maddie could get without telling an outright lie, which would upset Grace even more.

"Why not?" demanded Mrs Mountjoy. "Don't you think I have the resolution? I'm a lot lighter and steadier on my feet than you'd think. I've been doing my physiotherapy you know."

She made it sound as though her sole purpose in working to improve her mobility was to boost her chances of committing murder and escaping undetected.

"I know your resolution is equal to anything," replied Maddie, "and you've got ninja assassin skills that I can't even imagine. But I also know your answer to a blackmailer was 'publish and be damned' so it's not likely you'd kill a blustering bully like Douglas when you know he was about to be banned from the estate."

"That's true," admitted Mrs Mountjoy. "Violence is the last resort of the incompetent. Except occasionally when it's necessary in self-defence or, of course, in war." For a moment she seemed to look inwards, recalling the years towards the end of the war when she had been a very young guerrilla fighter in occupied France.

"And you're definitely not incompetent," said Maddie.

"Thank you, my dear." She nodded at Maddie's notebook. "So who else do you have on your suspect list?"

Maddie handed her the notebook and she held it at arm's length to read the list. "Why Jean Battle?"

Before Maddie could speak she answered her own question. "I deduce the murder weapon was a hatpin. What do you plan to do next?"

"We thought we'd check who amongst them has an alibi. Temp and Kyle have each other but I don't know if the police will think that's good enough."

"Nell went back to sing in the choir last night. You can ask her if Jean Battle was there and if Stan turned up."

Despite this suggestion Maddie got the impression that Mrs M. was disappointed with their progress.

"Do you think there's something else we should be doing?" she asked.

"Talking with people is always profitable, as long as you are careful not to arouse the anger of a very dangerous person. But there is something else worth considering. In my opinion, if the killer used a hatpin and they intended Douglas' death, they were either extremely lucky or they had some expertise and knew where to strike to hit a major artery."

Chapter 43

Maddie thought how obvious that should have been. "So you think hitting the fatal place would have been difficult?" Mrs Mountjoy was definitely an expert witness in matters like this.

"Not necessarily but death could have taken much longer. An inch or so astray and the weapon could have done far less harm, it might even have been deflected by the collarbone. I am surprised that so slender a weapon didn't plug the wound and prevent him bleeding to death so quickly."

"It had been pulled out." Maddie wondered if the killer had done that rather than Douglas himself.

"I see," said Mrs Mountjoy.

"Who would know where to stab?" asked Grace. "Do you mean a doctor or nurse?"

"Or somebody who'd had specialised armed combat training." Mrs Mountjoy gave a mischievous smile. "Or, as Maddie said, somebody with ninja assassin skills."

"So we need to do a background check on all our suspects," said Maddie. "What fun. At least it seems unlikely that Kyle has the knowledge to land a blow in the perfect place."

Mrs Mountjoy nodded. "We can only hope the police view it in the same way but Nell and I intend to set up Crowdfunding to cover his legal fees should it prove necessary. I know Freddie planned to pay but we think it would look better if we demonstrate that the community is behind him."

"Count me in," said Maddie.

"And me," said Grace.

"Thank you." Mrs Mountjoy heaved herself to her feet. "I'd better go now. Nell wants to go into

Portsmouth and I have said I'll go with her, so she won't feel she has to hurry home."

"Would you like me to walk back with you?" asked Maddie.

"No, thank you. I enjoy your company but I prefer to demonstrate that I'm capable of getting myself from Place A to B without assistance."

Grace looked embarrassed. "Oh! Mrs Mountjoy, I'm so sorry. I forgot to offer you a drink. How rude of me."

"Not at all," replied Mrs Mountjoy. "I arrived without warning and you've been very welcoming. But I would like one of those custard creams, such a satisfactory sort of biscuit."

"Of course," stammered Grace, and hastily proffered the plate.

After Grace had shut the door and returned to the living room, Maddie grinned at her. "I know you want to go and check on Rose but you'll have to put up with me for a few more minutes. I'm not going to risk being scolded for following Mrs M. too closely down the road."

"Of course you can stay. Would you like another cup of coffee?"

"How about a glass of wine? I think cross-examination by an interrogation expert like Mrs Mountjoy should be followed by alcohol."

"Oh, well, yes, of course. There's half a bottle left from yesterday's lunch."

"Perfect. Admit it, Grace, you need it too."

By the time they'd finished their wine and ascertained that Mrs Mountjoy was out of sight and presumably safely at home, the heavy grey clouds looked full and blowsy, ready to spill their load of icy rain.

"You need an umbrella," said Grace and picked one from the pile on her hall cupboard.

Maddie finished fastening her coat and eyed it dubiously. "Thank you, I guess." The umbrella was long and had a vicious looking spike on the end. Its dark blue colour might have been acceptable if it hadn't been covered with a bright pink logo belonging to a chain of upmarket hotels.

"My cousin gave it to me," said Grace. "She goes away on business trips quite often and stays at the sort of hotel that gives out free umbrellas to their guests."

Maddie thought that explained not merely the umbrella but also her aunt's family's eagerness for Grace to stay on permanently. Who could be more suitable as a companion for the old lady when her daughter and son-in-law were away?

There was no point is saying any of this. It would do no good and only upset Grace. She accepted the umbrella. "Thank you."

Once out in the bitter December weather, Maddie decided to cut straight across the grass of The Green towards the sheltered living flats and the nursing home. The pavement would be smoother but it took longer and she still hoped to avoid the necessity of actually opening the umbrella. Anyway, she didn't want to pass Hatty's cottage with its adornment of Scene of Crime tape fluttering in the wind.

Her mood wasn't helped by a text from Freddie informing her that Kyle had been taken down to the police station for questioning. He hadn't been charged but Freddie intended to have a first-class solicitor on stand-by. He added that he agreed that the Crowdfunding plan would show public support for Kyle but, in his opinion, the matter could become pressing at any time.

As she walked, Maddie texted a brief reply, thanking Freddie for letting her know and begging him to keep her informed, and all the time she kept whispering, "Damn! Damn! Damn!"

She passed the ancient oak tree, which still cast a ponderous shadow even though its mighty branches were bare. All her focus was on hoping the rain would hold off for another three minutes or so. A figure stepped from behind the tree trunk and blocked her way, and she only stopped just in time to avoid a collision.

"You! Maddie Summer! I want a word with you."

It was Jean Battle, her dark eyes gleaming viciously and her thin face twisted with rage.

"What do you want?" Maddie tried to sound calm but the memories of being attacked before were vivid in her mind and she could hear shrill panic in her voice.

"You set the cops on me, you evil bitch." She withdrew her hand from her raincoat pocket, holding a hat pin, which she thrust forward within inches of Maddie's face.

Chapter 44

"Not again! What is it with this estate?" Maddie didn't realise she'd spoken her thoughts out loud until she heard them bouncing through the air.

In the same moment she hoisted the borrowed umbrella and brought it down on her assailant's outstretched arm.

Jean Battle screeched and dropped the hat pin. Maddie stepped onto the pin, to ensure the woman didn't get hold of it again. At the same time she raised the umbrella so the pointed end was levelled at Jean Battle's chest. She was shaking but she felt a glow of triumph at her success.

After the previous attack, Mrs Mountjoy had told her that the prey had more hope if they could disarm the aggressor quickly while they were expecting their victim to be paralysed by shock and, having taken the initiative, be prepared to carry through.

"Thank you, Mrs M.," she whispered.

Not that Jean Battle was showing any signs of fighting back. She was holding her wrist and moaning as she rocked back and fore.

"Stop making that fuss," said Maddie. "You got what you deserve."

This silenced Jean Battle's whining. She looked at Maddie, hatred blazing in her eyes. "You hit me!"

"And I'll do it again if you try any other games. And next time I'll use the pointy end." Even as she spoke, Maddie realised that could have been phrased better. She felt a desire to giggle and had to swallow convulsively to control the impulse. This was no time for frivolity, or hysteria.

"You assaulted me. You've probably broken my wrist. I'm going to have you arrested." She moved her uninjured left hand towards her pocket.

"Stop right there or I'll break the other arm," commanded Maddie.

Jean Battle's hand froze in place. She backed away until she hit the tree trunk and could go no further. "You're crazy! You won't get away with it. Let me get my phone out before you make things worse for yourself."

"I'm crazy? This from the woman who jumped out at me and waved a murder weapon in my face."

"Weapon?" Jean Battle's gaze left Maddie's face and shifted to the hat pin, the end of which was just visible under Maddie's leather boot. She slumped back against the tree trunk. "What do you mean?"

So the police hadn't told her that one of her hat pins had been used to kill Douglas? If so, it wasn't Maddie's place to enlighten her. "More to the point, what did you mean about me setting the police on you?"

That reignited a small spark of temper. "Don't try and deny it! I know you told the cops that I was hunting for that Douglas fellow to have it out with him about walking off with my Art Deco hat pins. All I wanted was to get them back until I saw his cash. But you went and told them that I'd gone after him to kill him. Just to get your weird friend off the hook."

"Weird friend?"

"That Hatty woman. Don't tell me she's normal, always going on about talking to the dead. He was found dead in her house, wasn't he? But you'd throw me under the bus to save her."

Maddie would have willingly thrown Jean Battle under any vehicle that presented itself. It was a pity it wasn't bin collection day, a refuse lorry seemed about right for her. It was obvious she was using her words to wind herself back into a tantrum and Maddie was sure, in a slanging match, her opponent would come out the best.

She tried to defuse the situation, which wasn't easy when she still brandished the sharp umbrella. "I told the police that I'd heard that you were looking for Douglas to discuss some antiques he was buying from you. I never said or implied that you intended to harm him. If the police told you that they misled you."

Jean Battle looked sullen. "Yes, well it wasn't the police that told me. It was that Hatty woman. She's got a room over at the Main House. It's a bloody cheek, those rooms are for visitors. Anyway, I went along to see her and tell her what I thought of her, turning me into the cops like that, and she started crying and saying it wasn't her, it was you who'd told them."

"In other words, you bullied a vulnerable woman who's suffering from shock, and when she caved in you decided it would be better sport to carry on taking your nasty temper out on me. You really are a very unpleasant woman."

Two bright spots of scarlet flared in Jean Battle's pinched face. "You can't talk to me like that! You think you're something special, grabbing all the big parts in that show and bossing everybody around."

"You're welcome to spend all your time organising schedules and prancing round in a penguin costume, if you like. In fact we've got a vacancy for the snowman dance. Would you like to audition?"

"Me? Do something like that? What do you think I am?"

"You really don't want me to answer that." Maddie didn't attempt to hide her amusement.

"Don't you talk to me like that. You're nothing but a rich man's tart, we all know that." Carried away by temper, Jean Battle seemed to have forgotten the threatening umbrella.

Maddie hadn't seen that coming but she rallied quickly. "I think you'd better be very careful what you say, Mrs Battle. If I find that you've repeated that claim to other people you may well be sued for defamation of character and, as you are aware, my friend has enough money to ensure you pay in full for any damage you do to our reputations or any distress you cause."

A spasm of alarm twisted the woman's sour face. It made Maddie continue, "But I think you know about that already. A malicious gossip like you is bound to have ended up in court before now."

"You know nothing about me!"

"And you know nothing about me. But I still want to know why you threatened me with that hat pin?"

It was time to finish up. The umbrella was growing heavy and Maddie could feel her arm begin to shake.

"I didn't threaten you. It's not even sharp. The end is broken off. The police had the nerve to ask me if they were both broken when I sold them to him."

"And were they?" demanded Maddie.

"Of course not! They were both in perfect condition when he went off with them. That's why I was showing you that pin. I wanted to ask if you knew if Douglas Bartlett still had the other one on him when he was found or if I should keep on looking near where I found this one."

'Not on him but in him.' The words echoed sickeningly around in Maddie's mind. She didn't say them.

"You'll have to ask the police about that. Was this the other hat pin you let Douglas have?"

"Let him have is about right. He's destroyed all its value. I only hope I can get my money from whoever

222

inherits from him. And the other one's even better, a beautiful, enamelled, peacock feather. I wasn't that keen on letting him have that. Lovely it was." For the first time her voice softened. "I hope I can get that back."

"Where did you find this one?" Maddie nudged it slightly with her foot but still made sure it stayed trapped.

"Over in the shrubbery behind the Nursing Home. I'll have it back now."

"No, you won't. I'll let the police know I've got it. They may want to question you about where you found it. I suggest you go now. And stay away from Hatty, she's already upset enough." Maddie lowered the umbrella to leave sufficient space for Jean Battle to slide away.

"You bitch!" the woman eyed the edge of the hat pin that protruded from beneath Maddie's boot as if assessing whether to grab for it, abandoned the idea and stormed away.

Maddie watched her until she entered the Main Building. She felt herself shaking, the world was swirling round and fading in and out of focus. She took several deep breaths and braced herself. She said crossly, "Don't be so stupid! Snap out of it. You can't faint here."

It took a few minutes for her vision clear. At last she felt steady enough to bend down. She took a clean tissue out of her pocket and used it to pick up the hat pin. There would probably be plenty of fingerprints on it already but she saw no need to add hers to the mix. It was a silver hat pin, with an amber-coloured stone carved like a thistle contained in curved silver at the top. Maddie had no idea how long the spike should be, as Jean Battle had said, it was broken at one end, but it was still sharp enough to cause a nasty injury. She was uncertain whether the woman had really intended to attack her, but that didn't help to solve Douglas' murder or lessen her own fear.

Chapter 45

As soon as Maddie left, Grace tidied up, carrying the used china, glasses and spoons into the kitchen and putting the remaining biscuits back in their tin. Back in the sitting room, she plumped up the cushions, wiped down the coffee table and used a dustpan and brush to capture a few stray biscuit crumbs. She was more worried about Rose than she'd admitted, aware of how distressed she'd been about Douglas' deception and deeply regretting the loss of her beloved doll. Was her heartache strong enough to lead her to kill? Grace had to admit, to herself, that she wasn't sure about that. How did one know what any person would do if they were desperate? The answer popped into her head: she knew that Maddie might kill to protect someone she loved but never because of a possession, however dear. Grace couldn't be sure of that when it came to Rose, who had so little in her life to love. She wished that Freddie had abandoned the tactful approach and made time yesterday to tell Rose that he'd retrieved her doll.

As Grace thought about this she was tempted to hurry straight round to Rose's cottage. The strange, prickling feeling that her neighbour was on the brink of disaster couldn't be quelled. She told herself not to be foolish. She didn't believe in premonitions. She'd go to visit Rose after she'd washed up. It was forty-five years since Grace's mother had died but her directives for correct behaviour still ruled her life. One of these was that you must always leave your house immaculate in case some accident occurred and a stranger was the next person to enter your home.

The kitchen was soon tidy and Grace spent a few minutes trying to convince Tiggy that it was time to abandon his litter tray and venture into the garden to do his business. In response to her cajoling he strolled towards the open back door, sniffed the damp blustery air, gave her a look of ineffable contempt and returned to the sofa, where he sat washing his face. Grace submitted to the stronger will and locked the back door again. She excused her weakness by telling herself that Tiggy's decision was a good thing. She might be longer with Rose than she intended and he'd be shut outside. Anyway, if she decided to return to live with her aunt, Tiggy would have to become accustomed to life as a house cat. Her aunt and cousin were not animal lovers and had made it clear they didn't approve of felines roaming their immaculate gardens, terrorising the wild birds and digging in their flowerbeds.

Despite the overcast day, there were no lights on in Rose's cottage but Grace knew that didn't necessarily mean she was out. Rose was always worried about affording to pay her bills and never put lights on until it was evening, apart from when she was working in the spare bedroom, which, following Nell Mountjoy's example, she'd turned into a sewing room. Grace knocked and waited but the only sound from within was Snowy miaowing. The lack of response revived Grace's memories of standing outside this door several weeks ago when Rose had fallen and injured herself. Of course, that time Snowy had been shut outside and there had been other warning signs that all was not well. This time there was no reason to suppose that anything was wrong apart from Grace's nagging worry. She knocked again, more forcefully, all the time aware that nosy neighbours could be watching her every move. At any moment, Ron and Amy could scuttle across The Green to ask what was wrong and spread the news that Rose had gone missing and offer theories about what had happened to her. Ron was nothing if not inventive when it came to his neighbours' affairs.

Grace went through the side alley to the back of Rose's cottage, not with any great hope of gaining admission but wishing to avoid prying eyes. She got out her mobile and phoned Rose's number. No answer. She tried again and this time Rose responded.

"Hello? Grace? I'm sorry but I'm really busy at the moment. I'll call you later." The background sounds informed Grace that Rose was almost certainly in a vehicle, which she thought was being driven through heavy traffic.

"Rose, where are you?" she demanded.

"We're just heading into Portsmouth. I can't talk now. I'll be back in an hour or two. We're going to sort things out."

"But who are you with? Are you all right?"

"I'm with Stan."

"Stan!" That startled Grace. It also embarrassed her. Of course it was possible that, while she'd been away, Rose had started a relationship with Stan when he'd become involved in the Christmas show. But while Maddie and Freddie weren't in Ron's league, they usually knew the liveliest gossip about the residents of the estate cottages and they hadn't said a word about Rose and Stan.

"I'm sorry, I didn't mean to intrude. I didn't realise you were out on a … date," she stammered.

"Oh, Grace! No! It's nothing like that! If you must know, I went up to visit Stan's sister last night and he and I were talking and he said he was coming down to Douglas' shop today to confront him about Antonia's pendant. And I asked him if I could go with him. I know he, Douglas I mean, didn't legally steal

227

Guinevere Henriette but he did cheat me and I want to tell him what I think of him."

"But Rose, Douglas won't be there."

"Yes, he will. Stan contacted him yesterday, but Douglas was in a horrible temper and wouldn't talk to him. He said, if Stan wanted to talk business, he could come to his shop to do so today."

That wrong-footed Grace. It hadn't occurred to her that Rose didn't know about Douglas' murder. Rose lived near the other end of the row of cottages, on the same side as Hatty, and it was possible she hadn't seen the police cars and the scene of crime tapes. And she'd probably gone along to the road for her rendezvous with Stan in order to avoid Ron's surveillance.

"But, Rose, listen..."

"It's no good trying to talk me out of it. It's time somebody stood up to that horrid man."

"But..."

"I know you mean well, Grace, but I need to go now. If nothing else, I'll get to see my Guinevere Henriette one more time." She rang off.

Chapter 46

Grace tried to ring back but on the third ring her call was rejected. It was obvious that Rose was refusing to talk to her and she didn't know Stan's number. She stared helplessly at her phone. She couldn't believe how ineffectual she'd been. She hadn't managed to tell Rose that Freddie had already rescued her doll or that Doug had been murdered. Now Rose and Stan were in full battle mode and heading for Douglas' shop, apparently intent on demonstrating what excellent motives they both had for killing him. Of course, it was likely that the antique shop would be shut but that didn't mean the police wouldn't be there. A sickening image fluttered through Grace's mind: two unwary insects, a Daddy Longlegs and a moth, innocently approaching a sticky spider's web and being enmeshed in it.

She needed to contact Maddie, together they could work out what to do. She rang Maddie's number and waited in an agony of impatience until the answerphone message announced that Maddie wasn't able to take her call at the moment. Still mindful of her neighbours' watchful eyes, she stayed at the rear of the cottages and hurried down the footpath, through Maddie's rear garden and pounded on her back door. The silence that followed her barrage made it clear that Maddie was not at home. It seemed she was flying solo on this one. The phrase 'flying solo' startled her, it was more typical of Maddie than herself, but perhaps that was no bad thing.

Searching her handbag for her car keys, she hurried back along the footpath until she reached the side alley beside her cottage, went through it and jumped into the driver's seat of her car. The sight of

Ron Bunyan, fumbling with the latch of his front gate as he peered across The Green added fresh impetus to her movements. She turned the engine on, thrust the gear stick into first and was away before he had a chance to waylay her.

It was only after she was clear of the estate that another option occurred to her. It wasn't one she liked but, nevertheless, she pulled over and got out her mobile. The first number she tried went straight to the answer service. Reluctantly Grace tried the second number and this time the owner answered on the third ring.

"Mrs Mountjoy? Is that you?"

"It is."

"It's Grace."

"I know. The caller display showed that. What can I do for you?"

"Is Nell there? Could I speak to her." Grace knew how upset Nell would be if she involved her nonagenarian mother in a murder investigation.

"I'm afraid not. She's consulting with a new client about a major needlework project for a local charity that she's considering undertaking. I'm sitting in a cafe in Southsea waiting for her."

"Oh, I see." Grace felt her last hopes of rescuing Rose from her own folly fade.

"What's wrong, Grace? You sound upset."

"It's nothing. It was just you said you were going to Southsea but it doesn't matter."

"I'm sorry you don't feel you can trust me. May I take a message for Nell when she returns?"

"Oh dear! It's not that I don't trust you. I didn't want to worry you." Grace knew she'd made a total mess of this.

"I'm old, not dead, and I want to savour as much life as I can."

Grace knew she was beaten. "It's Rose, she's gone with Stan to Douglas Bartlett's antique shop. They plan to confront Douglas."

"In that case, they should have invited Hatty to accompany them."

"You don't understand. They don't know Douglas is dead."

Even as she explained this, Grace realised that Mrs Mountjoy was being sarcastic. She thought it wasn't surprising that Maddie and Mrs M. got on so well.

"Ah, of course. Stan doesn't live on the estate and Rose has never been what you'd call an observant woman. Of course, one of them could be the murderer, or maybe both, although they're not what I'd describe as a likely partnership."

"I don't know Stan but I can't believe Rose would so anything so violent."

"People are often not what others think them. But if you think they're innocent, I assume you're afraid they'll say something to the police to falsely incriminate themselves."

"Or do something. I'm afraid they might try to take back their property."

"Which in Stan's case, if Douglas stole his sister's pendant, would be a reasonable thing to do. He strikes me as a level-headed man. As a rule, I'd doubt if he'll act foolishly, but it depends on how upset he is about his sister's mental deterioration."

"I think he's very upset."

"In that case, it's fortunate that the cafe I am sitting in is only a few yards from Douglas' antique shop. I asked Nell to install me here while she's in her meeting but she didn't realise how close to the shop the cafe is. I think I'll stroll down and take a look at what's going on."

"But what will Nell think if she finds you missing?" Not to mention Grace's craven fear that Nell would blame her.

"That's not a problem. I'll leave a note in my wheelchair to tell her where I've gone. Then she won't have anything to worry about." She rang off.

For the second time that morning, Grace's protests were uttered to a blank, unresponsive phone.

Chapter 47

"Maddie! Oh Maddie!" The lilting voice made Maddie jump. She wrapped the hat pin in the tissue and thrust it into her pocket as Miriam Davenport minced carefully across the icy grass to join her under the oak tree.

"I wanted to ask you to join me for a cup of coffee but I couldn't while you were with that awful Mrs Battle and I waited until I was sure she had gone. Such an unpleasant person. Tell me, what were you doing? It looked as though you were about to poke her with your umbrella."

"We were discussing self-defence and how everyday objects could be used to save your life." As an excuse it was pathetic and Maddie waited for Miriam to tell her so.

"How interesting! You're quite a warrior, aren't you? I admire you very much. I've always been ridiculously sensitive and feminine myself, but that's how my dear hubby liked me and now my daughter takes good care of me. Not that I think Mrs Battle needs help with self-defence. A most abrasive woman. She was positively rude to the rest of us last night."

"Last night? Oh, you mean the choir. I wasn't sure she'd turn up for that."

"I'm sad to say she did. She arrived late and then was so offensive to everybody that we all got quite flustered." Miriam's delicately tinted lips were compressed so tightly they formed a thin line. "Unfortunately, dear Mrs Mountjoy had gone home. She wouldn't have dared behave like that if she'd been there. Nell did her best but she hasn't got the force of personality her mother has."

"Mrs Mountjoy's unique," agreed Maddie, wondering what rude things Jean Battle had said about Miriam's singing that had offended her. "So what time did Mrs Battle arrive?"

"I'm not sure. We were well in and doing quite nicely until she turned up and a fine old temper she was in when she did."

Which left it uncertain about whether Jean Battle could have had time to kill Douglas before she went in to join the choir.

"Did she stay to the end?"

"Yes, although we ended early. There seemed to be little point in continuing when it was so unpleasant. Mrs Battle has a very piercing voice and without the more robust male voices it became quite unbearable."

"No Freddie or Stan?"

"Dear Freddie stayed for a little while but Stanley didn't come. It's unlike him, he's usually so reliable."

"I think his sister isn't too well."

"I see, poor woman. Dementia is such a tragic condition. But I don't know why we're standing here in the cold. Do come and have that coffee with me and you can tell me all about last night. Poor Douglas. Such a charming man. Tell me, is it true his throat was cut with an antique dagger when poor Hatty discovered him on her doorstep?"

Maddie had a bad feeling that, as an interrogator, saccharine Miriam could be far more effective than acidic Jean Battle could ever be.

"Thank you, Miriam, it's really sweet of you, but I don't want to dwell on what happened last night. It wasn't very nice. And I'm sure your daughter would be very cross with me if I upset you when you're so sensitive."

In other circumstances, the chagrin on Miriam's face would have been laughable. Hoist with her own petard, she managed to conquer her pique and conjure up a sweet smile. "How thoughtful of you. I'm sure you're quite right, it would be too much for me. I phoned my daughter when I heard the news and she wants me to go and stay with her until it's all resolved."

"That sounds like a good idea. Are you going?"

"I don't think so. I should be here to support my friends and there's the show to consider. It must go on."

"I suppose so." Although, at the moment, Maddie would have been happy to abandon the whole thing.

"Do you know if dear Kyle is available today? Or is he at college? I'd appreciate another rehearsal if he has time."

This was a bit of information Maddie was willing to share. "I'm afraid Kyle has been taken to the police station for questioning. I really hope it's just a formality but sometimes the authorities go for the easiest target, and a young man who has just left Care is as easy as they can get."

"That's nonsense! I'm sure that charming boy would not hurt anyone. Is there anything I can do to help?"

"Freddie offered to pay for a lawyer but some of us thought it would show more community support if we Crowdfunded his legal expenses."

"I would certainly wish to be part of that. And I may be able to help further, I am acquainted with several eminent barristers, in fact my daughter's father-in-law is one of them. I am sure satisfactory representation can be arranged."

"Thank you."

"Now, about that cup of coffee."

"Would you mind if I took a rain check? I suddenly feel very tired. I think it's the shock from yesterday catching up with me."

Miriam beamed at her. "You poor dear. Of course you must go and rest. You go home and remember to use that umbrella before you get soaked through."

Chapter 48

Grace hurtled into Portsmouth at a speed that appalled her own cautious, rule-abiding soul. Of course, when she got there, she couldn't find anywhere to park, and ended up back-tracking to use the Waitrose car park. As she walked at her fastest pace back to the antique shop she thought that, if this was a fool's errand, at least she could stock her fridge and store cupboard with some high-quality goodies.

There was a CLOSED sign on the shop door but Grace tried the handle and pushed just the same. In her nervous state she exerted too much pressure and, to her surprise, the door opened and precipitated her into the shop.

"Sorry, we're closed!" announced an anxious voice.

Grace caught her balance and looked around her. The speaker was a plump, elderly woman, with grey, rigidly permed hair, respectably dressed in a dark skirt and pastel blouse. She looked flustered as she repeated, "We're closed."

"Grace! Oh, Grace! Thank goodness you're here." Rose hurled herself upon her, sending her staggering backwards.

Grace realised her worst nightmare was playing out. She was at the heart of an embarrassing public scene. Unwillingly, she put her arms around Rose and looked past her to see who else was in the shop. The shop assistant was standing on one side of a glass display case containing several pieces of jewellery. She was glaring at Stan, who stood on the other side. Mrs Mountjoy was seated on a wicker Lloyd loom chair with a price tag attached to the side. Grace hoped that it was substantial enough to bear her weight. The shop assistant seemed to have abandoned telling Grace to leave, so the priority was to discover why Rose was sobbing noisily and wetly down her neck.

"Whatever is the matter, Rose?" she demanded.

"It's my Guinevere Henriette. She's not here. This woman says she's been sold but I know that's not true. She's lying for him because she knows he's hidden her away because he knew I'd found out how he swindled me. I'm never going to see my Guinevere Henriette again."

"Do you know this woman?" demanded the shop assistant.

"She's my neighbour." Grace wondered if Mrs Mountjoy or the shop assistant told Rose and Stan that Douglas was dead.

"Well I won't have abuse like this. How dare she accuse me of lying? The doll was sold yesterday by my colleague. She'll be here in a few minutes and will confirm what I've told her. The woman's obsessed with that wretched doll. Coming here, making a fuss on today of all days."

Grace maintained a sympathetic, attentive expression but her main preoccupation was to get all of her troublesome charges out of here as soon as possible. Maddie had told her who'd been serving in the shop yesterday and Grace wanted to get everybody clear before Elouisa Briar appeared on the scene.

"This is all very unfortunate and I'm sure my friend will apologise to you when I've spoken to her and she's calmed down but I think it would be a good idea if we left now. I expect you'll want to shut up shop."

"No! I mean I don't think any of you ought to go." The shop assistant nodded towards Rose and Stan. "The police I spoke to when I called for help said to keep everybody here until the other officers arrive."

"Police officers? But why? Surely that's an over-reaction, even if Rose was rude to you."

"She was more than rude, she was threatening. But it's not just that. You get used to that. As poor Mr Bartlett always said, you get some foolish people who think they've been cheated even when they've had a very fair price." The shop assistant glared at Stan, who responded with a cold contemptuous look. Clearly flustered, she transferred her glower to Rose. "One of these two has stolen a valuable necklace from that display case and the rest of you could be accomplices. The police will find it when they search them."

Grace felt sick with apprehension. Knowing Rose and Stan's reasons for coming here, it seemed probable they'd attempted to steal back Antonia's pendant. What was worse, if Rose had the pendant, she was quite capable of panicking and slipping the stolen jewel to Grace. Fortunately, her handbag was firmly closed but her coat had wide pockets.

"Dear Lord, please help me." She made a silent but fervent prayer.

Her mobile started to ring, she took the opportunity to step clear of Rose's leech-like grip and check her pockets as she made a show of locating it. The Caller ID revealed that it was the person whose support she wanted most.

"Thank you, dear God," she whispered. That was a very prompt answer to her prayer.

Chapter 49

The sleety rain was getting heavier and, as Maddie made her way across the soggy grass, she took Miriam's advice and struggled to put up the umbrella. She suspected it was large enough to make her look like an odd coloured mushroom but she was grateful for its shelter.

Safely at home, snuggled into her favourite armchair in front of the gas fire, she drank coffee and treated herself to a bar of milk chocolate. She wasn't sure if the shock of discovering Douglas' body was responsible for making her feel so exhausted, or whether it was due to the fading of the adrenalin she'd needed to deal with Jean Battle.

When she checked her mobile she realised it was on Silent and she'd missed a call from Grace. She knew she ought to phone back or Grace would feel even more aggrieved. The problem with this was that, although Grace would be shocked when she heard what had happened with Jean Battle, she'd also point out that she'd said getting involved was a bad idea. At this moment, the last thing Maddie needed was a Job's comforter to make her feel worse. However, it wouldn't get any better for putting it off. She found the number, braced herself and summoned up her brightest tone to say, "Hi, Grace. Are you okay?"

"Maddie, I'd just been praying you'd phone me. It's all so dreadful!"

"What's wrong?"

"I'm at Douglas' shop in Southsea, but I think they're going to take us away very soon. At least, they may not take me, but I don't know what to do and whether I ought to try to go with them."

"Who's 'they'? And who are 'we'? And where are they going to take you?"

"Stan and Rose are here. And me of course." Grace lowered her voice, "And Mrs Mountjoy's still here. I'm worried about her, it's a dreadful experience for a lady of her age."

"Mrs Mountjoy! I don't understand! Who's going to come and take people away?" Time to enquire later why half the estate had been on a jolly without her.

"The police. I think they're going to arrest Rose and Stan."

"But you and Mrs Mountjoy are okay?"

"I don't know. The shop assistant is being very officious. I've no idea what she'll tell the police. And Elouisa Briar is due here any moment and I'm sure she'll make a terrible situation even worse."

Maddie thought it all sounded very odd but there was no use asking for more details when Grace sounded too stressed to be coherent. Anyway, too many people were listening to what she said.

Clutching her mobile, she bustled round her house, turning off lights and fires and checking doors and windows were locked. With her sane mind she knew they were but recent experiences were making her hyper-vigilant.

"Hang in there, Grace. I'm on my way," she said, heading into the hall.

No sooner had she rung off from Grace than her phone played out its jaunty tune again. She thought she ought to change her ring tone. 'Always Look On The Bright Side Of Life' had seemed like a fun idea when she installed it but today it was an added irritation. She was tempted to ignore the new caller, she'd got enough on her plate already, but the Caller ID declared it to be Freddie, which meant it could be important, even urgent.

"Hi, Freddie, is everything okay?" She put her phone on Hands Free in order to pull on her boots and coat.

"Very satisfactory, thank you, my dear. They are about to release Kyle. Just a few more paperwork formalities for him and his solicitor to deal with."

"That's great. Are they satisfied that he had nothing to do with Douglas' death?"

Freddie chuckled. "On the whole, I'd say they're profoundly dissatisfied, but that's more to do with their annoyance at being cheated of what they thought was easy prey. They didn't have anything to indicate that Kyle was guilty apart from the fact that Douglas attacked him yesterday but they didn't expect a kid like Kyle to be represented by a top notch solicitor, especially with an even more eminent barrister waiting in the wings. When it's a kid from a Care Home they regard having that sort of help as cheating. It spoils their fun."

This pretty well matched Maddie's own viewpoint but today had been rocky enough and she felt it wise to warn him. "I hope they can't hear what you're saying or you'll be in trouble next."

"Lèse-majesté, you mean? Or possibly lèse-constabulary." He laughed at his own joke, "I think they're wary enough at the moment to develop political deafness. Anyway, I just wanted to bring you up to date and to let you know that I'm taking Kyle out for lunch before we head back. We wondered if you'd like to join us. I phoned Tempest and she's getting the bus down."

"With our bus service she'll be lucky if she arrives in time for supper. I'm about to drive into Portsmouth and I'll keep an eye out for her to see if I can give her a lift. I'm afraid I can't join you for lunch. I'm on a rescue mission. It might be an idea to keep that

242

solicitor of yours on speed dial. It's probable that Stan and Rose are going to be arrested and possibly Grace and Mrs Mountjoy as well."

"What! Maddie, what's been going on? I thought you sounded stressed but I assumed it was because of yesterday. Tell me where they are and I'll see what I can do to sort things out."

"You're an absolute star, but I don't want you to get involved and especially you need to keep Kyle and Temp away from any more trouble. After all, we must have one cast member left to explain why the penguin, polar bear and Christmas tree are absent from the show because they're doing time."

"That's even less funny than my constabulary joke. Promise me you'll take care and that you'll phone me if there's anything I can do."

"Just look up recipes for baking cakes with files in the middle so that I can break out in time for Christmas." Maddie checked her bag for keys and purse, turned off the Hands Free and held the phone to her ear as she headed out of the door.

"Any cake I cook would be hard enough to demolish a prison wall even without a file in the middle. There's no other penguin in the world I'd rather go on the lam with but it would be better if you waited for better weather, living off the country is liable to be chilly for folks our age."

"You've been watching too many old gangster movies. On the lam indeed. But it's true there's nobody I'd rather go on it with than you." Certainly not Grace, who'd moan the entire time.

"I'm glad to hear it. Although I admit you'd be better off with Stan."

"Why Stan? If I'm going to hide in muddy ditches in icy weather I'd rather it was with a man I knew would give me a cuddle to keep me warm." Not a wise thing to say outside in the estate. The residents were masters at making bricks without straw and could create a whole edifice if they heard that.

"Really, Maddie! Such immodesty! I only meant that, before Stan trained as an accountant, he was Regular Army, a commando, so he'd be good at avoiding detection and living off the land."

"A commando," repeated Maddie thoughtfully. That certainly increased the likelihood of Stan knowing where to stab for maximum effect, and of all the suspects he was the tallest.

"I've got to go now," she said as she clambered into her car. "I promise I'll let you know what's happening and, Freddie, thank you."

"For what?" he asked.

She was tempted to answer, 'for being so kind, and sweet and generous, and for caring about me so much', but that was ridiculously mushy and would embarrass them both.

"For making me laugh," she said and rang off.

Chapter 50

The longer Grace had to wait the more she felt as if she was in a nightmare. This couldn't be happening to her. She wasn't a person who'd ever stepped outside the law. She sat on a hard wooden chair, surrounded by the varied artefacts in Douglas Bartlett's antique shop, one hand holding that of Rose, who sat beside her, trembling and sobbing. Grace longed to be back in her aunt's comfortable, uneventful household. She wondered why she'd ever imagined she was capable of moving out of her comfort zone. Why hadn't she minded her own business?

She kept her gaze fixed firmly on the ground beside her feet. She couldn't look around the shop with its expensive stock of ornaments and furniture and the display cases of antique jewellery.If she did somebody might think she was planning to steal something. More specifically, the shop assistant would suspect the worst. She kept throwing them wary glances, in between staring at the door, clearly longing for someone to arrive and break her vigil.

Grace found it even more difficult to meet the eyes of her companions. Not that anybody was trying to make eye contact with her. Rose clutched her handkerchief in the hand that was not holding onto Grace and she kept dabbing ineffectually at her eyes. Stan, was sitting opposite them, gazing solicitously at Mrs Mountjoy, still enthroned in her Lloyd loom chair. It worried Grace that Mrs Mountjoy was looking increasingly vacant, the way she used to before the doctors sorted out her medication. If getting involved in this unpleasantness caused her to relapse, Grace would never forgive herself and lots of other people who respected the old lady would blame her at least as much as she blamed herself.

Grace knew she ought to tell Stan and Rose the things they clearly didn't know, before the police arrived and they said something that could be interpreted as incriminating. Stan seemed to have himself well under control but Rose looked close to hysteria. The trouble was, Grace couldn't think of a natural way to casually mention that Douglas was dead, much less that he'd been murdered. Perhaps it would be better to open with the information that Guinevere Henriette had been rescued and Freddie would return her to Rose as soon as they could get together. Surely the time for tact was past? And perhaps good news about her doll would help to bring Rose out of her emotional state.

"It's not right, opening his shop on the day after Douglas died." Mrs Mountjoy's voice was tremulous and yet it seemed to echo round the shop. "That's what I came in to tell you ... it's a disgrace, opening poor Douglas' shop when he was murdered ... last night it happened ... killed on our estate in Clayfield."

The effect on her listeners was electric. Indeed, both Stan and Rose stiffened as though they'd grasped a live wire.

"I'm simply following Miss Briar's instructions," said the shop assistant plaintively. "Personally..."

She was cut off by Stan's incisive voice, "Is this correct? Is Bartlett really dead?"

This question, in its turn, was drowned out by Rose, who leapt to her feet and screeched, "Dead! He can't be dead!" She collapsed back onto her chair sobbing, and, catching her breath in a series of hiccups. "I'll never get Guinevere Henriette back now."

Grace stared at her in horror. She didn't register the shop door opening until she heard Elouisa Briar

246

demand, "What's going on? What are all these people doing here? And whatever's the matter with that woman?"

"She's been making a fuss about a doll she says Douglas bought, only she claimed he'd stolen it. She's been very rude and aggressive to me," replied the shop assistant.

"Why didn't you tell her to leave then?" demanded Elouisa. "You know that Douglas has a zero tolerance policy to abusive customers."

"I was going to insist that she left, and the man that was with her, but then I realised a valuable ruby necklace was missing from the display case and so I made them stay until the police arrive."

"I see, In that case you did right." Elouisa turned towards Rose. "It's no good making that fuss. I can assure you, you'll never get that doll of yours back now. I sold it yesterday."

"No!" whimpered Rose.

"Yes!" mimicked Elouisa, her eyes bright with malice. "Maddie Summers took a fancy to it and her lover bought it for her. Never mind, she lives near you, so maybe she'll allow you visiting rights."

"Maddie's got Guinevere Henriette?" Rose sounded dazed.

"Yes, it must be nice to have a rich boyfriend who'll buy you anything you want."

Grace could stand no more. Rose was behaving hysterically but that was no reason for Elouisa to be so cruel. "Rose, listen to me." She grasped Rose's upper arms, forcing her to turn towards her. "Freddie and Maddie did come here yesterday and bought back your doll, but not for Maddie to keep. They came to get it back for you because you were so upset. They had to buy it because Douglas didn't actually do anything illegal even though he cheated you.

247

Guinevere Henriette is waiting for you at Freddie's house. He was just trying to find the right moment to give it to you."

Rose stared at her. "Really? Maddie won't want to keep her for herself?"

"No. She helped Freddie to get her back for you. And Freddie isn't her lover. You know they're just friends."

"If you'll believe that, you'll believe anything," mocked Elouisa. "I saw the tarty way she was dressed and the way he couldn't keep his hands off her."

"That was naughty of them," conceded Grace. "They knew you were standing in for Douglas and what a troublemaker you are and couldn't resist teasing you. They were astonished how much nonsense you'd believe." She enjoyed the expression of outrage on Elouisa's face. She knew it was mischievous of her but Elouisa deserved it.

"What is this place? What am I doing here?" Mrs Mountjoy's querulous voice snapped Grace out of her satisfaction. She turned to look at the old lady and was shocked to see her heavily-veined hands were trembling.

"You're at the antique shop," she said gently. "Shall I phone Nell to come and get you?"

"Who are you?" Mrs Mountjoy's gaze was blank.

Grace felt sick. 'Oh dear Lord, what have I done?' she thought.

Chapter 51

"Mrs Mountjoy's ill." Grace spoke urgently. "I need to get her back to her daughter so she can get medical help for her. I'll get her wheelchair. She left it at a nearby cafe. Do you know where that is?" She hadn't noticed it when she hurried from the car park but she'd been thinking of other things.

"It's to the right. Next door but one," said the shop assistant. "Oh dear! What's wrong with her? She seemed all right when she came in."

"I heard she'd had some cognitive problems a few months ago. Maybe they've come back," said Elouisa.

"What should we do?" asked the shop assistant. "Should we call an ambulance? You're the one with nursing experience who knows about these things."

Elouisa frowned. "It could be a mini stroke, but her face hasn't fallen on one side and her speech is clear enough even though she's not making much sense. Mrs Mountjoy, can you raise your arms?"

Mrs Mountjoy stared at her and then did so.

"That seems okay," said Elouisa, "but I suppose we'd better call an ambulance, just to make sure."

"No ambulance! No hospital! I won't be shut away! I want to go home!" wailed Mrs Mountjoy.

"You won't be shut away. We won't let that happen." Stan stood up and moved to stand beside her, gently holding Mrs Mountjoy's shaking hands in one of his own large ones. "Somebody fetch that wheelchair and we'll get her out of here."

"I'll go," said Elouisa and set off at a brisk trot.

"But the police?" quavered the shop assistant.

"Don't worry, I'm not going anywhere until we've got to the truth about this absurd accusation and you've apologised," snapped Stan. "You can have no objection to this lady," he indicated Grace, "leaving the premises to place the poor old lady you've distressed so much in the care of her daughter."

"Of course not. I never said they should stay here in the first place."

Elouisa appeared, somewhat breathless, pushing Mrs Mountjoy's wheelchair. "The lady in the cafe said you're welcome to take her back there to wait for her daughter." She pushed between Mrs Mountjoy and Stan to assist the old lady to rise from the wicker chair.

Grace came to the old lady's other side, while the shop assistant bustled forward to steady the wheelchair. When Mrs Mountjoy was safely seated and a blanket tucked around her legs, she pushed her out of the shop. The only course of action she could think of was to do as Elouisa suggested and take Mrs Mountjoy out of this stressful environment. But, once they got to the cafe, whatever Mrs Mountjoy said, she was going to phone 999. Grace had already thought the last two days had been a nightmare but this felt like something far worse.

"I think it would be better if we go straight home, Grace. I'll phone Nell and leave a message that I'm with you and perfectly safe and well." The crisp, decisive tones of the old lady in the wheelchair bore no resemblance to the feeble mutterings of a minute ago.

Grace stopped dead and moved round to the front of the wheelchair. Mrs Mountjoy was still slumped down, head low, but when Grace bent to look into her face she winked and gave the flicker of a mischievous smile.

"You're all right?" gasped Grace.

"Yes, but let's keep on moving. They may be watching from the shop, and this rag-doll posture is very bad for my back. Perhaps you could ensure we take a route that doesn't tip off the antique shop people we have a different agenda."

Grace obeyed. She cast a quick look over her shoulder as they reached the cafe and, when she was sure they were unobserved, sped past and then took a side road which looped around so that they were heading back to her car without directly passing the antique shop.

As she did so she saw Mrs Mountjoy straighten up and speak into her mobile. "Hello, Nell. It's me. There's nothing wrong, my dear. You were quite right, I am bored and rather tired. Fortunately I've met Grace and she's giving me a lift home. I'll see you later, back at Clayfield. And, if you have time, do pick up some of those delicious cream pastries we both like so much. Be sure to get enough for Grace and Maddie too."

Grace concentrated on getting back to her car as quickly and smoothly as possible. Mindful that women over ninety are easily broken, she did her best not to jerk Mrs Mountjoy's chair, even though she was seething with anger and hurt at the way she'd been deceived.

When Mrs Mountjoy was safely established in her front passenger seat and she'd won the battle to fold and pack the recalcitrant wheelchair, Grace climbed into the driver's seat. She was clutching her car keys but made no attempt to start the engine. She was shaking and tears were pouring down her face.

"Oh dear, I see I need to apologise," said Mrs Mountjoy.

"Why did you do it?" gulped Grace, speaking between convulsive sobs. "It was a terrible thing to do. I thought ... I thought you'd..."

"Gone doolally again," Mrs Mountjoy finished the sentence for her. "I'm sorry I've upset you. I never intended that. Nor did I intend any disrespect to all those poor souls like Antonia who have not been as fortunate as I am. I don't know if it will make you feel any better if I tell you that I found the experience very unpleasant. I hope I will never really return to that time in my life again but it seemed the most effective way to get out of there before the police arrived."

"But why? I mean, why were you worried about the police? And, if you wanted to leave surely you could have just done so without behaving like that?" Grace was more or less in control again and felt cross and embarrassed about her display of emotion.

"Perhaps I am too fond of intricate plots," conceded Mrs Mountjoy, "but I thought it was essential that, if my presence was mentioned, it was made clear that I was negligible and pathetic, not somebody who could be part of any plot to stage a jewel heist."

"But what about me? Would they consider me negligible and pathetic? I wasn't acting a part." Grace had discovered another reason to take offence.

"Not at all. Rose is negligible and pathetic and she doesn't need to pretend. You are so upright, honest and respectable that nobody would suspect you of being an accessory to a crime. Even though, in a way you are."

"What do you mean? What have you done?"

"Do I have your word you won't tell anyone about this, apart from Maddie, of course."

"You have my word."

Mrs Mountjoy reached into the pocket of her thick wool coat, and allowed Grace a glimpse of what was held in her clenched hand. Grace saw the rich fire of a ruby and the sparkle of diamonds and gasped. "That's ... How?"

"I guessed Stan had reappropriated his sister's pendant but the shop assistant must be sharper than she looks and saw it was missing. When Rose was having hysterics, I managed to signal to him that I was on board. It's remarkable what can be conveyed by a sideways look and a discreet nod."

"So when he held your hand he wasn't comforting you, he was passing you the pendant. That means he knew all along that you hadn't been taken ill." Grace's sense of betrayal was back full force.

"Yes, but that was because he knew I was going to do something. You'd have guessed too if you hadn't been fully occupied with Rose. There was never any intention to deceive you."

"But when the police search Stan and Rose and don't find anything, won't Elouisa guess we've had something to do with it?" To herself, Grace admitted that 'we' meant 'I'. If Elouisa believed Mrs Mountjoy was incapable of deception, she'd suspect Grace of being Stan's accomplice?

"Don't worry. I suspect Stan has that covered. Once the real pendant's back round Antonia's neck nobody will be able to prove we've swapped it back. So, are you shocked?"

"No." Grace knew she should be. but this felt like righting a wrong, not committing a crime.

"Excellent. There's hope for you yet. Now be a good getaway driver and get us out of here."

Chapter 52

Even though she was on the look out for Tempest, Maddie almost missed her. However, a glimpse of a red jacket lurking behind the bus shelter alerted her in time. She pulled into the lay-by, beeped a cheerful tune on her horn and leaned over to open the passenger door. Tempest peeked out from behind the shelter, identified who was summoning her and sped across the pavement to leap into the car. Her whole demeanour was of a hunted animal.

"Do I understand you're on the run?" enquired Maddie.

"I don't know what you mean." She sounded defensive.

"I mean your whole attitude was of a bunny seeking sanctuary in the nearest rabbit hole. Not to forget you were lurking behind the bus shelter. I was looking for you and I only spotted you because I caught sight of your red coat." She checked her rear view mirror and pulled back onto the road.

"I'm glad I wore it then. I'd just been calling myself an idiot for not borrowing Kyle's camo jacket." The full import of what Maddie had said hit her and she demanded, "You said you were looking for me. Is something wrong?"

"Nothing new that I know of. Freddie phoned me and said you were travelling down to meet them for lunch and, as I have to go to Portsmouth, I was keeping an eye out to offer you a lift."

"Thank you."

"You're welcome. So, tell me, who were you trying to avoid?"

"My mum and Aunt Lou. I can't stand the way they keep talk, talk, talking. As if they're so wise and I'm a silly little girl. They both used to act like Douglas was the most amazing man in all the world. I know he's dead but I'm not going to pretend he was anything other than a nasty old bully."

Maddie considered protesting that a man who was at least fifteen years her junior was more middle-aged than old but that would achieve nothing and might derail the flow of information.

"Has he always bullied you, Temp? I mean, ever since he got friendly with your mum?"

"Not for the first few weeks. Then he was trying to win me round. He used to give me money to go out with my friends and at first I took it, even though I knew he was only being generous to get me out of the way so he could have Mum to himself. Even at fifteen, I could tell he didn't like me, even though he pretended to."

"I'd guess his pretence didn't last for long?" During her long teaching career, Maddie had known more than her fair share of deceivers and self-deceivers flaunting their phoney charm.

"No. Soon he just told me to get out whenever he didn't want me around and if I didn't, he'd hurt me. But Mum adored him. When I told her he kept bullying me, she said I was lying. And when I showed her my bruised shoulder after he'd shoved me against a wall, she said I'd done it myself."

Maddie didn't ask why Tempest had stayed living at home. The answer was obvious, she had no better options. When she was younger, if she'd appealed for help to the Social Services or confided in a teacher, the first thing they'd do was talk to Janetta, and that would have aggravated the situation. Now, at eighteen, the options weren't much better, even if she left college, the chances of getting a job that paid enough to afford accommodation and food weren't great.

"Kyle wanted me to move in with him," said Tempest, "but if anyone found out he was breaking the terms of his tenancy, he'd lose his bedsit and the bit of living money they give him while he's at college. I thought I could stick it out until we left college, that way Mum or Aunt Lou would probably pay their share for me to go to uni. Especially if I went for a course they approved of, like Performing Arts. I don't know what will happen now. It could be better or worse now Douglas is dead."

Maddie didn't blame Tempest for her indifference to Douglas' violent demise or to her mother's bereavement. One of Grace's favourite platitudes was that people reaped what they had sowed. In Maddie's experience this was rarely true but for Douglas and Janetta it might be. She could neither understand nor forgive a woman who prioritised the man she was sleeping with over her own child. Still it might comfort Tempest if she told her that her mother had showed some proper feelings yesterday. "In the committee meeting, I showed her pictures of your wrist and she stood up for you. She was very angry with Douglas about what he'd done to you, and so was your aunt."

Tempest shrugged. "You think so? It's more likely they were upset because you showed them up in front of everyone. They both hate it if people in the village think they're less than perfect. Especially Aunt Lou. She'd do anything to make sure Mum's dance school's successful. I don't believe Aunt Lou was worried about what he'd done to me. All she'd care about was Mum. It's always been like that."

"How odd." Maybe Grace was right when she said that Maddie was different to most other people. Her instinct was to protect the young and vulnerable.

"Aunt Lou's a lot older than Mum and their mother died when Mum was quite young, so Aunt Lou brought her up. And I never knew my father. Mum always claims it wasn't a one-night-stand but it certainly wasn't a long relationship. The strange thing is she didn't do what Aunt Lou wanted and get rid of me. Aunt Lou always said I'd ruined Mum's career. She's always been very protective of Mum and, of course, she paid out most of her inheritance to set up Mum's dance school, so she doesn't want it to fail."

When Maddie considered how much it must have cost to buy and convert the house near the village centre she thought that Tempest's last remark could win First Prize for understatement.

"That was very generous of your aunt."

"I think she felt guilty because the old lady who left her a small fortune didn't leave anything to Mum, even though she was as much her cousin as Aunt Lou was. Aunt Lou used to go to visit her, but she never said anything about it to Mum."

"I can see that could cause ill-feeling."

Tempest giggled. "It did! Mum hardly spoke to Aunt Lou for months, until she sold the big house in Southsea and most of the antiques and put it all into the dance studio. She only kept enough back to rent and stock her little shop. God knows what she'll do if that folds. It's hardly what you'd call a great money spinner but I'm not sure Mum will give her more than the nominal amount she's paying now."

Tempest sounded indifferent to her aunt's potential plight. Maddie hoped that the hardness in her that had been created by emotional neglect didn't

257

taint the rest of her life, especially in her relationship with Kyle.

"Was it when she was selling the antiques that she inherited that your aunt met Douglas?"

"Yes. It's funny, I've heard all about how he's cheated lots of people, but Aunt Lou got lots of evaluations and she said his were fair, even quite generous."

"Interesting. Maybe he started his cheating games more recently. Temp, there's something I've been wondering about for a while, does your aunt actually like you calling her Lou."

"Of course not. That's why I do it. I hate their pretentious playing round with names. They were originally called Janet and Louise. Considering Mum's obsession with The Tempest, it's a miracle she didn't call me Miranda."

"It would follow through with their desire to add 'a' to everything," agreed Maddie. "I gather you don't like the name?"

"I don't like the character. Aunt Lou always says I wouldn't be so wilful if Mum hadn't called me after a storm. If she's right and names do make a difference, I could have ended up a spineless, simpering goody-goody, blindly obeying her parent."

"And worse, you could have ended up in a relationship with a guy called Ferdinand," said Maddie, and was pleased to see Tempest laugh.

Chapter 53

Maddie dropped Tempest off at the entrance to Gunwharf Quays, relieved that Freddie and Kyle were planning to eat there rather than at any of the small restaurants in the vicinity of the antique shop. She didn't know why that area seemed to be exerting a magnetic force on all the residents of the Clayfield Estate and their associates, but she gave Tempest a firm warning that, however much Freddie pleaded, she was not to allow any of them to go anywhere near the antique shop.

Having established that, she set off to do the very thing she'd forbidden her friends to do.

She was fortunate enough to find a parking space in a side road quite near the shop. As she walked towards the shop she remembered her mobile ringing while she was driving. She checked it out, found a message on her answer service and accessed it.

"Maddie, it's Grace. Are you there? I wanted to speak to you because it's difficult to explain ... Oh, all right then. I wanted to tell you that I'm back home and I've brought Mrs Mountjoy with me, and it's all right, whatever you hear about her she's okay, but don't let anyone know that you know that. It's just I didn't want you to be worried the way I was. The trouble is, Rose and Stan are still at the antique shop and Rose is hysterical and Stan's done something very unwise, although I can't really blame him, and I expect the police are there by now, and Elouisa's there as well. And please be careful what you do and say. Perhaps you ought to come home, except that Rose is in such a state, and I'm so sorry I've involved you in this. ... Oh, yes. You ought to destroy this message as soon as you get it, in case it falls into the wrong hands."

The flurry of words ended as suddenly as it had started. Maddie stood in the middle of the pavement gazing at the phone in her hand. It seemed that Grace had had a total breakdown, at least when it came to coherent communication. She wasn't sure whether Grace was advising her to continue to the antique shop or to stay away. And as for destroying the message, did her deluded friend think they were in an episode of the original Mission Impossible and her mobile would ignite and self-destruct? She considered re-running the message, in the hope it made more sense the second time around, then decided life was too short to waste on a hopeless quest and deleted it.

Was there any good reason to go to the antique shop? The image of Rose in hysterics was off-putting, to say the least. She could understand why Grace was sorry for her but Grace was a person who needed to be needed. Maddie would help out anybody in distress but she was irritated by Rose's tendency to dissolve in floods of tears. Of course, Stan was in the mix as well and she liked him. But she was pretty sure he could look after himself. The thought of the tasty lunch Freddie would treat her to was very tempting, especially after the morning she'd had. There was no good reason she should carry on walking towards the antique shop, but she did. Like the Elephant Child, her 'satiable curiosity made her determined to find out what was going on.

When she arrived at the shop the door was locked and a sign announced it CLOSED. It seemed unlikely her nosiness would be satisfied, at least in the short term, nevertheless she tried tapping on the glass. The people in the shop all turned to look at her and Elouisa made an impatient gesture, indicating she should leave. At the same point, Rose's voice wailed, "Maddie! Maddie! Don't go! Don't leave me here!" The cry was shrill enough to make Maddie wince and she thought there must have been danger to the eardrums of the unfortunate people inside the shop.

After a short consultation, one of the police officers weaved his way through the muddle of people and antiques to reach the door and unlocked it. He eased it open a few inches and said, "Are you a friend of the lady who just called to you?"

"I'm one of her neighbours," said Maddie, unwilling to commit herself to greater intimacy than that.

She thought she heard the woman in the background mutter, "Not another one!"

"You'd better come in. Maybe you can calm her down." The police officer opened the door far enough for Maddie to squeeze in, then shut it as soon as she was clear. She wondered if he expected ravening hoards of looters to storm the shop.

"Maddie!" Rose was stumbling towards her, still sobbing gustily, arms outstretched.

Maddie recalled Rose's tendency to drape herself over anybody unwise enough to show her support. She grabbed a chair, plonked it down in front of Rose and steered her towards it. "Sit down, Rose, and stop making that appalling noise."

With Maddie's hand on her arm, manoeuvring her into place, Rose had no option but to obey the first part of the command but she continued to veer between sobbing and moaning, as she rocked back and fore.

Maddie stood beside Rose but evaded the groping hands that reached for hers. "Could somebody get a glass of water, please?" she said.

Elouisa picked up a glass from the counter and passed it to her. "We tried to get her to drink this but she refused."

"Well, now she's got the choice of drinking it or having it thrown over her," said Maddie. "Assuming the chair she's sitting on isn't a valuable antique with priceless upholstery?"

For the first time in their acquaintanceship she saw Elouisa smile at her. "Go ahead," she said, "be my guest."

"Thank you." Maddie took the glass and stood in front of Rose. "You're behaving very badly. It's your choice, you can either stop making that silly noise or I'll stop you. I'm going to give you until I've counted up to five. One ... two ... three ... four ... five ..."

Chapter 54

As Maddie reached five, Rose gulped and stopped whinging.

Maddie smiled triumphantly. "That's better. Now sip this water and concentrate on behaving like a civilised human being not a wailing banshee."

Rose's puffy, red-rimmed eyes glared at her reproachfully. "How can you be so hard?"

"It's my default position." Maddie turned away from Rose and saw the other occupants of the shop all gazing at her. Most of them looked admiring and Stan was openly grinning.

"Well done, Maddie," he said. "We thought we'd have to get a paramedic and have her sedated."

"Why on earth did you bring her?" demanded Maddie. "In fact what are you doing here at all?"

"Rose wanted to talk to Douglas about the doll he bought from her. She felt upset that he'd hiked up the price between buying and selling it but I didn't realise she'd get so emotional."

"A lot of fuss for nothing." Maddie looked down at Rose. "Freddie and I came down yesterday and he bought your doll back. It's safe at Freddie's cottage and I'm sure you can collect it whenever you want."

"But how can I ever repay him for rescuing my little Guinevere Henriette?" Rose clasped her hands together and prepared to emote again.

"That's between you and Freddie. I only came with him because he doesn't drive and because I'd seen the doll and could make sure he got the right one." Maddie kept her words deliberately dispassionate. "Okay, that's explained what Rose is doing here. What about you, Stan?"

"Somebody told me that there was a pendant here very like one my sister owns. I was curious and offered to drive down with Rose. Unfortunately, while I was looking at it, the shop assistant and Rose started to shout at each other. I was distracted. I'm sure I put it back on top of the display case but when things calmed down we couldn't find it and the assistant accused me of stealing it. She called the police but they took a long while to come. They've had me turn my pockets out and haven't found anything so now I assume they'll take us to the police station to search us properly."

At the last words, Maddie heard Rose start snivelling again. She had a bad feeling if Rose was being taken into custody she'd end up having to go with her.

"We've been here for hours," moaned Rose.

"It's not our fault that the police took so long to get here," snapped Elouisa.

"We're short-staffed," said the police officer. "There's been a serious incident in a shopping centre, several people hurt."

Maddie's eyes met Stan's and he gave a swift sidelong look under the display cabinet. Now she knew the next step in the game. "You'll want to get this sorted as soon as possible," she said. "Has anybody got down and had a good look around in case this necklace has fallen down somewhere?"

She saw Elouisa move forward and added hastily, "Perhaps one of the police officers could do it? If accusations of theft have been made it's better to have an independent witness."

Elouisa looked offended but the younger police officer got a torch out and kneeled down. After a tense minute of searching, he said, "Got something," and scrambled to his feet clutching a pendant. "Is this the missing item?"

Elouisa took it and examined it. "Yes, this is it. I can only apologise for my colleague's carelessness. It's quite unforgivable, accusing respectable customers of stealing and wasting police time." She cast a hostile look at the other woman, whom Maddie deduced was the shop assistant who'd noticed the pendant was missing.

"I'm so sorry." The woman began to cry, not noisily and messily like Rose, but quietly as if the happenings of the day had overwhelmed her.

This sort of person in distress, Maddie could feel sorry for. "No real harm's been done," she said. "I'm sure you were already in a terrible state after you heard the news about your employer. Somebody should have come and relieved you much earlier than they did."

"Thank you." The woman gave her a watery smile. "I am sorry I caused so much trouble. I don't know how it could have happened."

"Accidents do happen," said Maddie, who had a pretty good idea how this one had occurred.

"I do hope that poor old lady will be all right. I'll never forgive myself if the harm is serious."

"Old lady?" queried Maddie, feigning innocence.

"Mrs Mountjoy had a funny turn," explained Stan. "Grace took her home."

"I see." Grace's garbled phone message was getting clearer all the time. She smiled at the shop assistant. "If you give me a contact number I'll let you know how she's doing." She didn't want the poor woman to feel worried and guilty when what had happened wasn't her fault.

"Thank you. I am sorry."

The police officers had been talking to Elouisa, now one of them said, "If everybody's happy with the outcome, we'll be off now. Just take more care in future. Like I said, we're short-staffed."

The police officers left and Maddie said, "I'll be heading out too."

Stan grinned. "Just like Wonder Woman. You fly in, solve all the problems and fly off again."

Maddie had never thought of Wonder Woman as short, plump and elderly, but, as an image, it was more sexy than being a penguin. "See you at the next rehearsal," she said.

"Um, about Rose." Stan looked at the limp, damp, snivelling figure hunched in the chair.

"You brought her, you can take her home."

"You're a hard woman, Maddie Summer."

"You'd better believe it." Maddie smiled and headed for the door.

Chapter 55

"If we're going to have many more days like the last two, I'm quitting Clayfield and going on a retreat," said Maddie, stretching her feet, clad in reindeer slippers, towards the fire.

"You'll get chilblains if you do that," warned Grace, still primly upright opposite her. "And I can't believe you'd ever go into a nunnery."

"Of course I wouldn't! Heaven preserve me from back-biting nuns praying at me. I was thinking of a desert island, with all mod cons laid on and the family dropping in occasionally, because otherwise I'd miss them, but there'd have to be an embargo on them scolding me for taking risks."

Grace recognised that the remark about nuns was meant to tease her and refused to take the bait. She turned her attention to the latter part of Maddie's speech. "You can't blame your children for worrying. You told me you phoned as soon as you got clear of the antique shop to make sure none of your family had been at the shopping centre and they were all safe."

"I know. It's scary when you hear about random violence like that. Thank God nobody was killed but it's going to keep the police busy for a while."

"That doesn't mean you should keep investigating when you've already been threatened by a killer armed with a lethal weapon."

"At least I didn't spend my afternoon waiting for the police to arrest me as an accessory to a jewel heist. Anyway, nice though it would be to have one of the most unpleasant people on the estate arrested, we've got no proof Jean Battle's the killer."

"But she threatened you with a hat pin and we know that Douglas was killed with the other one, and they both belonged to her."

"Yes, but I'm not convinced Jean Battle knows that one of the hat pins was the murder weapon. From what she said, she was angry that I'd told the police she'd sold them to Douglas but I got the impression the police hadn't told her why they were asking."

"Bluff," said Grace.

"She's an evil-tempered old witch but I don't think she's stupid enough to threaten me with the same sort of weapon that she'd used to kill Douglas."

"Double bluff," said Grace. This sounded feeble even to her own ears. She met Maddie's quizzical eyes and they both began to laugh.

"Seriously," Grace continued, "I think we're going about this the wrong way. It's no good trying to decide who had a motive for killing Douglas. We don't have enough information to work that out, just lots of guesses about who might want to do so. When I was timetabling the rehearsals for the show earlier, I realised we ought to work out a timeline for when Douglas was killed and where people were at the time. I know we sort of discussed it this morning but we didn't put it down in black-and-white and turn it into a timetable." She frowned. "What's the matter? Why are you looking at me like that?"

"Sorry, I was amazed that, with everything that's been going on, you had the time and energy to sort out the rehearsals. You're so much more organised than I am."

Grace was tempted to accept the compliment but honesty forced her to say, "It was a displacement activity. Working on the rehearsal schedules had a sort of normality about it compared with the other things that have been going on."

Maddie chuckled. "If you think our Christmas show is related in any way to normality you're in an even worse place than I am."

"Do you agree that it was six-twenty when we got to Hatty's house?" Grace jotted it down, trying to keep on target although she felt a glow of pleasure at the implication that she had a share in the Christmas show.

"Yes, give or take a minute. And Hatty said it was about quarter past when she heard the knocking on her door, but we have no way of knowing if she's telling the truth, so you'd better put that down in a different colour because we don't know it for a fact. But if we trust her, it's close to six-fifteen that he was stabbed. We do know it was about five-forty when Douglas went storming out of the meeting."

"Five-thirty-seven," corrected Grace. "I noted it for our minutes."

"Excellent and I'd guess about five-fifty-five when you heard Jean Battle and her pal talking and Jean went off to confront Douglas."

A thought struck Grace. "I'm pretty sure that Jean Battle had only just arrived. Do you think she could have had a quarrel with him when he went to get the hat pins from her and killed him then?"

Maddie paused for a minute before answering, then she shook her head. "It doesn't seem likely. Even if you ignore my instinct that she didn't know a hat pin had been used to kill him, it would make no sense for her to kill him and turn up for rehearsal and then go off again. She'd have stayed in the hall to give herself as much of an alibi as she could."

"That's true," acknowledged Grace.

"And from what I've seen of her, if she's got a quarrel with someone she lets everybody in the vicinity know about it. I may be wrong, but I think if

269

she'd quarrelled with Doug in the fifteen to twenty minutes before you noticed her in the Main Hall, she'd have stabbed him there and then, not sneaked after him to stab him on Hatty's doorstep. Of course, it might have been different if she'd encountered him when she left the Hall to demand her property back."

"When she came back to join in with the choir rehearsal, she didn't arrive until well after six-thirty, so she doesn't have an alibi." Grace considered. "She was wearing a navy jumper and dark trousers. It's possible they wouldn't have shown any blood."

"The chances are she'd have worn a coat." Maddie leaned forward to consult Grace's list. "Let's tick off the people we know were in the hall the entire time: Freddie, Miriam, Ron and Amy, Jean Battle's friend, Lucy, the other two young musicians, Sam and Jenn, and half a dozen other choir people who, as far as we know, had no reason to kill Douglas. Anybody else?"

"Janetta and Elouisa, they were rehearsing their Snowflake dance until six-twenty-five and then they had to hand the children over to the parents waiting in the lobby. The choir were getting really irritable because Elouisa kept fussing and the children weren't out of the way until nearly six-forty."

"That's great detection. How do you know that?" asked Maddie.

"Ron sent Amy over this morning with a long letter complaining about being kept hanging around and hoping, if I was going to take over the role of organiser when there were others better qualified, I'd make a better job of it in future. Poor Amy looked so embarrassed." To Grace's surprise, she realised that Ron's complaint had irritated her but it hadn't dented her confidence.

"Miserable old bugger. What's really niggling him is that the police and paramedics didn't use sirens and he didn't hear them arrive in time to snoop. Still even Ron has his uses. He's given us a bit more of a timeline."

"And a list of which choir members were inconvenienced and for how long," added Grace triumphantly, picking up a piece of paper and waving it.

"Even better. Who'd have thought Ron could be so useful?" Maddie plucked the paper from Grace's hand. "Now let's get down to business."

Chapter 56

"So who else is there without an alibi?" continued Maddie. "I suppose one of the most probable is Stan. He's got a motive, he's very tall and he's an ex-paratrooper, so he's got the fighting skills. I like him but I suspect he's capable of killing if he thought it desirable."

Grace wanted to protest that murder should never be desirable but, before she could frame the words, Maddie continued, "I can believe he'd have the nerve to go to the shop the next morning and steal back his sister's pendant. And he's probably cool enough to fake surprise when it was announced that Douglas was dead. What I can't believe is that, if he's guilty, he'd take Rose with him on his heist."

"Perhaps he needed a distraction while he swapped the pendants," suggested Grace, "but it would be a wicked thing to do, to take someone as vulnerable as Rose into that situation."

"Although she'd be good at the distracting bit, when I got there she'd been driving everyone to distraction for hours. I know you've got a soft spot for her but you've got to remember she's got no alibi for Douglas' murder and she was absolutely obsessed with that doll and bitterly angry about having been cheated. It may have brought back memories of what her husband did to her."

"Oh dear! I can see that's true, but do you really think she's capable of murder?"

"I think when she's in hysterical mode she'd capable of just about anything."

Grace sighed. "I'm afraid you may be right." She wanted to argue that, if Rose had killed Douglas, she wouldn't be capable of pretending to being shocked when told of his death. But Rose had spent years living with a husband who had defrauded many unfortunate people before he vanished abroad. Grace suspected that when it came to self-preservation, Rose could play a good game of deceit.

"While we're talking about your friends, I presume that Joel's out of it?" said Maddie. "And for that matter the couple in the end house next door to him. I can't help wondering if Douglas played his games on them."

"I don't know about that but I do know they were all going to a Literary Society meeting yesterday, so that should cover the time when Douglas was killed."

"I thought Joel had given up that game?" Maddie grinned. "I guess he slipped back into his old pretentious ways while you were away."

Grace felt flustered and suspected her face was turning red. When Joel had first moved into the estate, a few months ago, she'd hoped that he would become more than just a friend, She still felt embarrassed when she remembered how foolishly she'd acted. "Actually, Joel invited me to go to it but I told him I was already committed to helping with the show. What's relevant is that if they were all together at the Literary Society we can rule them out as suspects."

"You can do a bit of undercover work tomorrow to confirm their alibis." This time Maddie kept a straight face but Grace could hear the mischief in her voice.

"There should be no problem with that." She couldn't control her tendency to blush but she could control her voice.

"You're no fun anymore," complained Maddie. "So what about Mrs Mountjoy and Nell? According to Ron's list, Nell was back waiting to work with the choir by around five past six, which gives her half an alibi but it's for the more likely time. I'm no doctor but

I can't believe Douglas survived very long with a wound like that, let alone being able to stagger to Hatty's house and knock on the door."

"You're right, of course." Which meant they'd been wasting their time worrying about the first half hour when Douglas had stormed out of the committee meeting.

"If it was an Agatha Christie book, the killer would have propped him against Hatty's door and rigged up a way to knock on the door automatically when they had an alibi, but I guess that's not feasible." Maddie sounded regretful. "Or, if it was a tale of the supernatural, one of the spirits Hatty has summoned could have risen up to smite Douglas."

"If you've quite finished?" said Grace.

"Sorry, I got carried away. Back to business. Mrs Mountjoy hasn't got an alibi but I really don't think it's her. Even if we assume she's strong enough to stab him and fast enough get away without being seen or leaving a trace, if she went out to meet him it must have been with the intention of killing him. She'd have taken a weapon with her, not relied on getting a hat pin away from him."

"The same could be said regarding Stan. Or Kyle or Tempest, assuming that one of them is covering for the other. Does that make sense?"

"Maybe not, but I know what you mean. I suppose that means the murder was unpremeditated."

"Which brings us to the most obvious suspect. I take your point that she's not tall enough but she's the person who was found with the body, on the doorstep of her own cottage. We need to talk to Hatty."

"I agree but that's not going to happen until tomorrow. I phoned her mobile when I got back from Portsmouth and got no answer, after a few tries I phoned the Nursing Home to check up on her and the nurse told me she was so distressed they'd sedated her."

Grace frowned. "Are they qualified to do that?"

"The nurse said they got the doctor who'd come in to check on another patient to look at her and prescribe something."

Grace stood up and smoothed her blue tweed skirt, wishing that wool, however well tailored, didn't crease when she sat down. Maddie's jeans were more practical but they weren't her style, a smart pair of trousers were as far as she would go. "I'll go home now. We both need an early night."

It wasn't until they were in the hall and she was buttoning up her coat that she plucked up the courage to ask the question that was worrying her. She thought it was a fair observation but she hated it when Maddie accused her of being judgemental.

"I don't mean to be unkind but do you think it's suspicious that Hatty is still so overwrought? Do you think it might mean she was involved in Douglas' death? I know about her fear of snowmen but all the same..."

To her relief, Maddie showed no sign of thinking her question over critical. "It was obvious she was deeply shocked last night but I understand she was coming round quite nicely today, then the nurse told me she got in a state again. I'd guess Jean Battle had a go at her."

"That woman is abominable. I really hope she's the murderer." Grace felt shocked at her own vindictiveness.

"I agree, as long as she gets caught and suitably punished. But, in the meantime, I take some satisfaction from the fact that she's walking around with her arm in a sling having spent several hours in the Walk In department at St. Mary's Hospital."

Grace couldn't share her gratification. To provoke a possible killer seemed unwise.

"Why are you looking so disapproving?" demanded Maddie. "You said she's an abominable woman."

If Maddie hadn't thought of the danger, Grace was not going to enlighten her. Instead she said, "I hope she's not going to make trouble for you. She could charge you with assault."

"She wouldn't get very far with that and she knows it. I've still got the hat pin she threatened me with and I've handled it through a tissue to make sure it's got her prints on it, not mine. Anyway, I guess she doesn't want to lose her image as the toughest kid on the block. Apparently, she's telling everyone that she slipped on an icy path and fell. The Manager may decide to pay out for more sand and an extra workman to make the paths safer but that's a good thing as far as I'm concerned."

Maddie bent down and picked up the umbrella that she'd left leaning against the wall beside her front door. She smiled at Grace. "I appreciate all the gifts you've given me but, at the moment, this one rates as the best. I'm keeping it close at hand for the foreseeable future, although, if you want to borrow it to walk home I'll be willing to lend it."

"I'm grateful for the offer but there's no need." She grasped the handle of the capacious shopping bag she'd deposited in the hall when she arrived and removed another umbrella, shorter than the one she'd bestowed on Maddie but with an equally menacing point. "I've got a couple more at home. My cousin is determined to collect freebies whenever she goes on business trips."

"I guess they come in handy for beating off the opposition in a taxi queue," said Maddie.

"You're probably right." Grace knew that her cousin, Althea, was the sort of person who always insisted on getting her money's worth, including the acquisition of superfluous umbrellas. "After you told me about what happened yesterday I decided to arm myself with my own umbrella."

Laughing, Maddie raised her umbrella, holding it high as if it was a sword. Greatly daring, Grace lifted hers to cross it, wondering why only Maddie could bring out the frivolity in her that she'd thought was dead and buried long ago.

"The Dynamic Duo ride again," announced Maddie triumphantly.

"Both for one and one for both," replied Grace, who, even in a moment of great silliness, strove for grammatical accuracy.

Chapter 57

Maddie woke early, her mind buzzing with a long checklist of people to see and questions to ask.

Yesterday evening, soon after Grace had left, Tempest had phoned from Freddie's to say that Jenn's parents were away and she'd invited Tempest to go home with her, as long as Maddie didn't need her and she was really grateful for everything Maddie had done and how very kind she'd been.

Maddie had assured her that was fine, struggling to conceal how delighted she was. She liked Tempest and it was only in the darkest moments of paranoid fear that she thought the girl had been complicit in Douglas' death, but it felt great to have her house to herself. And, in the eyes of the world, it would be thought less strange for Tempest to be staying with her friend and fellow musician than lurking in Maddie's spare room.

After a quick text conversation with her daughter to check all was well, Maddie had felt the tension leave her as she powered down. She was relieved that Libby hadn't heard about Doug's murder. If she had, she would probably have abandoned their holiday and headed straight home.

It sometimes amused and sometimes irritated Maddie when people like Joel talked about being an introvert, with the tacit implication that she was an extrovert and thus had a tougher, coarser personality. She wondered what he'd say if she told him how often she felt that long hours surrounded by demanding vociferous people drained her, until she felt like there was nothing of her left. She'd often been tempted to inform Joel that an unwillingness to undertake anything that had the potential to be tedious wasn't the same as being an introvert. But it wasn't worth quarrelling with one's neighbours, unless, of course, they attacked one with lethal weapons.

As she showered and dressed she ran through the list of people she had to see today. Foremost there was Freddie. They'd spoken on the phone yesterday but hadn't managed to get together. He'd been a rock the last few weeks and she didn't want him to feel neglected now Grace had turned up again. Next she wanted to make sure Mrs Mountjoy was still okay. When she'd got back from Portsmouth, she'd phoned and Nell had assured her that Mrs M. was fine, but sometimes stress set in later. Also she wanted to check if Stan's sister had got her pendant back and whether it had made any difference to her state of mind. Last but not least, she had to talk to Hatty as soon as she'd slept through her sedation. Hopefully, she was calmer now. She wondered how much sense the police had got out of Hatty. Maddie had a bad feeling that, if they were forced to abandon pinning the blame on Kyle, they'd go for the next easiest option, the strange woman in whose hallway the victim had been discovered.

In the kitchen she put the kettle on and texted Mrs Mountjoy. Her reply came through swiftly. It was subtle and succinct and made Maddie smile.

First task ticked off, she was trying to decide whether the tastiness of scrambled egg was worth the effort of cleaning the saucepan afterwards when a knock on her back door made her jump. She peered through the kitchen window and saw Freddie smiling at her. He was clutching a handsome poinsettia in a gilded pot and a large paper bag.

She opened the door and he beamed at her. "Good morning, I hope I'm not calling too early."

"Not at all, you're just in time to join me for breakfast. Assuming you haven't eaten, that is?"

"Not only have I not eaten, I've brought breakfast with me. Croissants and pain au chocolat from the village bakery." He handed her the plant pot and paper bag and bustled into her hall to take off his hat and coat.

"Delicious." Maddie put the eggs back in the fridge, joyfully abandoning them for a far less healthy treat. "You're out and about early this morning."

"I made a pot of tea and realised the food cupboard and fridge were bare, at least of milk and anything else a man of my age wanted to eat for breakfast. I'd miscalculated how much young people eat. Not that I'm complaining, they're excellent company. Kyle offered to go shopping for me but I thought it better for him not to show himself on the estate at the moment, at least not by himself. One or two of the more judgemental residents can be rather strident about him and we've got a couple of reporters hanging round. I expect they'll be coming round knocking on doors quite soon."

"Oh wonderful! Let's hope they don't interview Ron. Is it all over the media by now?" She'd put off checking the News but, if Doug's murder had made the headlines, she needed to be prepared to reassure her children. And, of course, the more publicity the more likely it was that Grace would decide to leave Clayfield and go to live with her aunt.

"There's not much so far. The headlines seemed to be full of celebrity scandals and suspected arson at a landmark pub and a child going missing."

"Oh no!" She'd rather their latest murder was all over the front pages than that a child had been harmed.

"It's okay, they've got him back again, but they're still investigating who took him," said Freddie.

"That's a relief. Do you want to get Kyle and Percy and bring them over for breakfast?" Maddie put the oven on to heat the croissants and filled the kettle to make coffee.

"There's no need for that. I dropped into my place with milk and groceries before I came over here. He and Percy are perfectly happy watching a dog training DVD I bought years ago when Percy was a pup. Mind you, I wouldn't like to hazard a guess about which one thinks they're training the other."

"My money's on Percy. Although, to be fair, Kyle did a brilliant job on training Miriam." She touched the soft red leaves of the poinsettia. "Thank you for this. It's a real herald of Christmas."

"I'm glad you think that. There hasn't been much Christmas cheer about here lately. I'm sorry I ever got you involved in this wretched show."

"It's not your fault, I could have said no." Although they both knew it wouldn't have been easy. "We'll just have to take a tighter grip on things from now on." Assuming the show didn't collapse if one of its major performers was arrested.

He smiled. "That's inevitable now Grace is taking control. Anyway, I've got some good news."

"What's that?"

"Jenn and Sam came round yesterday evening and Jenn happened to mention that she'd phoned Tempest while the snowflakes were rehearsing."

"That's around the time that Douglas was probably killed but with mobiles it doesn't prove anything even for Temp, let alone for Kyle."

"Jenn could hear Kyle's voice in the background talking to Percy and, at one point, Jenn had to stop talking to do something and Sam took over and was talking to both Tempest and Kyle. And, what's more, they both heard my living room clock, the one that annoys you so much. Jenn heard it chime the three-quarter hour before six and quarter-past and half-past six and Sam heard it do six chimes on the hour.

"And, as far as we know, Doug was stabbed between six-ten and six-fifteen. I admit, as alibis go, that is the most complex I've ever heard. I'm not sure the police will be convinced but I am. Why didn't Temp mention this before?"

"She said she didn't think about it because she didn't think it would prove anything. Like you said, it's a mobile and she'd disconnected the app that lets people trace her whereabouts."

"Let me guess, her mother kept tracking her."

"Exactly. Janetta kept phoning and texting last night but Tempest wouldn't reply. I think one of her reasons for going home with Jenn was so that her mother wouldn't guess where she is. Now, tell me what you got up to yesterday. I thought about coming round to see you but I didn't want Grace to think I was muscling in on your double act."

"You're my friend too and Grace will have to like it or lump it. She's the one who disappeared for weeks while you stayed around."

"And turned you into a reluctant but very sweet penguin," said Freddie.

"Don't be sloppy. You'll put me off my delicious breakfast."

Chapter 58

While they ate she told Freddie all about what had happened yesterday, omitting only Stan's jewellery swap in the antique shop. She trusted Freddie but it wasn't her story to tell. They had polished off the last crumbs of croissant and Freddie was still expressing his horror at the thought of Jean Battle threatening her with a hat pin, when they heard somebody knocking on Maddie's front door.

Maddie thought that best case scenario, it was the postman with some of the many Christmas presents she'd ordered online: worst case it was a nosy reporter. She checked though the side window beside her door and discovered it was Janetta Briar. She sighed and put the security chain on before opening the door.

"Hello, Janetta. What can I do for you?"

"My daughter, is she here?"

"No."

"Oh God! What can I do?"

Janetta looked white faced and drawn and her appearance was far less immaculate than usual. Maddie could have felt sorry for her but she still hated the way she'd let Tempest down.

"I knocked at Freddie Fell's house. His dog was yapping and I'm sure someone was there but nobody answered, even when I called through the letterbox. Look, it's really difficult talking through this tiny gap. Please open the door."

"Sorry, after all that's happened I feel safer with the chain on. Temp isn't staying at Freddie's."

"And you don't know where she is?"

"I haven't seen or spoken with Temp since early yesterday afternoon." The words were accurate

283

although the suggestion was false. "I'm sure she's okay, she just needs some space."

"That's what Elouisa said. She said I should leave her alone and she'll come home when she stops sulking and needs money or if she has a fight with that Kyle boy. I know she's right but I'm worried. After what happened to Doug, I want my little girl safe at home." She started to cry.

"I expect I'll talk to her some time today and I'll tell her you want to speak to her." That was as far as Maddie was prepared to go.

"How can you be so hard? I've lost poor Doug and now my daughter has disappeared."

"I thought you'd lost Douglas already. You broke up with him at the committee meeting."

Janetta's tears dried up as swiftly as they'd appeared. She glared at Maddie. "I was upset with him that he'd been a bit rough with Tempest but we'd have made it up. I'm sure he was provoked. Tempest has never appreciated how much I've sacrificed for her. Now she's all I've got left."

"You've got your sister." Maddie wasn't buying into Janetta's 'poor little me' act.

"It's all Elouisa's fault! If she hadn't ignored Doug's text when he asked her to come and open her car for him to get his things, he wouldn't have been hanging round this horrible estate. I need my daughter to comfort me. You're a mother, I thought you'd understand."

"It's because I'm a mother that I can't understand how you could have let her down so badly."

"Oh!" Janetta turned on her heel and flounced along the path, although it was icy enough to turn the strut into an undignified skid.

Maddie shut the door and turned to look at Freddie, who was waiting in the sitting room doorway,

284

discreetly out of sight. "Coward, hiding there behind the door." She grinned at him.

"I'd have jumped out to save you if you'd been in any danger but I thought it was better not to give the gossip-mongers any more ammunition. You know there's a lot of people who'd decide that me being here for breakfast meant we'd spent the night together."

At least that explained why he'd come to the back door rather than the front. She didn't have the heart to point out that such covert behaviour was more likely to arouse suspicion than quell it.

"As if I care what our neighbours think. I guess I must be a hard woman. Three people have said so in the last twenty-four hours, four if you count Miriam saying that I'm a warrior. Although I think Stan was joking, at least I hope so."

"When most people say you're hard it's because you don't suffer fools gladly. I like the idea of you as a warrior though. I didn't think Miriam had so much sense."

"I don't think she meant it as a compliment," objected Maddie.

"Well I do." He pulled her towards him and hugged her.

Chapter 59

Despite Freddie's claims that he was no good at baking, Maddie had to admit he was good to have around the house. He insisted on washing up, even though only a fraction of the dishes had been used at breakfast, and did it without implying she was a slut, the way Grace so often did by her sighs and reproachful looks. When all was tidy, he insisted she kept the pain au chocolat in case she fancied a snack later on.

"You've got to get out of this habit of buying excess food and leaving it at other people's houses to be eaten up," she told him with mock severity. "You're doing terrible things to my waistline and even worse damage to Grace's conscience."

"Your waist looks fine to me and I don't think I've done anything to Grace's conscience, have I?" He looked puzzled.

"You lumbered her with a fridge full of Chinese takeaway leftovers. She didn't get round to doing anything with them and now she knows she ought to bin them but she was brought up with the words 'Eat up. There are little children starving in the Third World'."

"Oh dear!" Freddie chuckled. "I'll make sure I don't do that again."

"I don't want to be inhospitable but I'm going to check on Hatty. I feel bad that I've neglected her."

"Of course." Freddie put on his coat and hat and departed via the back door in what he doubtless considered a subtle manner.

Maddie smiled as she locked the back door and, bundled up against the weather, went out the front door and round The Green towards the Main Building.

"Maddie!" She spun round and saw Stan striding towards her, clutching two bouquets of roses.

"Good morning. You're here very early. Is everything all right?"

"Absolutely fine. My sister's nurse phoned me to say Toni is much more settled today. She was particularly pleased that, when they offered to put on her pendant, she was happy to wear it again. The nurse was so pleased about her progress that she wanted to share the news."

"That's good." Maddie hesitated, uncertain how to phrase the question she wanted to ask in an oblique enough manner. "Did the nurse have any idea why your sister had changed her mind?"

"Not really. She told me that people with my sister's condition often have irrational fancies and I mustn't get upset if she changed her mind tomorrow and refused to wear it." He smiled. "But I don't think she will."

"Nor do I," agreed Maddie.

"I was just about to call at your house. I bought you some flowers to say thank you."

"Thank me for what?"

"For the excellent advice you gave me."

"I'm glad I've been useful, but what advice was that?"

"You told me to make more effort to spend time with my son and his family, so on impulse I phoned and invited them all to let me treat them to the pantomime. We had a wonderful time. It really bridged the gap that had formed between us since my wife's death. Chloe, that's my daughter-in-law, admitted she thought I wasn't interested in the children. I tried to explain that I've never been any good at showing my feelings. My wife was the people person and I'd never had to make the effort before. I asked Chloe to bear with me while I learned."

"It sounds like you've made a pretty good start already." Maddie tried for a nonchalant way of asking the next question. "So what time exactly were you out with your family?"

"I helped Chloe by picking the kids up from school soon after I left you. I took them for burger and chips then home to change." He grinned. "I've got an unimpeachable alibi for the time of Douglas' death, although I must apologise for not informing you I was going to miss the rehearsal."

"I guess I wasn't subtle enough? But I'm really pleased to hear you're in the clear."

"Of course, in a book that would mean I was the guilty party."

"I've got an alibi too, so I'm not going to go for that sort of plot." She could have left it there, but there was something she really wanted to know. "Speaking of plots, do you mind if I ask you something? Why did you take Rose with you yesterday? She's not exactly the sort who keeps her head when all around are losing theirs."

"Believe me, I wish I hadn't. She was making a minor costume repair for me just after our rehearsal. I happened to mention that I'd phoned Douglas and I was going to meet him in his shop to confront him and she asked for a lift. When we were in the shop, I hadn't intended to do anything other than talk to him but when I realised he wasn't going to turn up the imitation pendant was burning a hole in my pocket. It should have been simple but Rose moved towards the jewellery display cabinet just at the wrong moment. If it hadn't been for the magnificent Mrs Mountjoy I'd have been sunk. I hope she's not too exhausted. I bought her some roses too."

"I texted her this morning and she said she was fine. She said she'd visited your sister yesterday and had successfully used her ninja invisibility skills."

"Her what?"

"That's when she fades into the background by looking so old and frail that nobody notices her."

"I've seen how talented that impersonation is. This estate contains some truly remarkable ladies, especially you, you're very special, my dear." He smiled down at her as he proffered the red roses.

Maddie craned her neck to peer up at him. The fifteen inch height difference made it hard to read his expression but she got the distinct impression that Stan was trying to chat her up.

Chapter 60

Tiggy was still being skittish about going out and Grace felt all the familiar sensations of guilt that her neglect had so circumscribed his life. Of course, if she decided to go and live with her aunt, it would be better if he was content to stay indoors, but even thinking that made her feel more mean.

She was trying to tempt Tiggy out into her back garden when she heard somebody walking along the footpath that flanked her low, wooden fence. She hurried to hide behind her narrow garden shed. The thought of being observed laying a trail of sardine along her garden path was too embarrassing.

From her refuge she saw Freddie hurrying along the footpath, carrying a large bag that bore the local baker's logo and a beautiful poinsettia in a gilded pot. She waited until she heard a gate click further down the row of cottages and the sound of Freddie requesting and gaining admission. It didn't need the skills of a great detective to work out who Freddie was visiting so early in the morning, bearing gifts. Grace felt a familiar pang of jealousy. It wasn't the same as when she'd been jealous a few months ago because Maddie had attracted Joel when she'd hoped he'd like her. She had no desire to win Freddie's attentions but she hated the feeling that he and Maddie were excluding her. The idea that Maddie had found a new best friend and detective partner really hurt.

Her mood wasn't improved by the discovery that, while she'd been preoccupied, Tiggy had ventured out to consume the sardine pieces and, having scoffed the lot, was back in her kitchen doorway miaowing loudly for her to bring the tin back inside and donate the rest.

In the kitchen she made tea and toast and waited hopefully for her phone to ring with an invitation to join Maddie and Freddie. Of course, she wouldn't accept a share of whatever indulgent treats Freddie had been carrying in that bag, but a cup of coffee and a discussion of the investigation would be a reasonable way to start the day. Her phone remained obstinately silent.

At last, looking out of her kitchen window, she saw Freddie, sneaking back along the path. At least, in her mind he was sneaking, even if other people didn't notice it. She pulled herself up sharply. Was she really beginning to think like Ron Bunyan? Well, sneaking or not sneaking, whatever they'd been up to, they didn't want to include her. Well, there was one thing she could do and one person who was always grateful for her company. She was going to visit Rose.

She was already bundled up for braving the December chill when the memory of yesterday's discussion with Maddie returned to her. She'd tried to deny that it was reasonable to suspect Rose but the fact remained that it would be foolish to go to visit anybody on their list without telling Maddie or Freddie what she was planning to do. Swallowing her pride, she got out her mobile, wrote a quick text and sent it to Maddie. Surely that was precaution enough? If she abandoned visiting her neighbours for fear they were killers the decision about her future would be made.

At first she thought Rose wasn't going to answer her knocking but, after she'd patiently tapped on the door at regular intervals for two or three minutes, the door inched open and Rose allowed her to enter.

"Good morning." Grace spoke as cheerily as she could, determined to get some positive response from the limp, pallid, red-eyed woman in front of her. "I

291

thought I'd stop by and see if you're okay." It occurred to her that this was one of the few times she'd visited Rose without bringing her a small gift, some cat food for Snowy or a cake or pot of home-made soup, all tactfully offered in a way that alleviated her poverty without offending her pride.

"I didn't think you'd come. I thought you'd be angry with me too." Her voice was as plaintive as her demeanour.

"Why should I be?" Grace could think of nothing else to say.

"Because I was upset and I spoiled Stan's plot by walking to the display cabinet just when he was stealing that necklace. He shouldn't have taken me with him if he planned to do a thing like that. It was wrong to involve me."

Grace thought it was certainly a stupid thing to do. She couldn't imagine a worse conspirator. "Did he ask you to go with him?" It wasn't relevant but she was intrigued.

"Well, no. But he should have refused to take me if he planned to steal things."

It was definitely time to nip this story in the bud. "You know Stan didn't steal anything. Maddie told me what happened after I left. You were there when they found the pendant where it had fallen on the floor."

"I can't remember. I was too upset. You went and left me and Maddie was unkind."

Even though she was cross with Maddie, Grace had to admit the justice of her warning that the more support she offered Rose the more she'd demand.

"Mrs Mountjoy needed me more than you did, and Maddie did what she thought necessary to stop you having hysterics and making yourself ill."

"Maddie was so angry with me," snivelled Rose.

"I don't think she was angry. If anything she was bored."

Grace couldn't believe she'd said that, it was a comment worthy of Maddie herself. Nevertheless, it seemed to do the trick. Rose stopped whinging and stared at her, a puzzled expression on her face.

"Have you been over to get your doll back from Freddie?" she asked.

This produced a fresh bout of reproach. "How can I? It was kind of Freddie but I can't bear the thought that everybody knows and pities me because I'm so poor. Everybody's laughing at me behind my back."

Grace was beginning to feel that Maddie's cold water threat was fully justified. She rather wished she had a glass to hand.

"Nobody's laughing at you. Although they will if you don't pull yourself together. Of course, those who know are sorry for you that you had to sell your doll to pay for Snowy's veterinary treatment and even sorrier that Douglas cheated you. Freddie was happy to help and he can afford to do so, but if you're too proud to be grateful and accept your doll back gracefully, I suggest you thank him and tell him to put it in an auction to get his money back."

This long speech left Grace breathless and feeling that she'd been cruel but it had its effect. Rose gazed at her in horror and said, "I didn't mean to be ungrateful. Oh, my poor little Guinevere Henriette! Is it too early for me to go and see Freddie now?"

"I'm sure it's not too early." If Freddie was awake enough to visit Maddie, he could certainly deal with Rose.

"Would you mind coming with me? It's going to be so difficult," begged Rose.

"Of course I'll come." Although she shuddered at the sort of scene Rose could create.

"I'll just smarten up. I look such a mess."

Rose fluttered away and Grace sat down to wait. At least Rose caring what she looked like was a positive sign.

In fact, restoring Guinevere Henriette to her doting owner was not the ordeal Grace had anticipated. This, she had to admit, was thanks to Freddie's tact and kindness. Fortunately, he owned one of the larger cottages, which meant they could use his dining room, while the four young musicians, who seemed remarkably at home in Freddie's cottage, stayed tactfully in the living room. It was hard to tell if they found the garrulous, tearful old lady and her stern-faced companion funny but Grace was grateful that they were polite enough not to let their laughter show.

When Rose had finished thanking Freddie and hugging Guinevere Henriette as she showered her with thankful tears, she made her move to leave. Grace followed, trying to think up a plausible excuse why she was unavailable to accompany Rose back to her cottage to witness the reuniting of Guinevere Henriette and Jemima Jane.

"Would you mind staying behind for a minute, Grace?" asked Freddie. "There are one or two committee matters I wanted to consult you about."

"Of course," replied Grace, profoundly grateful. "I'll see you later, Rose."

"Actually, it wasn't about the show," admitted Freddie, as he shut the door after Rose's departure and ushered Grace into the sitting room. "I wanted to tell you that Kyle's alibi for the time of Douglas' murder is confirmed. Jenn was talking to Temp on the phone and she could hear Kyle playing with Percy in the background and the television on and my clock chiming in the background. So he couldn't have been out of the house murdering anyone. I was so pleased I dropped in to tell Maddie the good news first thing."

"That is good news," agreed Grace. She smiled at the two girls. "It's lucky you were talking all that time."

"They're women, of course they talk," teased Sam.

"That's the sort of sexist remark that could shorten your career," threatened Jenn. "But yes, we were talking all the time, apart from ten minutes when I had to take one of the littlest snowflakes to the loo. The poor little thing had wet herself and I had to sort her out and get her some new knickers from the spare stuff that Janetta brings in case of emergencies."

"But I was talking to Kyle and Temp while Jenn was gone," said Sam. "So she's the only one without a full alibi."

Jenn stuck her tongue out at him. "All I've got is a tearful five-year-old and a pair of wet knickers to bear out my story," she agreed. "It's a good job I've got no reason to kill Douglas, apart from him once treading on my foot and sending me flying when he was showing off what he called dancing and then he dared to swear at me and call me a clumsy little cow."

Kyle grinned at Freddie. "A new motive for you to consider. Who was pissed off with being trampled by a fat snowman and wanted him out of the show?"

Chapter 61

Clutching the roses, Maddie continued towards the Main Building. She'd been tempted to ask Stan to leave the flowers on her doorstep but, if her talk with Hatty took longer than she planned, they'd be destroyed by the cold. Anyway, the chances were high that Ron was glued to his front window, binoculars at the ready. Maddie had told the truth when she said that gossip didn't worry her but she saw no reason to give the scandalmongers fuel for their campaign. Of course, she could take the flowers back home herself. It would only take five minutes but she had the bad feeling that something or someone would turn up to divert her from her errand.

The Nursing Home was part of the renovated Main House and there were two ways of accessing it. You could go inside and pass the Main Hall, residents' lounge and the rooms designed for Craft Activities, or round the outside of the building until you reached the door which allowed access to the immaculately modernised rooms of the Nursing Home. Either route took you to the Nurses Station where you had to state your business and sign in.

Maddie wasn't a frequent visitor to the Nursing Home but, as soon as she said who she'd come to visit, the woman on the desk beamed at her. "I'm so glad she's got somebody to support her. She seems to be a very lonely soul."

"I assumed she likes it like that. She's turned down all the invitations to join groups or even come round for tea, not just from me, Nell Mountjoy said she'd invited her too."

"Perhaps she's shy."

"Maybe." That wasn't the vibe Maddie had picked up on, although she was sure that Hatty was camouflaging something beneath her mystical posturing,

"Just sign here and go on up. It's Room 19 on the Top Floor."

"Thank you."

Faced with the choice between stairs and lift, Maddie chose the slower option, despite the ache in her hip. As she plodded upwards she realised this was a delaying tactic. The words, 'Won't you walk into my parlour,' echoed through her mind. She really hoped she wasn't making a fatal mistake by going alone to visit Hatty but she had the feeling it was the only way to get her neighbour to open up.

She arrived, slightly breathless, outside Room 19 and knocked on the door. There was no answer but she was sure she'd heard a soft shuffling sound from inside the room. Was it her over-active imagination that conjured up the picture of a frightened creature in hiding?

She knocked again and called, "Hatty, it's me, Maddie. I want to check you're okay."

There was a clock mounted on the wall at the end of the corridor and Maddie watched a full minute tick past before she tried again. "Please, Hatty, open the door. I'm worried about you."

The handle turned and the door opened to reveal Hatty, looking even more shabbily eccentric than usual, swathed in a motley collection of cardigans and shawls, and clutching an indignant, wriggling, Persian cat. She didn't speak but stepped back in mute invitation for Maddie to enter. Maddie did so, aware of the unappealing smell of stale clothes and a cat litter tray that needed emptying. "Hello, Toly," she said, stroking the big cat's neck, "you're honoured, they don't usually allow animals in the Nursing Home."

"They didn't want to but they made an exception after the police asked them to let me keep him," explained Hatty. "He kept going back to my house and they said he was contaminating the evidence."

"If I'd realised, he could have stayed with me, although I guess I'd have found it hard to keep him inside. Anyway, I expect he's been a comfort to you?"

Hatty nodded and hugged the squirming cat even closer to her.

With the feeling of burning her boats, Maddie came right into the room and shut the door behind her. "How are you?" she asked.

"I don't know." Hatty backed towards the bed and sat down. Toly wriggled his way free and strutted over to jump on the windowsill, surveying the cold, blustery day as if he was longing for the freedom to explore it.

Maddie sat on the armchair and waited for Hatty to say more.

"Frightened," said Hatty at last. "I don't know what is happening or why."

Her fixed stare alarmed Maddie. Up until now she'd thought of Hatty as eccentric and deluded but this seemed to verge on something more dangerous than that. Maybe the voice she'd heard wasn't that of someone trying to scare her but was in her head.

"I don't think you're my enemy. Are you?" whispered Hatty.

"No! I'm your friend. I want to help." Maddie put so much reassurance into her voice that she feared she sounded totally insincere. "It would help if you told me what was going on."

Surely Hatty couldn't be responsible for the theft of the snowman costume or for the carrot nose Grace had found in her garden? For her to take part in such an elaborate farce made no sense. That meant the snowman hadn't been a figment of Hatty's imagination. Maddie found that thought comforting.

Her hands tightened on the bunch of red roses. She'd forgotten she was still clutching them. With a mental apology to Stan, she held them out and said, "I've brought you some flowers."

Hatty stared at the flowers. "For me?" She sounded incredulous. "Nobody has ever given me flowers before." She leaned forward and tenderly stroked the vivid petals.

"Take them," urged Maddie. She wasn't afraid of Hatty anymore, just filled with pity.

Hatty did so and then looked at them helplessly. "I haven't got a vase."

"Put them on the table. They'll be fine there for a little while. I'll ask a nurse to bring a vase when I leave."

Now she'd got through to Hatty, she was determined to keep her on track. "Hatty, I want you to listen to me. I'm not saying there's no such thing as spirits and I'm not dissing what you believe, but I am certain that the snowman that's been tormenting you isn't a ghost. It's somebody in a snowman costume that they stole from where we store them between rehearsals. It's somebody who wants to scare you, possibly to frighten you away from your cottage."

"But why?" At least Hatty wasn't dismissing the idea out of hand.

"Perhaps there's something in the cottage they want to get access to." Although, in that case, if the object hadn't arrived with Hatty, she couldn't explain why they hadn't taken it when the cottage was unoccupied between tenants.

"No. It's not the cottage. They want me to go right away from here."

"How do you know that? Come on, Hatty, tell me."

Maddie watched as Hatty took a deep breath, she could almost see her arranging her thoughts.

"The first time it happened was when you asked for people to audition for the show. It was the second call for people to audition and I thought I'd give it a try. I didn't want a big part, or anything like that, but you wanted the Morris dancers and people for the choir. I like dancing and singing and I thought I could get to know people, maybe make some friends." A tear trickled down her cheek and she wiped it away.

"What happened?" asked Maddie.

"I was just pushing the door to the Main Building open when someone whispered in my ear, "Do not go in! The dancing snowman will kill you if you do. Leave this place forever or you will die."

"You didn't see who it was?" As she asked, Maddie knew it was a foolish question. If Hatty had seen who'd spoken, she wouldn't be so convinced she'd been threatened by a ghost.

"There was nobody there. That's when I knew it was a warning from the Other Side."

"Just accept, for one minute, that it wasn't a ghost, it was a living person trying to frighten you. There are pillars on each side of the front porch and lots of shrubbery. A quick moving person could soon get out of sight. Did you look there?"

Hatty shook her head. "I just ran home as fast as I could and shut and bolted the door."

Which, if it had been a spirit, was a totally pointless act. Maddie struggled to be patient.

"I know about the two times you told me you saw the snowman in your house, and that you heard its voice a couple of times. Did it appear or speak any other times that you didn't mention?"

Hatty hung her head, staring down at her plump, work-worn hands, which she was twisting together in her lap. "It was in my house three other times. It always said the same thing, 'Leave this place or you will die.'"

"Why didn't you tell me?"

"You're the only person here who's been nice to me. I didn't want you to think I was mad."

Maddie was torn between exasperation and pity. "I don't think you're mad but I'm sure it's nothing to do with spirits or the Other Side. Tell me, did you have your doors bolted when this snowman appeared?"

"I don't think so."

"That confirms it. Somebody very much in this world wants to scare you away. We've got to work out who and why."

Chapter 62

"I don't know why anybody would want to get rid of me. I'm a very ordinary person, leaving aside my gift of contacting the departed," said Hatty.

Maddie was only too willing to permanently leave aside Hatty's vocation as a medium. "Did you tell anybody other than me about your fear of snowmen?"

"No. Most people think it's a silly thing to be afraid of."

"So if the person who threatened you when you were going to audition knew about your fear, they must have known you before you came here. Are you certain you don't recognise anyone from your past?"

"No. Of course, I don't know many people. You and your friend are the only people who've actually come into my house, apart from that man, the dead man, when he pushed his way in asking about antiques."

Maddie accepted that, at the end of the row, Hatty didn't have an unlimited a view of her neighbours but still she persisted, "What about walking around The Green?"

Hatty hesitated. "I did think that tall girl who was back and fore between your house and Mr Fell's looked familiar but when I saw her face I knew I was mistaken."

Maddie scoured her memory. She was certain all four of the young musicians had been early for the auditions. In fact, one of the Performing Arts tutors had accompanied them to make sure all was as it should be. "I'm pretty sure Tempest didn't threaten you that day you almost came to the auditions. The thing I don't understand is, if you thought a ghost was threatening you, why didn't you leave the estate?"

"I couldn't afford to. It would take me ages to sell this house and while I was trying I couldn't buy anywhere else and I couldn't get back on the waiting list for social housing." As she said this, she flushed an ugly, blotchy red.

"I thought you said you lived in a big house in Southsea?" Maddie felt sorry for her but she couldn't let this pass, not when it could be the heart of the mystery.

"I did live there," mumbled Hatty, "but I lied about owning it. I lived in a big house as carer for an old lady. She promised me she'd leave me something in her will so I could buy a little flat somewhere. With a bit of cleaning work and my sessions as a medium I could have managed quite nicely until I got my pension. I don't need much to get by. And she told me she'd leave me this very special vase, it was Chinese and she said I should keep it as a nest egg because it was worth a lot. But she didn't leave me anything. This second cousin of hers turned up out of the blue and she left everything to her."

"It was unkind of her to break a promise like that."

"It was because the spirits told her too."

"Of course the bloody spirits had to get in on the act," muttered Maddie. Fortunately she spoke softly enough that Hatty didn't hear. Then, at her normal volume, "What do you mean 'the spirits'?"

"My old lady believed in a medium's powers. She really wanted to get through to her late husband. I tried and tried but I couldn't contact him. But this cousin had great powers. On the third attempt she managed to reach him and then, I understand, it happened many times again. The spirit of her husband commanded my poor old lady to leave everything to her cousin, Rosalinda. She sobbed when she told me.

She was so sorry. But she couldn't go against her husband's wishes."

To Maddie it was a clear case of undue influence but it wouldn't make Hatty feel any better if she convinced her that her 'dear old lady' had been duped and she'd been swindled out of her inheritance. "You said you understood the husband's spirit had appeared several times. Weren't you there when it happened?"

"No, I only attended the first two attempts to reach him. Rosalinda said my presence was draining her powers. She said two mediums in the same room diluted the psychic energy, so I had to go away, right out of the house."

"What was this clever cousin like?" demanded Maddie.

"She was impressive, tall and slim with wonderful red hair. When she first came to visit my old lady she wore a very elegant business suit and her hair was wound up on the top of her head and she wore an enormous, very stylish hat. But when she came in her spiritual capacity she wore her hair loose with jewels wound through it and had these glorious silk robes. She was magnificent."

Maddie thought how odd it was that Hatty showed no envy of the medium who'd outshone her. The spiritualist angle was a clever way to lull Hatty's suspicions that she'd been duped. It also occurred to Maddie that large hats and extravagant outfits would make it hard for Hatty to identify the woman if she saw her dressed in ordinary clothes.

"She had an American accent," added Hatty.

Which added absolutely nothing to the mix at all. For a con artist, an American accent would be easy to assume.

"And the old lady you lived with had never heard of her until she turned up?"

"Well, no. Except she didn't just turn up, she wrote first, but my old lady had never heard of her. She wasn't pleased when she got the letter but it was all above board, she checked on the family tree, and when they met and realised how in tune they were, she was very happy about it."

"So how long ago was it since the old lady died? And what was her name?"

"Her name was Mrs Justice and she died just over three years ago."

"And what happened then? Did this Rosalinda throw you out?"

"She did want to sell the house soon after the will was approved. My old lady's solicitor wasn't happy because it had been done on a will form, not like the one before that he'd done for her, but he couldn't find anything wrong with it, however cross he was. Rosalinda told me she was sorry, she'd have liked to give me something to mark all my years of devoted service but she couldn't risk angering the spirit of Mr Justice by disobeying his commands. She couldn't even give me a reference because she said she didn't know me well enough. At first, when I left the house in Southsea, I had to sleep in shop doorways. The house that the council wanted to demolish was a squat."

Chapter 63

The words 'mean-spirited bitch' echoed through Maddie's mind, but she didn't say them. "One thing I don't understand, if you had nothing and ended up in a squat, how did you afford a cottage in Clayfield? Did Rosalinda relent?"

"Oh no! She sold my old lady's house and all of her lovely furniture and antiques and went back to America." Hatty blushed again and Maddie thought she changed colour more often than a chameleon. "I won some money on the premium bonds. I had them ever since I was a girl. They were a present from my grandmother when I was twenty-one and I couldn't bear to cash them in."

"That's brilliant luck. Why are you embarrassed about it?"

"This is an estate for professional people. I'm not the right sort of person to come here."

"Don't you believe it. We're not really as snobby as you seem to think."

"I know! I mean I know you're not, and Mrs Mountjoy and her daughter were kind when I met them one day walking round The Green. But I couldn't tell anyone about not having anywhere to live. As it is, lots of people haven't spoken to me, And the other day your friend looked so disapproving, even though she was kind enough to patch me up."

"Don't worry about that, disapproving is Grace's default expression. You should see the sort of looks she gives me."

Hatty managed a tremulous smile.

"That's better. I don't want to upset you again but I need you to tell me what happened on the night that Douglas died."

Hatty was silent for so long that Maddie thought she wasn't going to answer but then she said, "There's nothing to tell that I haven't said before. I was watching television and I heard somebody knocking on my door. I didn't want to answer it. I just wanted to be left alone. But someone banged harder and I went to the door. I unbolted it and took the chain off but then I stopped and looked through the little window and saw a snowman standing there. I was so afraid that I felt faint. I shouted 'go away'. Then I heard a strange noise, sort of a cross between a gurgle and a groan, and the door burst open and the snowman fell into the hall, almost on top of me, and..."

"Back up a second," interrupted Maddie, "how come the door opened if you didn't open it?"

"The catch isn't always reliable."

"I see, so when Douglas' weight lurched against it, it burst open?"

Hatty nodded. "I think so. He fell against me and I went back and back until I reached the stairs. I felt his blood sticky on my hand. I don't know why I couldn't do anything. The police thought I should have done something. They didn't say so but I knew. I saw the way they looked at me."

Could Douglas have been saved if Hatty hadn't frozen? Maddie didn't think so but she didn't know and it wasn't any use thinking about it.

"You were in shock. It wasn't your fault."

"It was because he was a snowman, you see, and he was dead," Hatty continued to try to excuse herself, or maybe to make sense of it.

"Try not to think about it," advised Maddie. "When this business is all cleared up and the police have finished with your cottage, if you're willing to go back there, we'll clean it up and get you some new furniture, and we'll make sure you get to know people properly." She stood up. "I'll be off now. I'll ask the nurse to bring you a vase."

At the nurse's station she asked about the vase and also if they had any spare, clean, paper bags and a pair of plastic gloves. Suitably equipped, she went outside and started her search.

It took quite a while to find the objects she was looking for, but she was grateful that the sludgy ice was melting, otherwise it would have been a hopeless task. At last she found what she was seeking, not far from where she'd guessed they might be, in the shrubbery that bordered the car park behind the Main Building. She rummaged in her bag and found the stubs of two well-used pencils and used them to mark the spot. She used her phone to photograph her finds in situ and, wearing the plastic gloves, picked them up. After a brief moment to gloat about her clever deduction, she placed them in the paper bags and stowed these carefully in her fabric bag. Now she had to do the responsible thing and turn her findings over to the police. The problem with this was that she'd have to explain why she'd been searching the shrubbery at the crucial place. She considered inventing a sighting of a lost kitten but that wouldn't tie in with the careful preparations she'd made to preserve the evidence. She wished she could tell them what she'd deduced but she didn't believe they'd take her seriously. In fact, she wasn't sure she believed it herself. Logic told her the identity of Douglas' killer and intuition backed up her deductions but one insurmountable fact stood in the way. She really needed someone as a sounding board. She got out her mobile and phoned Grace.

Chapter 64

"The game's afoot, Watson!" announced Maddie, striking a suitably dramatic pose.

"I thought it was Hercule Poirot who gathered all his suspects together to reveal the culprit, not Sherlock Holmes," objected Grace.

"True, and I haven't got the right sort of figure to carry off a Holmes impersonation and even my nearest and dearest can't claim that I'm musical enough to play the violin. Poirot's my best bet. Do you think I should buy a false moustache?"

Grace sighed. Maddie had been infuriatingly bouncy all afternoon, ever since they'd got together to pool their information and Grace had supplied the one key detail which sealed Maddie's case. Grace would have been proud of her contribution if she hadn't been so worried about what Maddie was planning to do next.

"Couldn't we just do what we've scheduled and have a meeting to discuss the adjustments we need to make to the Christmas show?" she asked. "Do we have to go through with all these dramatics?"

Maddie shook her head. "Don't you see, we can't finalise any plans for the show until we know there isn't a killer in the cast? What if they strike again?"

Grace couldn't suppress the shiver that ran down her back. "Surely not? Why should they?"

"If somebody has a secret they're desperate to keep they may go to any lengths. This person has already gone to ludicrous lengths to cover up what they've done. We don't want any more violence."

"But real life isn't like crime fiction. Do you really think they'll simply confess? Or do one of those absurd chases, like they do on TV?"

Maddie chuckled. "That would be rather fun. In fact, it's given me a brilliant idea. Could you tell everybody to collect their costumes and wear them for the meeting? You can say that Nell wants to check them for fit and signs of wear."

"Maddie! No!" protested Grace. "You know that's a bad idea." Nevertheless, she started to compile the email, including Maddie's request.

Three hours later, Grace surveyed the main hall, populated with Christmas characters, and shuddered. Of course, there were a few non-performers, like herself, Nell, Rose and Elouisa, who were dressed in everyday clothes but the overall impression was of a fairytale world gone mad.

"Why are there two people dressed as penguins?" demanded Janetta. "Surely one of them is enough?"

"More than enough," agreed Elouisa.

"Maddie has been having trouble with her arthritis so she thought it would be wise to rehearse an understudy," explained Grace. "Fortunately, Nell had made spare costumes for Maddie, Freddie and Stan. So Maddie got her friend to come along and see how she felt about helping out."

"Oh, I see. Poor thing. Understudy is such a dreary role. Always the bridesmaid, never the bride. What's her name?" said Janetta.

"Queenie," said Grace. She was fascinated by the contrast between the two sisters. Janetta in her white, sparkling, floating dress and Elouisa clad in her customary black polo neck jumper and black trousers. They were the perfect archetypes of the pantomime fairy queen and wicked demon king.

"I see my daughter over there. I must speak to her." Janetta sped across the hall to where Tempest had just entered accompanied by Kyle, Sam and Jenn.

Elouisa lingered. "Why are other performers allowed spare costumes when my sister hasn't been offered one?" she demanded. "It's disgraceful when she's the only professional performer you have in your pathetic little show."

Grace felt her temper fray to snapping point. "I understand that Maddie, Freddie and Stan paid for the materials for both their costumes and for those of the student performers but your sister preferred to adapt one she'd worn previously. However, I'm sure, if she wants another costume, you can afford to pay for it from the profits you made from the children's costumes."

Elouisa flushed but stood her ground. "If this is a rehearsal, why didn't you allow any of the little snowflakes to attend? After all, they are the highlight of this show."

"You're slipping, Elouisa, you missed out the insulting adjectives," said Maddie, coming up behind her. "And the reason we didn't invite the children is because this isn't a rehearsal, it's a meeting to discuss whether we should hold a show at all when there's a killer on the loose." She raised her voice, "Will everybody take a seat, please. We've got a lot to discuss."

Everybody obediently took a place in the circle of chairs. Grace watched as Janetta tried to seat herself next to her daughter but Tempest moved away so that Sam and Jenn were on one side of her and Kyle on the other.

With a guilty start, she remembered Maddie's instructions and pushed through the performers to make sure she was seated beside Queenie, the substitute penguin. Mrs Mountjoy was seated on Queenie's other side, looking remarkably majestic and solid.

Maddie remained standing. Despite her short stature and the comic effect of her penguin costume she dominated the room. Not for the first time, Grace thought she must have been a superb teacher.

"Thank you all for coming. First of all, in case any of you think you're seeing double, let me introduce Queenie. Like all great stars, I need an understudy, and she's kindly agreed to stand in if my arthritis cripples me, but that's only if we all decide to carry on."

There was a murmur of greetings to Queenie, who bobbed her head shyly in response.

"Why shouldn't we carry on?" challenged Jean Battle. "We've put a lot of hard work into this show."

"I'd have thought the reason was obvious," retorted Maddie. "A murder has been committed on this estate and the murderer's still at large. We have to decide if it's safe for our performers and our audience."

"And any of our performers could be arrested and hauled off to prison at any point," added Freddie, with what Grace suspected was mischievous intent.

A gasp rippled around the room.

"But surely that woman whose house Douglas was in killed him?" said Janetta.

"No she didn't," said Maddie. "She was unfortunate enough to be caught in the crossfire."

"In that case, I think we should cancel the show. At least we should take out the children's part of it. I can't be responsible for all those little children to be put at risk. I'd like my daughter to withdraw as well, but I know she'll do whatever she wants to do." Janetta looked across at Tempest and stretched her hands out in appeal. Tempest made no response.

"I agree," said Miriam. "I can't have my grandchildren coming to a place that's so dangerous.

And, although I love singing and don't want to let anybody down, I know my daughter would say I mustn't take any risks."

"Nonsense!" snapped Elouisa. "I'm sure nobody else is at risk. I don't want to speak ill of the dead but Douglas had a lot of enemies."

"That's true," agreed Maddie, "for a start, there's all the people he cheated over antiques. Apparently he was very clever about it, gaining people's confidence by making a fair or generous offer on some minor items and then ripping them off when it came to something valuable."

"I didn't kill him!" Rose jumped to her feet. "I know you think I did it, but I didn't! I was upset about Guinevere Henriette but I wouldn't kill him, even after what he did."

A startled silence greeted this outburst, followed by Ron Bunyan enquiring in a hoarse whisper, "Amy, what's she on about? Who the heck is this Guinevere Whatsit?"

Chapter 65

"Sit down, Rose, and stop making a fool of yourself," said Maddie. "We've heard enough about your wretched doll. You're not the only person Douglas conned, and some people for a lot more money than you lost. Isn't that right, Freddie?"

"It certainly appears to be the case," said Freddie, "I saw a Chinese vase in his shop that I thought was very rare. I took a photo of it and asked an expert I know to confirm its value and I was right. Apparently the old lady it belonged to knew it was worth a lot but after she died Doug bought it from her heir for a few thousand when it's worth at least a million."

"And he was capable of stealing valuables and replacing them with something worth a fraction of the value," said Stan, which Grace thought was reckless of him, considering what had happened yesterday.

"I always said he was a wrong 'un. Didn't I tell you so from the start, Amy?" announced Ron Bunyan.

"Yes, Ron," agreed his wife.

"I reckon, if it's dangerous, we ought to cut our losses and give up," continued Ron. "It's a pity, though, I put a lot of hard work into those balls."

A blank silence followed this statement. Grace thought, considering the circumstances of fraud violence and murder, surely that was the most inappropriate thing anybody could say and felt shocked that she had to fight to hold back her laughter.

Tears were trickling down Janetta's cheeks. "I knew he could be ruthless in business matters but I never thought he was actually dishonest. Is that why he was killed? Because he cheated the wrong person and they wanted to be revenged?"

Grace felt sorry for her but she reminded herself that this was a performer, skilled at portraying the emotions she wished to persuade her audience she felt.

"He cheated lots of people and caused a lot of hurt, but that's not necessarily why he was killed," said Maddie. "You remember what he said when he was leaving the hall?"

"Something about making us sorry, but he was in a temper, it didn't mean anything."

"Oh, I think he meant something very specific," said Maddie, "and somebody took him seriously. So seriously that they killed him to prevent him speaking out."

"All this nonsense about secrets and revenge! If that crazy woman who talks to ghosts didn't kill him, it was that boy who's been in Care that you make such a fuss of," snarled Jean Battle.

"Fortunately, Kyle has an alibi," Maddie smiled sweetly and added, "Unlike you Mrs Battle. I found the ends of those broken hat pins, you know. They were in the car park, just about under the window of your flat."

"How dare you suggest I killed him?" Jean Battle's voice rose to a screech.

Maddie clearly took that as a rhetorical question because she said, "The person Douglas was talking about doesn't seem to have worried about him knowing their secret, at least not until he got angry and threw out a threat."

"You keep talking about a secret but not what it is. I bet you've got no idea." Jean Battle wasn't giving up her onslaught yet.

"Actually, I have. A very rich old lady was scammed by a person who claimed to be her relation and persuaded her to sign a will in their favour. There was only one person who might have recognised this imposter and there was little chance of them ever meeting again because the fake will left her destitute. It must have been a shock when she turned up here and our fraudster has been going all out to frighten her away."

"What did they do to frighten her away?" Grace already knew the answer but Maddie had asked her to help keep the momentum going.

"They dressed up to prey on her phobia and they threatened her with death if she joined in any activities on the estate. And when Douglas said he was going to speak out, they killed him on her doorstep."

Grace saw enlightenment dawn on most of the listeners and decided to say the name out loud. "So the person who might recognise the fraudster is Hatty?"

"Poor lady!" exclaimed Freddie. "How brave of her not to run away."

"Very brave, very desperate," said Maddie. "Because of the scammer, she was left without anything or anywhere to go."

"But isn't doing all this rather excessive?" said Tempest diffidently. "If it was a few years ago would this lady actually recognise the scammer?"

"The ironical thing is that she probably wouldn't have. The person always wore a wig and fancy dress, but the way a person moves can be more distinctive than a face. Still, for good measure, I did some sketches of what certain people would look like with red fuzzy hair."

"This is absolute nonsense!" Elouisa sprang to her feet and stormed towards the door.

Mrs Mountjoy raised her hand. The door opened and two uniformed police officers stood there.

Elouisa spun round and took a few steps back into the hall, her face twisted with rage.

Before she could go any further, the understudy penguin rose to her feet. She was visibly shaking as she waddled towards the centre of the circle of chairs. The effect should have been comic but, somehow, it wasn't. Maddie moved to stand on one side of her and Grace stood up and hurried to her other side as she reached up and tugged off the head of her costume.

"Hello, Rosalinda, remember me?" said Hatty. "I certainly remember you."

Chapter 66

"So that's it, all sorted" said Maddie, "and just in time. My daughter's home and wants me to go Christmas shopping." She beamed around the select group of friends. "Luckily, the news was full of other stuff and she didn't pick up on our little local murder."

The meeting in the Main Hall had broken up and now it was just Grace, Freddie, Stan and herself who'd gathered with Nell and Mrs M. in the Mountjoys' sitting room.

Freddie chuckled. "Little local murder indeed. What are you going to tell Libby when she finds out?"

"The truth. After all, I took all the precautions I could and I haven't been in any real danger."

"No danger! What about that awful Battle woman threatening you?" protested Grace.

"I admit I was worried for a few seconds but I was armed with your trusty umbrella. And you must admit, today I took all the precautions I reasonably could."

"It was impressive the way those police officers arrived right on cue," agreed Stan. "How did you manage that?"

"I realised the police were fully occupied with those shootings in Portsmouth and the missing child investigation and the arson, which is probably why they failed to search the entire grounds for the broken end of the hat pin that was used to stab Douglas. Fortunately, the magnificent Mrs Mountjoy has connections in high places and made a phone call requesting police back up." She raised her tea cup to toast her hostess.

"Just somebody whose grandfather I happened to know many years ago. So kind of the dear boy to remember me," said Mrs Mountjoy.

Maddie noted she was doing her harmless old lady act again. Mrs Mountjoy's past was a secret she shared with only a few close and trusted friends.

"But how did you know the murder weapon had lost its tip? Surely the police didn't share that information, however friendly Mrs Mountjoy was with somebody's father?" protested Stan.

"The police are very selfish about sharing their clues," agreed Maddie. "So I worked it out by my own brilliant powers of deduction."

"Brilliant and modest," murmured Grace.

"That's me," agreed Maddie cheerfully. "I could do a Sherlock Holmes and tell you to work it out for yourselves and then sneer when you get it wrong, but you might get it right and that would spoil all my fun." She fended off Freddie as he leaned over to remove her plate with its chocolate eclair. "Okay, I'm getting there. Jean Battle waved the second hat pin at me after she found it in the grounds and I knocked it out of her hand. When I looked at it, I wondered how it got broken and I decided maybe somebody had tried to force a lock."

"What lock?" demanded Grace. "I mean, which lock? Before the meeting, you told me whom you were going to try and trap but you didn't elaborate."

"Oh excellent grammarian," teased Maddie. "I have to keep some secrets to maintain my illusion of omnipotence. Anyway we were running short of time. There were lots of locks it could have been used on but I remembered about Douglas being dressed in his snowman costume."

"Of course! His clothes and wallet were locked in Elouisa's car."

"Exactly. Janetta said he texted Elouisa, demanding that she came to unlock it for him. Janetta said she ignored the text and I think she believed that. But Elouisa must have slipped away while Janetta and the children were on the stage. If one of the little ones hadn't needed the loo nobody would have realised she'd gone. She was always there in her dark clothes in the shadows and no-one noticed her."

"So what happened?" demanded Freddie.

"My guess is she was too late to stop Douglas attacking the lock on her car boot, He'd failed to open it and had broken the points off both the hat pins, thrown them down and stormed off. There was red paint on the broken points, so he must have scratched her car. Jean Battle found one hat pin the following day but I think Elouisa had already found the bigger one and, in a fury, she went after Douglas."

"I'm confused," announced Stan. "Did she kill him because he damaged her car? I know I'm being stupid, but what has her pretending to be the relation of that old lady who left her lots of money got to do with it?"

"The police had a problem getting their heads around that too," admitted Maddie. "At least, they had no problem with the scam, they're used to that sort of thing. It was all the theatricals that flummoxed them, especially trying to scare Hatty away from the estate by posing as a snowman."

"I don't get that either," said Stan, and Freddie and Grace both nodded in agreement.

"Why would anybody do that?" asked Grace.

"For fun," said Mrs Mountjoy, "and because she could. She was an actress who'd always wanted the starring role. If nobody else would offer her one, she'd create her own. Also, the excitement of being in danger of discovery became addictive."

Maddie nodded. "She'd always sublimated her desires to those of others. She gave up an acting career to become a carer for her mother. After her mother died she carried on looking after her young sister. She lived through Janetta and was determined she should be a success. That was why she was so bitter about Tempest. She resented her very existence, which, in her mind, had prevented Janetta from reaching the heights she believed she should attain. And, to make matters worse, Elouisa and Janetta both believed that Temp was mucking up her own career by being in a relationship with Kyle."

"Is that why she stole Kyle's bike and left it in the field behind Hatty's house?" asked Freddie.

"I'd guess it was both spite and convenience. She needed an unobtrusive way of reaching Hatty's house and what could be better than a bike along a footpath that's almost unused in winter? She'd stolen Kyle's snowman suit too. So any suspicion would lead back to him."

Maddie sighed. "It only occurred to me a few minutes ago that I could have solved the whole snowman thing on the first day when I noticed that Elouisa had a sore nose. She said it was an allergy but I bet it was because Hatty had thumped the snowman hard enough to remove the carrot nose."

"I was with you and I never thought of that either," said Grace.

"I presume it was because Elouisa was a carer that she heard about Hatty's old lady?" said Freddie.

"I think so," said Maddie. "When I questioned Hatty about who else came to the old lady's house, she said agency carers would come in once a week when Hatty had a day off and she remembers the old lady talking about one called Lulu. It amazes me that Hatty isn't bitter about her old lady. She waited on her for years, six days a week, and yet she went back on her promise. The old lady liked talking about her family but Hatty told me she was too busy looking after the old tyrant and her house to pay much attention. The tyrant bit is my interpretation, not Hatty's."

"I presume that Elouisa was Lulu and she did listen to the old lady?" said Grace.

"I'm pretty certain that's so." Maddie smiled at her. "The thing that made me think of it was Hatty saying the long-lost cousin was called Rosalinda."

"The obsession with sticking 'a' on everything," said Mrs Mountjoy.

"So where did Douglas come into it?" asked Freddie.

"When Elouisa had got possession of the house and everything else the old lady had left her, she decided to sell off the contents. In between carer jobs she'd worked in his shop. I suppose she thought she knew the value of things well enough that he wouldn't be able to cheat her. I think he was in a relationship with her until he met her prettier, younger sister. But the Chinese vase seems to have been too much of a temptation for him. Of course, Elouisa didn't find out that she'd been cheated until Freddie spotted it when we visited Doug's shop. She was stunned, then she was furious. It was one thing setting up other people to be conned, quite different when he did it to her."

"Me and my big mouth," mourned Freddie.

"Don't beat yourself up about it," said Maddie. "She was happy not just to act as a scout for Douglas, tipping him off about antiques he might want, but also to help to pressurise people to sell. Rose confirmed it was Elouisa who'd assured her she wouldn't get PDSA treatment for Snowy."

"Elouisa's rage may have had many roots but I think the thing that really clinched Douglas' fate was

322

his veiled threat in front of us all to be revenged," said Mrs Mountjoy.

"Yes," agreed Maddie. "I don't know if he knew about her snowman impersonation but he must have known about her scam and who Hatty was. When she didn't come to open her car boot, he went storming off to tell Hatty everything. And when Elouisa saw her damaged paintwork and realised what he was going to do, she chased after him, lethal hat pin in hand."

"Do you think she meant to kill him?" asked Grace.

"I have no idea but I bet she'll claim it was an accident, either that or self-defence."

"So was her motive fear he was going to blow the whistle? Or the Chinese vase? Or that he'd ditched her for her sister? Or that he'd scratched her car?" asked Freddie. "I'm confused."

Maddie grinned at him. "Join the club. My guess is it was a combination of everything. When it comes to her motive it's what you might describe as 'an embarrassment of riches'."

Chapter 67

Walking back around The Green, Freddie fell into step with Maddie and said, "What do you want to do about the show? Do you think it's better to call it off?"

Maddie thought of all the hard work that had gone into the preparation and how disappointed the performers and their families would be, as well as the good causes they'd be letting down. "I'm up for it if you are. After all, we can't waste Ron's balls."

Freddie chuckled. "Mrs Mountjoy's already said she's happy to carry on. That lady's like you, a fighter through and through."

"She's far braver and more resilient than I'll ever be. I'm pretty certain that Miriam won't want to miss her Que Sera moment in the spotlight and we can patch together the choir. What about Stan?"

Freddie raised his voice to reach Stan, who was walking ahead with Grace. "Oy, Mr Polar Bear! Are you still up for being the nimblest dancing bear in Hampshire?"

"Definitely." Stan grinned at them. "Just tell me the next rehearsal time and I'll be there." He waved goodbye and loped away with his long-legged stride.

"We may have to do without Janetta and her snowflakes but if the kids are willing to provide the music we should be able to put on a half-decent show."

"They're over at my cottage, why don't we go and ask them? Although, I'm afraid Tempest's very shocked. In her wildest dreams she'd never imagined her aunt could be a killer."

"We can give her time to decide what she wants to do but it would be good if we could find out if the others are willing to appear." Maddie shouted, "Grace,

I'm going to Freddie's to speak to the kids. Do you want to come?" They didn't actually need Grace at this juncture but Maddie didn't want to make her feel left out.

Grace looked back at them. She was frowning and Maddie expected to be reproved for being too loud in Clayfield's hallowed grounds. Then the cross look vanished and she called back, "I need to feed Tiggy. Come round when you're ready, if you're not too tired."

She walked on towards her cottage and Freddie said, "Let's cut across The Green." He offered Maddie his crooked arm, which, contemplating the icy grass, she willingly accepted.

When Freddie opened his front door they were greeted by the whirr of a vacuum cleaner.

"Do you think they're cleaning?" asked Freddie.

"Don't get your hopes up, they're probably trying to incorporate the hoover sound into some new musical composition," chuckled Maddie.

"No, we really are cleaning," said Sam, peering out from where he was polishing the case of Freddie's handsome grandfather clock, which in Maddie's opinion took up far too much of the hallway. "Kyle said he ought to move out tomorrow and Jenn told him he couldn't leave the place looking a total tip. Jenn's the domesticated one out of us four."

"He means I'm the only one who's not a total slob," retorted Jenn, appearing in the doorway. "I hope that's okay with you, Mr Fell? I didn't mean to take over and interfere with the way you do things."

"I appreciate it." Freddie beamed at her. "But it's Freddie you know, not Mr Fell."

"Thank you. I know you said to call you that but Temp's aunt said it was disrespectful. Kyle said to ignore her but the rest of us felt awkward about it."

"Point for debate," said Maddie, "should one take lessons in etiquette from a probable murderer? I'm with Kyle on that one."

Jenn giggled. "I guess you're right."

"How's Tempest coping?"

"Okay, I think. Confused rather than upset. It's not the sort of thing you expect to happen, is it?"

"Can you get everybody together in the sitting room? We want to ask about the show," said Freddie.

Five minutes later they were all assembled, sitting in a row on Freddie's super-sized sofa. It occurred to Maddie that, for a small man, Freddie went in for mega sized furniture, which might explain why he'd gone for one of the largest, most commodious cottages on the estate.

"Are you okay, Tempest?" she asked.

"Yes, I think so." Despite this reassurance, she looked pale and strained. " I never loved Aunt Lou and I know she didn't like me, but it's strange to think she'd do such awful things. Do you think my mother knew?"

"I'm sure she didn't." Janetta was a performer but Maddie didn't believe she could counterfeit the shock and disgust that were evident when Douglas and Elouisa's dishonest practices had been revealed, or her anger when she finally accepted that Douglas had bullied Tempest. And her horror seemed genuine when she realised her sister had killed her lover. Janetta was undoubtedly vain, shallow and selfish, all the faults that Elouisa had engendered in her, but Maddie felt sure she had no idea about the darker side of her sister's life or the truth about her lover.

"We wanted to know if you're all willing to carry on with the show?" asked Freddie.

"I am. It's not much thanks for all you've done for me," said Kyle. "I never had anyone on my side the

326

way you've been, not older people I mean. You make me feel different about myself."

Maddie smiled at him although she could feel tears welling in her eyes.

"I want to go ahead," said Jenn.

"And me," said Sam.

"What about you, Temp?" Kyle put his arm around her.

"I'd like to, if you still want me. I mean after what my aunt did, I'll understand if people don't want me to take part."

"We want you," Maddie assured her, "and if anybody complains we'll set Mrs Mountjoy onto them."

"Maddie's scary enough, let alone Mrs Mountjoy," teased Kyle. "Don't worry, Temp, with them on our side we can't fail."

"Thank you." Tempest smiled tremulously and then turned to hide her face against Kyle's shoulder.

"We're more or less up and running. I haven't checked with the choir yet but Mrs Mountjoy will whip them into line."

"What about the kids' dance?" Tempest emerged from Kyle's embrace to ask the question that Maddie hadn't wished to bother her with.

"We're happy to have them. I suppose it depends on whether their parents are willing and whether your mother is willing and able to perform," said Maddie.

Tempest was silent, indecision obvious on her face. At last she said, "It's not fair to the kids to make them miss out. If Mum doesn't want to do it, I can dance with them. I've rehearsed with them. But we'll need Mum's agreement to use the choreography."

"If she wants to save her dance school, she'd be a fool to refuse your offer. Thank you, Temp. Do you want to phone her or shall I?" said Maddie.

"You, please. I know I've got to contact her at some point but not yet. Jenn says I can stay at her mum's until Kyle and I can get a place together."

"I'll do it," said Freddie firmly. "She despises me but she probably hates you, Maddie."

"Well, I did get her sister arrested for murder. Okay, Freddie, use your famous diplomatic skills to get the snowflakes on the stage."

"Not in front of an audience." Freddie took out his mobile and bustled out of the room.

He returned five minutes later. "She's very upset but she agreed to let Tempest take her place. She'd like to speak to you, Tempest, but I told her you'd call her when you're ready."

"Thank you. I'll need to speak to her soon to sort out some liaison with the parents but I've just thought of another problem, her dress won't fit me, even if she'd lend it to me."

"That's a shame. You won't be shedding sequins everywhere," said Kyle sarcastically.

"It's not a problem, I'll talk to Nell," said Maddie. "I'll let you all know when we have a rehearsal schedule. Goodnight, everybody. I hope you sleep well."

Freddie accompanied her to the front door and, to her surprise, put on his coat again. "I'll walk with you across the grass. I don't want my leading lady to slip and literally break her leg."

They walked across The Green in companionable silence until Freddie said, "I'm sorry I got you so deeply embroiled with this show. I thought it would be good for you after the shock you had and Grace going off the way she did, but I could have been wrong."

328

"No, you weren't wrong. I'm glad you pulled me out of my depression. Thank you."

"I understand that now Grace is back you won't need me as much."

Maddie suppressed a sigh. It seemed that, as well as reassuring Grace, she had to do the same for Freddie. It didn't matter. If people cared about you, you had to value them. She stood on tiptoe and kissed Freddie on the cheek. "I'll always need you," she said.

Chapter 68

Grace was watching through her window for Maddie's return. When she saw her friend kiss Freddie she felt a foolish pang of jealousy and her old feelings of being excluded crept up on her again. Well, it was her own fault for running away.

Freddie left Maddie on her doorstep and two minutes later Grace's phone rang. "Do you want to come over? I've got wine. You can bring Tiggy if you want."

Once again, Grace put on coat and shoes and hurried along the path, carrying an indignant Tiggy under her arm. She settled in Maddie's cosy sitting room, sipping a very pleasant Merlot while Maddie placated Tiggy with a saucer of mashed sardine.

"I've been thinking," announced Maddie, sitting down opposite Grace.

"That sounds ominous," said Grace.

"I want to do something to help Hatty. I know she's a funny one but she's had a really bad time."

"What are you thinking of doing?" Grace hoped Maddie wasn't contemplating joining in a séance and, if so, she wouldn't try to involve her.

Maddie's mischievous look told her that she'd read her mind and her answer confirmed this, "Don't worry, she's not going to try and contact the ghosts of those who died in that cottage. I think her close encounter with a dead snowman has rather put her off that sort of thing."

"I'm glad to hear it. What are you planning to do for her?"

"For starters, I'm going to encourage her to join the choir for the show and ask everyone to make her welcome. Of course, if she's still snowman phobic, she may have to shut her eyes while they're dancing, but maybe confronting her fears will be good for her."

"Maybe." Grace was not entirely convinced that it was safe or desirable for Maddie to practise psychological therapy without proper training but, she had to admit, joining the choir seemed like a good way to integrate Hatty into the estate. "Has she got a nice voice?"

"I'm not sure but I do know it carries well."

Grace remembered her first introduction to Hatty invoking the spirits and was uncertain whether to shudder or to smile.

"Do you think she'll be willing to join in? After such a bad start on the estate, she may feel too embarrassed and shy. Not everyone's a performer." Grace could sympathise with that.

"This is a woman who has spent years going into trances and yodelling to the spirits to come and join her. Don't tell me she's shy," said Maddie caustically, "Anyway, I've got a cunning plan, I'm going to ask her to join us as a favour to me, because we desperately need some more voices in the choir. And that has the virtue of being true."

"It would be better to have a few more singers," agreed Grace.

"Yes, I've persuaded Amy to join us. She's got a lovely voice but she didn't offer before because she was afraid that would mean Ron would insist on joining too."

"Oh no!" exclaimed Grace. Ron's singing voice closely resembled a particularly off-key fog horn.

"It's okay. When he phoned me to inform me of the treat in store for us, I told him his voice was too powerful for singing as part of a group but we'd be happy to offer him a solo spot."

"And that makes it better? He'll clear the Hall. You might as well set off the fire alarm."

"You underestimate me." Maddie looked at her reproachfully. "I described the rigorous rehearsal schedule, which would be especially demanding for a solo performer who was coming in at the last moment. He soon decided it would be too much for him."

"You are brilliant," admitted Grace, "and exceptionally devious."

"I'll take that. Brilliant and devious just about sums me up. Are you going to join the choir to help make up the numbers?"

"Me? No! It's really not my sort of thing." Even during hymn singing in Church she was careful to never raise her voice above the rest of the congregation and usually played safe by simply mouthing the words. Eager to change the subject, she said, "What else were you thinking of doing to help Hatty?"

"I want to help her change her cottage," said Maddie. "She can't stay in the Nursing Home guest room for much longer and her cottage will feel more like home if she puts her mark on it. I'll try to persuade her to get rid of some of that dingy old furniture and I'll help her paint the rest."

Grace thought that the combination of Maddie's artistic flamboyance and Hatty's passion for crystals and dream catchers could result in a very unusual décor, but she was willing to do her bit.

"I'm not as good at sewing as Nell or Rose but I could help make some new curtains, or alter them if we find any nice ones in a charity shop."

"That would be great."

"I don't know if you've guessed, but I've decided not to leave." Grace felt absurdly shy as she confessed.

"I'm glad." Maddie grinned at her. "I've been so busy I haven't finished your Christmas present yet and it will be a real pain to pack and post."

"I've already got yours wrapped and ready in my spare room. And things for your family too."

Although having an excess of spare time wasn't really much to boast of. Grace remembered the long hours each evening, sitting alone in her suite in her aunt's house, watching television and knitting Maddie a multi-coloured, chunky jacket, and felt a surge of happiness that she was never going back.

As if to emphasise the point, Tiggy climbed onto her lap, kneaded himself a nest, curled up and settled down to sleep, purring softly.

"Seriously, I'm glad you're staying. I missed you when you were gone and, more important, it's time you stopped thinking your mission in life is to care for everyone who demands your help. You've spent enough of your life running after other people. It's time you thought of yourself."

Maddie leaned over to refill Grace's glass. "Having said that, I've got a favour to ask of you. We're going ahead with the show, so will you organise us?"

"Of course!" Grace rummaged in her handbag and got out a notepad and pen. "Tell me what you've got planned."

Maddie obediently listed what she and Freddie had put together.

"We'll need a replacement snowman," said Grace. "Have you any suggestions?"

"I thought you might like to take that on," said Maddie, her voice bubbling with mischief, "I've spoken to Nell about running up a new costume." Her voice trailed off into a strangled squeak as the giggles she was suppressing burst through. "Welcome home!"

For several seconds, Grace maintained her outraged expression, then she too started to laugh. "It's good to be here," she said.

About the Author

Carol Westron is a successful short story writer who now writes crime fiction, children's fiction, articles and reviews. She is an expert on the Golden Age of Detective Fiction and has given papers at several conferences. Her four contemporary police procedurals and her first Victorian Murder Mystery are set in the south of England, as is the stand-alone cosy crime, This Game of Ghosts.

Her new cosy crime series, which starts with The Curse of the Concrete Griffin, is also set in Hampshire, in Clayfield, a fictional village a few miles north of Portsmouth.

Printed in Great Britain
by Amazon